Paul Thomas, bor
Wellington, New Ze
journalist and spor
a bestselling series featuring maverick Maori cop
Tito Ihaka, of which *Death on Demand* is the latest.
These include *Dirty Laundry* (aka *Old School Tie*,
1994), *Inside Dope* (1995) and *Guerrilla Season*
(1996). *Inside Dope* was the winner of the Ned
Kelly Award for Best Crime Novel.

DEATH
ON DEMAND

Paul Thomas

BITTER LEMON PRESS
LONDON

BITTER LEMON PRESS

First published in the United Kingdom in 2013 by
Bitter Lemon Press, 37 Arundel Gardens,
London W11 2LW

www.bitterlemonpress.com

First published in New Zealand by
Hachette New Zealand Ltd., 2012

© Paul Thomas, 2012

A CIP record for this book is available
from the British Library

ISBN 978–1–908524–17–1

Typeset by Tetragon, London

Printed and bound in Great Britain
by CPI Group (UK) Ltd
Croydon, CR0 4YY

To Georgie, Harry & Susan.
And to my mother.

PROLOGUE

WARREN
Greytown, fourteen years ago

Females had always found him hard to resist. When he was small, his aunts and cousins cooed and fussed over him, telling him how gorgeous he was. His older sister was like a second mother: she spoilt him, couldn't stay mad at him, wouldn't let him leave the house without a hug. Other kids, their sisters called them retards and wouldn't touch them without rubber gloves.

At thirteen he had a growth spurt, and suddenly wasn't a cute little boy any more. Now his aunts went on about what a handsome young man he was becoming. When the phone rang in the evening half the time it was girls wanting to speak to him, which made his old man huff and puff. Once he overheard his sister on the phone: "Forget it, bitch," she said. "He's way too young for you. I don't give a shit that his balls have dropped, he's still only fourteen. Let me explain something: I worry about my sweet little bro. I worry about him getting pimples and an attitude and turning into a dropkick; I worry about him getting in with a bad crowd and leaving school with nothing to show for it; I worry about all sorts of things. But most of all I worry about my slut friends getting their slutty little claws into him and putting him off girls for good."

Around that time his parents had a party. He helped out pouring drinks, picking up empties, slipping coasters under glasses left on the sideboard. This woman he hardly knew kept staring at him. Next time he came by with a bottle of Sauvignon Blanc, she waved her empty glass. He went over. She manoeuvred him into a corner, standing right in front of him with her back to the room. It was weird: she was his mother's age and spoke to him like adults usually did, asking pointless questions – "So what's your favourite subject?" – and not listening to his replies, but she kept touching him, squeezing his bicep and stroking his forearm. Her face was so close her breath warmed his cheek. Her leg pressed against his.

He squeezed past her, saying he had to get some more wine. She followed him into the kitchen, eyes bright, lips curved in an unsettling smile. She pushed him up against the bench. Her mouth fell open as she reached out to pull his face down to hers. He tasted wine as her tongue flailed around inside his mouth. Footsteps in the corridor made her pull away. A guy came in looking for beer, and as soon as they started talking he slipped out the back door and ran down the street to a friend's house. He didn't tell his mates; they gave him enough shit about being a pretty boy as it was. Besides, they would have thought it was gross, some old bag sticking her tongue down your throat.

She was really friendly next time he saw her. Thinking about it that night, he decided it was probably because he'd kept his mouth shut: in Greytown gossip circulated at the speed of sound. He was tempted to knock on her door one morning after her husband had left for work just to see

10

what would happen, but there was a fair chance it could backfire, big-time. He was curious, but not that curious.

He wasn't academic, but he was worldly by the standards of Greytown teenagers and had grown up with an older sister. He lost interest in girls his age pretty quickly. He tended to lose interest in girls younger than him before their friends had finished asking him to ask them out. He gravitated towards older girls, but the smart, sparky ones took off as soon as they'd left school, whether to go to university or embark on life's big adventure.

Craig and Donna came up from Wellington to run one of the cafés which had sprung up along the main street. They rented the house next door while the owners, empty nesters, went travelling for a year. There was a party every weekend, which ruffled his parents' feathers, but he got on fine with them and scored a part-time general dogsbody gig at their café.

He got on particularly well with Donna, who he guessed was in her mid-twenties. She'd lived in Sydney for a couple of years and bummed around Asia, sleeping on beaches, smoking weed, doing Buddhism for beginners. The problem with the girls he went out with was that they didn't know how much was enough, so they showed too much thigh or too much tit or were too eager to please, trying to swallow you whole when they kissed or sucking your dick without being asked and probably without wanting to because they didn't want to be labelled cock-teasers. He actually didn't mind a bit of cock-teasing; it added to the fun, gave you something to look forward to. Donna made them seem very young: indiscriminate, compliant little herd animals. She had a way of triggering a rush of longing with just a look, a sideways smile, a murmured aside.

Not that he had great expectations. For a start, she was a woman and he was a boy. A good-looking, rapidly maturing one perhaps, but still a boy. Secondly, she was living with a guy. She laughed when he asked if she and Craig were married – "Oh yeah, that's me: good little wifey" – but they seemed as much of a couple in their interaction as most of the husbands and wives he'd observed. And while Craig treated him okay and took the piss in that blokey way, he had the look of someone you wouldn't want to cross.

His bedroom window looked out onto his father's vegetable garden and into next door's spare room, where Craig had set up his weights. One day he was idly watching Craig pump iron in front of a mirror with his shirt off when Donna appeared in little shorts and a tight singlet. He kept watching, but closely now. Suddenly Craig got up off the bench and came over to the window. He gave him a weak grin and a wave; Craig held his expressionless stare for five seconds, then squeezed out a thin smile. Next day at the café Donna told him he should feel free to come over for a workout if he ever got the urge. He blushed and started to apologize, but she grazed a fingernail down the side of his face. "It's okay, baby," she murmured. "It's cool."

He sometimes wondered what she made of Craig's habit of laying a heavy dose of charm on any attractive woman who came into the café. This particular day he was behind the counter watching Craig do a number on this woman from Carterton who'd started coming in on her own pretty regularly. Suddenly Donna was standing right behind him, resting her hand on the small of his back.

"Look at that wanker," she said. "He thinks he's irresistible. You could teach him a thing or two."

He turned his head to look at her. She was so close they were almost bumping noses. "What about?"

She gave him a lazy smile. "Oh, you know, how to look at a woman. Raw lust doesn't do it for most of us, any more than being taken for granted. We like to see a little tenderness."

Then without warning, without saying goodbye, without a word to anyone, Donna and Craig were gone. It was the shock of his young life: he was used to deciding when a relationship's time was up, as opposed to having it decided for him. Whatever there was between him and Donna was undeclared, unfulfilled and at least partly in his head, but it was more real and more significant to him than any number of teenage pairings with their juvenile rituals and matter-of-fact sex. And while there was an element of fantasy, it was a fantasy she'd encouraged. He hadn't imagined that. He was crushed that she could leave him desolate, without a word or gesture to acknowledge the depth and purity of his infatuation.

It turned out that they'd skipped on a raft of unpaid bills, including several months' rent. His mother went into I-told-you-so mode, insisting she always knew they were fly-by-nighters, there was just something about them, good riddance to bad rubbish. His Donna thing hadn't gone unnoticed by his contemporaries. Boys who'd had to make do with his sniffling cast-offs and girls he'd ignored or casually dumped delighted in telling him that he'd made himself look ridiculous, having a crush on a grown-up woman who obviously didn't give a shit.

His old man, of all people, was the only one to shed any light. Donna and Craig were chancers, he said, drifting from place to place looking for an arrangement, a set of circumstances, which worked for them; when it didn't materialize, they moved on. Because they never stayed in one place long enough to form real relationships, it didn't bother them to run out on their debts or abandon people who thought of them as friends. That set his mother off again: they were common criminals, she snorted; it was just a matter of time before the police caught up with them and they got what they deserved.

He hardly slept that night. Now he got it. Why would they stay in Greytown? What would keep them there? It was a place you had to get away from, and that's what they'd done. No explanation, no apology: when it was time to go, just disappear without a trace. That way you could start again somewhere without having to worry about the past – people who'd passed their use-by dates, pain-in-the-arse complications – stretching out its long, bony arm to tap you on the shoulder.

Another couple, gays this time, took over the café. It was just drudgery now, but he stayed on because he needed the money for what he had in mind. A week before the end of the school year, he got a letter, care of the café. It was from Donna. She was sorry for taking off like that, but things had got messy and they'd done their dash in Greytown. He had to get out of there, she wrote, or he'd end up just another drongo stuck in a shit job, living a shit life. If he made it to Auckland, he should check out the Ponsonby café and bar scene: if she was still there, they were bound to bump into one another sooner or later. There was a PS: "Burn this and don't tell anyone you've heard from me."

His plan firmed up. His parents were spending Christmas and New Year in Mount Maunganui with relatives; a couple of his mates were going down to Wellington to watch the cricket test at the Basin Reserve. He told his parents he was going to the cricket and would crash on the floor of a friend of a friend's flat; he told his mates he'd ride with them down to Wellington but peel off to go camping in the Sounds with his sister and her boyfriend.

His mates dropped him off on Lambton Quay. He lugged his bag to the train station and bought a ticket to Auckland. He left without warning, without saying goodbye, without a word to anyone.

ADRIAN, CHRISTOPHER, FRASER, JONATHON
Waiheke Island, six years and three months ago

These boys' weekends went back fifteen years. Before going their separate ways they'd settle on the when and where for the following year, taking it in turn to make the arrangements. They had a week to square it with work and home, then it was set in stone. Come what may – children's big sporting moments, favourite nieces' weddings, suicidal colleagues, parents-in-law on life support – they were committed, immune to persuasion, pressure or emotional blackmail. It was the annual boys' weekend. It was a tradition.

There were four of them. Two met at boarding school; the other two had flatted together during their student days. They'd connected through marriage: two – one from each pairing – were married to women who'd been best friends since Brownies. They coalesced in Auckland in the mid-1980s, drawn together by history, a love of games and a shared world view, essentially an in-your-face, you-only-live-once materialism. They were white, well-off, respectable married men who liked letting their hair down in controlled conditions.

It began with a relatively low-key golf weekend in Taupo. They stayed at a mid-range motel, went out for a meal and a few drinks, played Wairakei on the Saturday, had an early night, teed off again first thing Sunday morning, and were home in time for the Sunday night roast. As they were having a sandwich before the drive home, the property developer (Christopher) suggested they should do it again next year. The dentist (Adrian) pointed out that there was more than one decent golf course in the upper half of the North Island. The businessman (Jonathon) said, why limit ourselves to the upper half of the North Island? The lawyer (Fraser) said, why limit ourselves to golf?

They'd had weekends in the three other main centres organized around All Black tests. They'd done the rugby league grand final in Sydney, the Aussie Rules grand final in Melbourne, and the Adelaide Grand Prix. They'd done wine tours of Hawkes Bay and Central Otago. They'd even done a tramp in the Marlborough Sounds, but the decadent variety with husky youngsters to carry their backpacks to the next luxury lodge and a hot bath, a five-course dinner and a soft bed.

There were two rules, which had never been articulated let alone formally adopted: the weekend's main activity, its ostensible *raison d'être*, had to be something which held little or no appeal for the wives so they wouldn't feel they were missing out. Secondly, there would be no shenanigans involving other women, whether as a group or individually. That way, when pressed for details or a few illuminating snippets, they could look their wives in the eye and invoke the principle that what happens on tour should stay on tour.

This year it was the Hauraki Gulf on a chartered launch, fishing optional. They gathered at Westhaven on Friday afternoon. After loading the supplies, they headed up to Kawau where, in keeping with tradition, they got drunker than they'd been since last year's boys' weekend. In the morning they swam to clear their heads, had a late breakfast of whitebait fritters and Bloody Marys, then motored down to Waiheke for a long lunch at a vineyard restaurant.

They rolled out of the restaurant at five, and went up the eastern side of the island to a private bay where one of the businessman's mates had a weekender. They went ashore, lit a fire in the courtyard fireplace, and got to work on the case of Syrah they'd bought at the vineyard.

Over the years, the wine they consumed had got steadily better and their consumption had steadily increased. That reflected a paradox: as they'd become more prosperous, more secure, more embedded in their circumstances – more content, one might think, looking in from the outside – the boys' weekends had become more of a relief from their everyday reality.

And after a decade and a half of *in vino veritas* without a single breach of confidence, these weekends were also a chance to let off steam, to say out loud things that normally stayed inside their heads. For instance, Fraser, who was now an MP, took the opportunity to tell racist jokes. Like the others, like many Pakeha of his age and background, he was instinctively mildly racist, but in public life and in his infrequent interactions with Maori, Polynesians and Asians, he bent over backwards to present as Mr Multiculture.

The openness extended to their private lives. This tended to mean that the two happily married men – Jonathon and Christopher, the property developer turned consultant – had to listen to the two unhappily married men – Adrian and Fraser – moan about their marriages and brag about their affairs. These bore out the banal truth that proximity is the greatest aphrodisiac – Adrian had been through a string of nurses, receptionists and hygienists; Fraser's late-night trawls of the Beehive had landed a few research assistants and members of the press gallery – although in the telling their lovers were invariably pretty, lubricious, and gratified. Whenever Christopher and Jonathon compared notes back in Auckland, they'd conclude that their friends were full of shit. Their scepticism was borne out when one of the press gallery catch changed jobs to become an unsightly presence on the six o'clock news.

They were sitting in the courtyard drinking Syrah and smoking the Cuban cigars which Jonathon, by some distance the richest of the four, always provided.

"I've got a joke for you," said Adrian, who now spent most of his working life in Sydney maintaining the ivory grins

17

of newsreaders, models and trophy wives. "It's a fucking classic."

"Is it dirty?" asked Fraser.

"Not really," said Adrian. "But there's more to life than dirty sex, you know."

Jonathon laughed. "Coming from you."

"Exactly," said Fraser. "And, anyway, who says there's more to life than dirty sex?"

"The Pope?" suggested Christopher.

"Well, he would, wouldn't he?" said Fraser. "You know why the Pope showers in his undies? Because he doesn't want to look down on the unemployed."

Adrian groaned. "Oh, please. You know how old that joke is? I heard it from my scoutmaster. He was trying to seduce me at the time."

"When you say 'seduce'," said Jonathon, "that implies some reluctance on your part."

"Au contraire," said Adrian. "He just wouldn't take yes for an answer." The others guffawed. "Now, you want to hear this fucking joke or not? Okay. A businessman rushes up to the ticket counter at some American airport. He's in a panic because the last plane to Pittsburgh is about to depart. As he opens his mouth to speak to the woman behind the counter, he notices that she's superbly endowed in the knocker department. 'Yes sir,' she says, 'what can I do for you?' The guy's still eyeballing her stupendous norks. Without looking up he says, 'A return ticket to Tittsburgh please.'"

"Half an hour later, on the plane, he's still mortified by his faux pas. The guy in the next seat can see he's a bit uptight and asks if he's okay. 'I just had the most horrendously embarrassing experience,' he says, and explains what happened. 'Tell me about it,' says the other guy. 'I know how easy it is to get your words mixed up when you've got something on your mind. At breakfast this morning I meant to say to the wife, 'Darling, would you pass the marmalade,' but you know how it came out? 'You fucking cunt, you've ruined my life.'"

The joke met with a mixed reaction. Jonathon shrugged as if he didn't really get it; Fraser emitted a low, appreciative chuckle; Christopher spluttered a few times then let out a roar, like a motorbike kick-started on a cold morning.

"Settle down," said Jonathon. "It wasn't that bloody funny."

"Actually, I wouldn't have thought it was your sort of joke," Fraser said to Christopher. "Twenty-five years of married bliss and all that."

Christopher dabbed his eyes. "You like racist jokes, but you're not a racist – or so you keep telling us. And since when was I going on about wedded bliss?"

"Maybe not this time," said Adrian, "but you'd have to admit it's been a bit of a theme over the years."

"Yeah, well, that was then," said Christopher.

"If I didn't know better," said Jonathon, "I'd say that sounds like trouble at mill."

Christopher shook his head crossly. "I thought I married the girl next door, not bloody Wonder Woman." He stood up. "The shithouse calls. I might be some time." He went inside.

"Well, I'll be fucked," said Fraser, eyebrows aloft.

Adrian said, "Are you two thinking what I'm thinking?"

"I'm not thinking about sex," said Jonathon, "so probably not."

"I reckon he's got something going on."

"What do you mean?"

"A bit of stray," said Adrian, "a bit of crutch, a bit of what makes you throb in the night."

"You think he's having an affair?" said Fraser.

"Don't be daft," said Jonathon.

"You've got to admit," said Adrian, "that was way out of character. Like a whole different person."

"Give the man a break," said Jonathon. "His life's been turned upside down – that's got to take a bit of getting used to."

"Jesus, it's been a while now," said Fraser. "Besides, what's the big deal? It wouldn't take me too long to get used to my wife making a shitload of money."

"Nor me," said Adrian. "Then she could fuck off and fend for herself. There's something's going on there, you can put the ring around it. You guys see more of him than I do so maybe it's harder for you to pick up, but I sensed it the moment I laid eyes on him at Westhaven."

"You know what I don't get?" Jonathon asked Adrian. "If things are that bad at home, why don't you just split? Okay, she'll walk away with half, but you're the most expensive fucking dentist in Australasia: you'll make it all back and more in ten years."

"Fuck that for a game of soldiers," said Adrian as Christopher rejoined them. "I haven't sweated my balls off all these years to hand the bitch half of everything I own on a silver platter. And I don't want to work for another ten years either. In five years tops I want to be an ex-dentist kicking back in Noosa."

"Suit yourself," said Jonathon. "Don't get me wrong, I'm pleased you don't want to do that because I happen to like your wife. But if the relationship's as poisonous as you make out, you could retire to the Riviera and still be unhappy."

"He's got a point," said Fraser.

"Pity this isn't America," said Christopher. "You could just look up Dial a Hitman in the Yellow Pages."

Adrian extended his arm across the table for a high-five. "Right on, brother."

JOYCE
St Heliers, Auckland, six years ago

It all boiled down to self-discipline. Sure, being organized helped, but a lot of what people called organization was really self-discipline: having a structure to your life; sticking to your plans and routines regardless of what circumstances and other people threw at you. Having a few brains helped too, but less than you'd think. Look at her: nobody's fool, no question about that, but certainly no Einstein. She came across plenty of people who were brighter than her. For that matter some of her employees were brighter than her. So how come they worked for her and not the other way round? How come she was more successful than all those brainboxes out there? Two words: self-discipline.

She did her stretches at the bottom of the drive, glancing up at the dark mass of the house.

Where would their lovely home be without her self-discipline? Gone west, that's where.

Self-discipline had got her through a degree while holding down a full-time job. Self-discipline had enabled her to raise two well-adjusted, high-achieving kids while working part-time. And self-discipline had been the key to building a thriving business from the ground up when their comfortable little world was on the verge of falling apart.

It was 5.59 a.m. She shook the traces of sleep-stiffness from her arms and legs, set her watch and eased into a jog. Within twenty-five metres she was moving at the brisk tempo she'd maintain for the next three quarters of an hour.

Self-discipline had enabled her to roll back the disfiguring effects of childbirth without resorting to cosmetic surgery, like some people she could mention. To heck with that: this body was all her own work. And pretty darn trim for fifty-one if she said so herself, as she often did when she inspected it in the full-length mirror in her walk-in wardrobe.

Self-discipline got her out of bed at 5.40 every second morning to go for a run. Even on mornings like this when the chill turned your nose red and your fingers white and it would be so easy to sink back into that big, soft bed. Even if she'd been up late getting on top of her paperwork, or cleaning up after a dinner party while her husband was upstairs snoring his head off. Assuming he was capable of negotiating the stairs. Even if she had a rotten cold, because you couldn't let a little bug rule your life. Every second morning, without fail, she was down at the gate stretching by 5.55 and on her way by six. You could set your watch by her.

Her route never varied. What was the point? It was exercise, not sight-seeing. Mind you, she'd be doing the old eyes-right when she passed a certain house that had just gone on the market, a snip at $8.7 million. Dream home was right. Dream on. Not that they couldn't have done the deal. Since the business took off, getting money out of the bank was the least of her worries – they were almost offended that she didn't want more. Once bitten, twice shy, though. She had nothing against bankers – well, nothing much, anyway – but she didn't want them owning a chunk of her home. When you own it outright, no one can take it away from you.

If it was up to her husband, they'd be moving in next week. He still didn't get it even though it was his over-confidence and, let's face it, lack of self-discipline that had landed them in the poop in the first place. Oh well, he was what he was and that leopard certainly wasn't going to change his spots. Besides, she wouldn't have fallen for him if he'd been a different person, more like her. They were a classic case of opposites attract. No, it wouldn't happen next week, but it would happen. And the first he'd know about it would be when she tossed him the front-door key and said, ever so casually, "Darling, you know that house in Lammermoor Drive that we were so keen on…"

People couldn't believe she went jogging without an iPod. What a waste, drifting through this precious, uninterrupted time with your head clogged up with music. This was when she did her best thinking.

Maybe she would have checked before crossing the road if she hadn't been preoccupied with the looming confrontation with her increasingly distracted personal assistant. Maybe she would have noticed the car if the driver had had his headlights on. But there was so little traffic at that hour of the morning in those leafy suburban streets.

By the time the engine noise did penetrate her cocoon of concentration it was too late. She was in the air for several seconds, her body a bag of shattered bones, her limbs as limp as a rag doll's, because death was instantaneous.

ROGER
Ponsonby, Auckland, three years ago

Jesus, who'd live in the suburbs? Stuck in traffic twice a day and sipping sparkling mineral water while the rest of the crew got shit-faced. As opposed to this: a ten-minute walk from SPQR to his front door, seven if he took the shortcut through the old bakery site. He could do it on autopilot, and often did.

At least Phil didn't do the stuck record thing tonight, thank fuck. He just didn't get it. You couldn't really blame him. People who grew up poor craved financial security – it was their Holy Grail. They lay awake at night fantasizing about getting that big break and never having to worry about money again.

So when they were offered a truckload of coin for the company, Phil couldn't think past the thrill of seeing telephone numbers on his next bank statement and the fuck-you call to Mum and Dad. Hey, guess what? Your dropkick son who left school at fifteen and still smokes dope is a dead-set millionaire. Not a theoretical, if you sold everything you owned and lived in the in-laws' spare room-type millionaire, but a real fucking millionaire. Keep buying the Lotto tickets, man.

Phil wasn't thinking about what a pain in the arse it would be having to answer to other people after twenty years of being your own boss. Shit, it would be bad enough reporting to the guys in London, but at least they had an industry background and seemed to accept that making films and TV programmes wasn't always and only about the bottom line. That dipstick in Sydney, though... As far as he was concerned, if it didn't have celebrities with big tits, forget it.

Phil couldn't – or wouldn't – see how soul-destroying it would be jumping through hoops and kissing arse to get the green light for projects that right now they could decide on over a long lunch. And while the guys in London weren't dipsticks, they weren't Kiwis either. How fucking hard would it be to get London excited about uniquely New Zealand stories?

There'd be paperclip-counters always looking over your shoulder, insisting on proper budgets and timesheets and fully documented expense claims. There'd be some sanctimonious bloody company code of conduct that would knock the fringe benefits on the head. For Christ's sake, half the fun of being in the fucking film industry was the hot chick factor.

Take the new girl; he certainly intended to. Man, did she spark up in the bar just now when he was talking about hanging out at Cannes with George Clooney and Brad Pitt. It crossed his mind to ask her if she'd mind popping back to the office to help him get out a pitch document, but experience had taught him the value of patience. Give her a while to get her head around the idea of fucking the boss who was old enough to be her father. Besides, when the time came he wanted to put his best foot forward and he was a few glasses of red past that point.

Sure, it was different for Phil: like all the other old hippies, he probably wanted to send his kids to private schools. But he knew the score. Shit, whose bloody idea was it to have that legal agreement that both of them had to approve any change to the shareholding structure?

It was a shame Phil had his tits in a knot but he'd get over it. He always did. It wasn't as if it had been sweetness and light and never a cross word between them, especially the last couple of months. But at the end of the day, they complemented each other. As a partnership they had credibility and runs on the board; if they split up, they'd just join the queue of hustlers and wannabes and bullshit artists hawking their half-arsed ideas to anyone who'd sit still. So Phil would get over it. He had to. He had no fucking choice.

Once he'd got over it and they had a serious, edgy project on the go, he'd remind Phil that he'd saved them from a fate worse than death: working for the man, coming in every day to do shit they'd be embarrassed to put their names to, being bad-mouthed behind their backs as pretenders who'd talked the talk but sold out the first time a big cheque was waved under their noses. And Phil would thank him for it.

In a couple of weeks the new girl would be ripe for the plucking. No, he wouldn't use the old "Can you work late tonight?" gambit, tried and tested though it was. The casting couch – as Phil called it – in his office had seen plenty of action over the years, but it was really designed for wham, bam, thank you ma'ams, not that they didn't have their place in the scheme of things. But if you were contemplating something more than a one-off Friday night quickie, repeat business as it were, home was the go: the outdoor fire, the spa under the stars, the super-king bed that seemed to bring out the beast even in the good girls. But even though he'd be pawing the ground, he'd have to remember not to come this way. Fuck, it was dark. No wonder that last chick freaked out and bailed on him.

He froze when the arm snaked around his neck and a male voice snarled in his ear: "Take out your wallet and drop it on the ground." The choke hold tightened. "Do it, fucker." As he pawed feebly at the hip pocket of his jeans, he was swung around. A gloved fist slammed into the middle of his face. He reeled backwards, blood filling his mouth. Through the firestorm of pain and terror he saw a hoodie, saw a knife blade flash, saw nothing else.

EVELYNE
Remuera, Auckland, nine months ago

They were two of a kind, she thought: stubborn old bitches.

She looked down at the golden Labrador lying at her feet. Wag just pipped her age-wise, fifteen dog years being ninety-plus in human terms according to some chart her daughter had found on the Internet. They were really just hanging on because the alternative – slipping away into oblivion – was even less appealing.

They still had their marbles, thank God, but were a couple of physical wrecks. Now and again the woman who did her shopping and cleaning tried to interest Wag in a walk around the block, but after fifty metres or so she'd just lie down on the footpath and refuse to budge. A far cry from the days when she followed you around like a shadow until you gave in and got the lead, then dragged you through Cornwall Park practically ripping your arm out of its socket.

As for her, the stairs were her Berlin Wall, a barrier to the outside world. Going down was manageable but, Lord above, getting back up. Her son's solution was for her to move into a ground-floor apartment or a "unit" – what an evocative term for home, sweet home – in a retirement village. Not on your Nellie, buster. She'd lived here since 1968 – they'd actually signed the contract the day the *Wahine* went down – and moving now would seem like a repudiation of the best years of her life and the memories that sustained her. She wasn't going anywhere; they'd have to carry her out in a wooden box.

Her solution was much more elegant: install a basic kitchen upstairs, convert one of the spare bedrooms into a living-cum-TV room, *et voilà*: the stairs were no longer a problem because there was no reason to go downstairs. Someone asked her if she ever got bored being restricted to one floor. What a daft question. Housebound was housebound: what difference did it make how many rooms your world had shrunk to? Besides, boredom was as much part of old age as loneliness and infirmity, although it didn't get as much recognition.

By and large she'd learned to live with loneliness. The only way she was going to see her husband was if he was waiting for her on the other side. Much as she'd like to believe that, and much as she'd like to think her decades of conscientious church attendance would be rewarded, she wasn't taking it for granted. If there was an afterlife, she hoped her mild scepticism wouldn't be held against her.

She always went along with her friends' suggestions that she must miss the entertaining, but that was for their benefit – they'd probably be offended if she disagreed. In fact, she didn't miss it at all. It was something she and her husband had done together. He loved planning a dinner party, putting together a menu, organizing the food and wine, and his enthusiasm rubbed off on her. And in those days she had a decent appetite and liked a glass of wine or three. Now she ate like a bird and a second glass of wine left her feeling as if she'd been sandbagged.

She missed her daughter and grandchildren – and son-in-law up to a point – but they lived in Brussels. Their visits every second Christmas were, by some distance, top of her ever-diminishing list of things to look forward to. Her son and daughter-in-law lived on the North Shore. Of course she enjoyed seeing them but, if she was absolutely honest, it wasn't the end of the world if he rang to say they were too busy to make it over that week. Maybe she was being unfair but, when they did come, she always got the feeling they'd spent the drive over working out why they couldn't stay for very long.

The truth was the relationship hadn't been quite the same since she'd politely but firmly rejected her son's suggestion that he should take over the running of her financial affairs. It was for his own good, not that he could see that. Despite ample opportunity he had failed to demonstrate that he'd inherited his father's astuteness in money matters. A couple of her husband's friends, who did share his astuteness in money matters, were happy to look after her affairs and had done a very good job of it. Unlike some other widows she knew, she'd come through the recent financial turmoil relatively unscathed. When the time came her son could do as he pleased with his share of the inheritance, and if he didn't, his wife certainly would. The look on their faces that time she jokingly suggested she might leave a decent whack to the SPCA… Clearly there were some subjects one simply didn't joke about.

Goodness gracious, what was that racket? Wag really was on her last legs if she could sleep through that. It was one of those dreadful radio people being inane at the top of his lungs. Why were they so proud of being imbeciles? It sounded as though it was coming from downstairs, but her help had left hours ago and anyway wouldn't have dared to put talkback on at that volume. It had to be some kind of electrical fault or power surge. Oh well, nothing else for it but to venture downstairs for the first time in months.

Leaning on her walking stick, she made her way to the top of the stairs. What a God-awful din. She thought of trying to find the earplugs she'd used to block out her husband's snoring. He, bless him, had claimed it was all in her mind.

She lurched forward, losing her balance. The landing rushed up to meet her. Her last thought was to wonder if the loud click that seemed to come from inside her head was the sound of her neck breaking.

LORNA
Parnell, Auckland, one month ago

She had to clasp the cup in both hands to stop it spilling, and it clattered in the saucer when she put it down. The man at the next table was staring at her. She could feel his prying gaze roam over her like a torch beam. She could almost hear his eyebrows clench as he observed her burning cheeks and shaking hands and the mess she'd created – the puddle of milk, the dusting of sugar. She trapped her hands between her thighs, where they couldn't shake and couldn't be seen, and looked straight ahead. Everyone in the café must be looking at her, thinking, what's going on there? What's up with the woman of leisure in the Trelise Cooper outfit and the Blahnik shoes?

It was a good question. What the hell was she doing there? Why was she, a sensible, enviable, middle-aged married woman who'd hardly done a reckless or wilfully foolish thing in her life, sitting there summoning up the nerve to go into the apartment building across the street and have sex with a man she barely knew? Why would anyone in her position and in their right mind even contemplate it?

Because while her husband doted on her (which, in his mind, was proof of love), he wasn't really interested in her as a person. He was solicitous, respectful, indulgent, but never sought her opinion on anything beyond trivial domestic or social matters, and struggled to conceal his indifference whenever she volunteered it. He was happier to go to work than get home, happier to hook up with his male friends than stay with her.

Because there was more to life than lunches with other ladies who lunched, and tennis, and yoga classes, and charity work (socializing by any other name), and overseas holidays, and supervising the gardener.

Because the children had left home.

Because she was ashamed of not having done more with her life, in the sense of using her ability and exposing herself to a wider range of experiences and challenges.

Because it was too long since she'd had an adventure.

Because she was bored.

Because she wanted to have a secret, something thrilling and forbidden she could relive second by second when she woke up at three in the morning.

Because when it was over she could walk away, knowing there would be no aftermath, no repercussions.

Because there was no risk.

She finished her coffee. Her hands had stopped shaking. She placed her palms on her cheeks. They were warm as opposed to hot, which meant pink as opposed to crimson. Pink she could live with.

She stood up and walked out of the café, not caring if people were staring at her, feeling the first, faint stirrings of arousal.

CHRISTOPHER
St Heliers, Auckland, two weeks ago

He'd always wondered how he'd react if it came to this. Pretty well as it turned out, assuming you subscribe to the code of the stiff upper lip. Quite the stoic, in fact. He hadn't swooned or broken down or got angry; he'd sought clarity on the time frame and, as the condemned often do, thanked his sentencer. The specialist had admired his courage, belated acknowledgement that he was a patient rather than a case study.

It was a different story at home, of course. He'd thrown up, he'd howled and ranted, he'd soaked his shirt front with tears like equatorial raindrops. When the crying jag had run its course, he stared at himself in the mirror above the basin. A Latin phrase he hadn't used or thought of since boarding school popped into his head: *Morituri te salutant* – those who are about to die salute you. He seemed to remember it was what the gladiators said to the emperor before hacking each other to bits for his entertainment.

He sat beside the pool drinking $300 cognac. Buggered if he was going to leave that for the wake. When the sun went down he went inside and passed out on the sofa. He woke up in a room stuffy with sun, having slept for fourteen hours. He couldn't remember the last time he'd managed ten; probably not since his student days. It was a fine time to regain the knack of sleeping in.

He thought about telling his friends, but that could wait. There was nothing they could say or do and he wanted to put off being treated as an endangered species for as long as possible. They would ask, "Have you had a second opinion?" This was the second opinion – and third, fourth, fifth, and sixth. The best people in the field in Australasia, doyens and Young Turks, safe pairs of hands and pushers of the envelope, optimists and pessimists, had read the notes and studied the images. They were unanimous: It's inoperable. It's terminal. Time is very short. We are very sorry.

He would put off telling the kids for as long as possible too. They were both overseas and there was no point in disrupting their busy lives any earlier than necessary. That was how he rationalized it anyway. The real reason was that their grief would be intolerable.

He thought of getting in touch with his ex, just out of curiosity really. Would she feel guilty about the way she dumped him, without warning or sympathy? Would she offer to nurse him? He suspected the answers would be no – she simply didn't do guilt, that one – and yes. She'd probably want to be involved, not because he meant anything to her, but because she would respect the fact that he was dying. But he wouldn't have that. No matter how bad things got, he wouldn't have that.

There was only one person he yearned for, one person he wished he could cling to in the night, but she was out of reach. He'd made sure of that.

TITO IHAKA, JOHAN VAN ROON
Wairarapa, yesterday

Well, would you look at this, thought Johan Van Roon as he nosed his car through the trees into a space between two grimy utes. It was a classic summer scene. A cricket match was in progress on a converted farm paddock, a natural oval bordered by a long, curving stand of macrocarpas on one side and a stream on the other. Brown hills undulated across the horizon. Late afternoon was becoming early evening, and the burn and dazzle of Wairarapa summer had receded to a benign, golden glow.

Van Roon got out of his car, almost planting his boat shoe in a fresh cowpat. Yep, classic Kiwi all right.

He jumped the stream at a point where it narrowed to not much more than a metre, and negotiated a low wire fence to join the scattering of spectators on the boundary. Some boys were having their own game with a plastic bat and tennis ball, while a couple of toddlers tottered like drunks among the female support crew spread over several picnic rugs.

A classic scene, perhaps, but not one in which Van Roon had ever expected to see Tito Ihaka. Yet there he was at square leg, typically the only fielder not wearing a cap or floppy hat. Unless Van Roon's eyes deceived him, Ihaka had shed some weight. It wasn't that he was a shadow of his former self, like the ex-fatsos in diet adverts who pose beside life-sized cardboard dummies of their old, blubbery selves, but there was definitely less of him.

Next over Ihaka was stationed on the long-off boundary, not far from the spectators. Van Roon wandered across. Ihaka was too focused on what was happening in the middle to notice him.

"You've been down here too long, mate," said Van Roon. "I suppose you've taken up pottery as well."

Ihaka glanced over his shoulder. "Detective Inspector Van Roon. What brings you…?" The rest of the sentence was drowned out by a group bellow from the middle. Ihaka's head whipped around. His team-mates were trying to alert him to the imminent arrival of a skier. Ihaka got a sighter, unhurriedly positioned himself and took the catch with a minimum of fuss, the ball seeming to nestle gratefully in his meaty grasp.

The other fielders converged. After a minute or so, Ihaka extracted himself from the back-slapping huddle and walked over to Van Roon. "If I'd fucking spilled that," he growled, "you'd be face-down in a cowpat right now."

Van Roon retreated to a wooden bench a few metres back from the boundary. Nothing's changed, he thought. Ihaka might have spent five years in this backwater, he might have lost a bit of weight and taken up a team sport (and a pretty white, middle-class one at that), but under those cricket whites was the Tito he knew and loved – and had sometimes regretted ever setting eyes on.

A few minutes later Ihaka came on to bowl. Van Roon expected him to try to bowl faster than was sensible for a man of his age and build. In fact, he shuffled in off half a dozen paces and rolled his arm over as gently as if he was bowling to an emotionally fragile eight-year-old in backyard cricket. While his slow-medium trundle seemed, to Van Roon's admittedly untrained eye, to sit up and beg to be flogged to all corners of the ground, it proved too crafty for the opposition. In quick succession three batsmen launched violent swipes and were either clean bowled or caught in the deep. With the youngster bounding in from the other end chipping in with an athletic caught and bowled, the game ended in a clatter of tumbling wickets.

The fall of the final wicket was the cue for a round of hugs and high-fives. Van Roon wished he'd brought a camera:

he knew people who'd pay top dollar for photographic evidence of Ihaka participating in mass man-love, however sheepishly.

The players came off the field, the teams shook hands, chilly bins were looted. Van Roon sniffed the beguiling aroma of sausages on the barbecue and wondered how long he'd have to wait for Ihaka. But less than five minutes later he came over with a bottle of beer in each pocket and a sausage wrapped in white bread and smothered in tomato sauce in each hand.

"So how do you like Wellington?" he said, parking his backside with a thump which made the bench shake and Van Roon think that maybe his eyes had deceived him after all. "And spare me a five-minute bleat about the weather."

"Who needs five minutes?" said Van Roon. "The weather sucks, end of story. Apart from that, Wellington's great."

"And the job?"

"The first few months were interesting in the sense that nightmares can be interesting. It seems to be getting less interesting, thank Christ. And you?"

"What about me?"

"How's it going over here?" said Van Roon. "I mean, it's been five years, right? I didn't think you'd last six months."

Ihaka shrugged. "Time flies when you're asleep. You didn't drive over the Rimutakas to watch me play cricket, so what's up?"

"Missed you too, mate. McGrail wants to see you."

"What the fuck for?"

"He didn't share that with me," said Van Roon. "Said it was confidential."

Ihaka grunted derisively. "What did he say?"

"That he wants you up there ASAP." Van Roon rummaged in the pockets on his cargo shorts and produced a folded sheet of paper. "Your flight details."

Ihaka scanned it. "I'm on a flight first fucking thing in the morning."

Van Roon nodded. "He said – and I'm not making this up; he really did use these words – 'time is of the essence'."

1

Now and again, during what he sometimes thought of as his exile, Tito Ihaka would wonder what he'd be doing at that moment if he'd actually remembered to forget his cellphone.

When the fateful call came, five years earlier almost to the day, he was in a Ponsonby Road bar striving to maintain a Mandela-like air of twinkle-eyed magnanimity as he waited for a woman he'd known for less than half an hour to finish apologizing for what her ancestors had done to his ancestors.

There'd been a time when it amused him to see how many of Maoridom's current social and economic ills he could browbeat contrite Pakeha into accepting the blame for, and how outrageous his demands for redress had to be before they baulked. But white liberal guilt wasn't as much fun as it used to be. In fact, it bored and sometimes even irritated him, all that vicarious shame and retrospective moral certainty over what took place in another time and a different world.

The woman had moved on to imported diseases. She was clearly a bit of a flake, but a certain amount of flakiness had to be expected in that neck of the woods. And she was a cutie all right, standing there gnawing her lower lip and showing off her pierced belly button and a scoop of active cleavage. Ihaka's strategy, based on several optimistic assumptions, was to hang in there nodding gravely for a few more minutes, get another margarita into her, then steer her onto the subject of race relations in the here and now and exactly what conciliatory gestures she was prepared to make to atone for the rapacity of her forebears.

When his cellphone rang, Ihaka automatically plucked it from his jacket pocket. He apologized and went to put it straight back, but the woman wouldn't hear of it. "Answer it," she said. "Please. Do it for me. It's bad luck not to. I really believe that."

"Where the hell are you?" rasped Detective Sergeant Johan Van Roon, once Ihaka's protégé, now his equal, and his closest – some would have said only – friend in the police force. "Did you really think no one would notice you're not here?"

The woman was already surveying the room. Being familiar with the dynamics of the bar and pub scene, she assumed Ihaka would shortly be walking out of her life. But there were plenty more fish in the sea, and she was confident of landing one. She doubted he'd put up much of a fight.

"So how's the party going?" said Ihaka finally.

"Well, it's warming up," said Van Roon, "but then it's been going for three bloody hours. Look, I know he's an old woman, but Christ almighty, Tito, the bloke's put in fifty years."

Senior Sergeant Ted Worsp was retiring after fifty years on the force, having made more comebacks than tuberculosis. He'd been on the brink of retirement for well over a decade, but some interfering prick would always find a little task or project for him, some bullshit community-policing role or a cold case over which he could make an ineffectual fuss. Little or nothing would be achieved, but anyone who happened to ask could be assured that something was indeed being done.

And now that he'd clocked up the half-century, his departure was being marked as if the greatest crime-fighter since Wyatt Earp was bowing out. Everyone from the District Commander down had gathered to give him a big send-off. Everyone except Ihaka.

"Ah, fuck," said Ihaka. The woman interrupted her reconnaissance to give him a deadpan, raised-eyebrows look. It was a look of such pure cynicism that he had to wonder if the whole bleeding-heart thing had been an act. Maybe she didn't really give a shit about Maori obesity and the diabetes epidemic. I suppose I should be flattered, he thought.

He shrugged and grimaced to indicate that the caller was being difficult and half-turned away. "I suppose Boy and Igor are there?"

"Of course they're here," said Van Roon. "Is that what this is all about?"

Three months earlier Ihaka's boss Detective Inspector Finbar McGrail had been promoted to Auckland District Commander.

Over the course of the thirteen years they'd worked together the pair had established a strange, symbiotic, much talked-about relationship. A lot of the gossip that swirled around Auckland Central Police Station concerned McGrail's tolerance, even indulgence, of Ihaka. For a time the popular theory was that McGrail was doing it under sufferance: he had to cover for Ihaka and turn a blind eye to his disregard for protocol and procedure because Ihaka had something on him. Maybe it was the same dark secret that had compelled one of the Royal Ulster Constabulary's rising stars to resign abruptly and emigrate to New Zealand. Sceptics pointed out that McGrail probably got the fuck out of Belfast because he was on an IRA hit list. They also asked how Ihaka, who'd never ventured further afield than Sydney and was hardly a student of international affairs, would know more about McGrail's Northern Ireland past than the recruitment team who vetted him before bringing him to New Zealand.

The rumour-mongers then tilled more obvious and fertile ground: McGrail was a devoted husband and father and a lay preacher in the Presbyterian Church, but behind that pillar of the community façade he was obviously some kind of sleazebag or pervert because people who wore their virtue on their sleeves always were. Ihaka must have found out that McGrail consorted with under-age Oriental prostitutes or rent boys, or visited a dominatrix once a fortnight to have his nuts slapped around with a fly swat.

What gave this version of the theory legs was the catch-22 cynicism – the more virtuous McGrail appeared, the more likely he was to have a depraved secret life – and the fact that even Ihaka's most fervent detractor (and there was hot competition for that title) had to admit he had a nose for deceit and human weakness. It took a few years, but eventually even the hardcore cynics came to accept what those who believed the evidence of their own eyes had argued all along: Ihaka didn't have anything on McGrail because there was nothing to have; McGrail really was as straight and above-board as he appeared to be.

The truth was both more complicated and more prosaic. In his dry Ulster way, McGrail quite enjoyed confounding other people's expectations, but it was hard-headed calculation rather than contrariness that led him to cut Ihaka a liberal amount of slack. Yes, Ihaka was unkempt, overweight, intemperate, unruly, unorthodox and profane, none of which featured on McGrail's checklist of what constituted a model citizen, let alone a police officer. But when it came to operating in the cruel and chaotic shadow-world where the wild beasts roam, he was worth a dozen of those hair-gelled careerists who brought their running shoes to work and took their paperwork home.

McGrail's promotion forced Ihaka to do something he'd been putting off for years: think about his future. He was well aware that the likelihood of McGrail's replacement granting him the same licence was remote, if not non-existent, so he had four choices: he could take the view that all good things must come to an end and adjust to the new reality – i.e. toe the line, pull his head in, and join the queue to kiss the new boss's arse; he could seek a transfer; or he could leave the police force.

Or he could put his hand up for McGrail's old job. Realistically, he was a long shot. He hadn't bothered keeping count of all the toes he'd trodden on, but took it for granted that someone had. He assumed that few among the top brass shared McGrail's appreciation of his particular attributes, and suspected that even some of those who did felt the risks outweighed the rewards. In other words, he wasn't seen as officer material.

He consulted McGrail, who reinforced those perceptions, wondering out loud whether being a detective inspector mightn't really suit him anyway. "Maybe not," replied Ihaka, "but if the alternative is being some wind-up toy's bumboy..."

As was his custom, McGrail didn't respond directly to Ihaka's vulgarity, restricting himself to a slight upward tilt of his right eyebrow. After thirteen years, Ihaka was a highly proficient interpreter of his boss's body language and subtle shifts of expression: he took this to mean that he was being a prize ass, and that the meeting was over because McGrail had better things to do than listen to the braying of a prize ass.

Ihaka got to his feet. "Well, thanks for that. Your enthusiasm is infectious."

McGrail's thin lips twitched briefly, indicating that he found Ihaka's comment hilarious. "Actually, Sergeant," he said to Ihaka's back, "I can offer some practical advice. The hit-and-run. You'll need to have a strategy in place to neutralize that issue, because they'll certainly tackle you on it."

The hit-and-run, as everyone but Ihaka referred to it, had taken place a year earlier. A middle-aged woman on an early-morning jog had died after being hit by a car. The car, which had been stolen from the Auckland Airport car park, was dumped and torched in South Auckland. Everything pointed to it being a boy racer, but Ihaka's renowned gut instinct told him otherwise. He suspected the woman's husband had something to do with it, and wanted him to be the focus of the investigation even though there was no concrete evidence to support this theory.

After six fruitless months McGrail decided to downgrade the investigation and redeploy resources. Ihaka wouldn't let go. The husband hired a politically connected, media-savvy QC who got to the minister. Word came down the pipe to McGrail: bring your attack dog to heel.

Which he did, with unusual vehemence. (McGrail's normal mode of censure was impassive sarcasm, mild only in the delivery.) It was one of the few times in their long relationship when he seemed to take Ihaka's lone-wolf behaviour personally. What Ihaka didn't know was that McGrail was closing in on his goal of becoming Auckland District Commander and lay awake at night running through scenarios which could prevent that happening. Almost all of them involved Ihaka.

Ihaka paused in the doorway. "Oh yeah, the hit-and-run," he said, making the speech marks sign. "They'll make a fucking meal of that. Any brilliant ideas?"

McGrail's expression became even more dubious. "As in turning the negative into a positive?" He shook his head. "That's probably a bridge too far. If I was in your shoes, I'd focus on damage limitation."

It all went pretty much exactly as McGrail had anticipated. Ihaka never got around to devising a strategy to neutralize the issue. When it came up at the interview, instead of dealing with it quickly by admitting error and declaring that he'd learned from the experience, he said he still thought he was right. The panel chairman observed that Ihaka seemed to be missing the point, which was his unprofessional conduct rather than who was right and who was wrong. With all due respect, replied Ihaka, although respect wasn't evident in his demeanour, that mindset was another example of priorities being arse-about-face.

McGrail's replacement was a detective sergeant from North Shore, Tony "Boy" Charlton, who was six years Ihaka's junior.

It was bad enough being overlooked, worse that he now had to report to the guy who'd got the job, but what Ihaka really couldn't stomach was that Charlton was everything he wasn't – youthful, good-looking, polished, politically adept, destined for stardom. He was going all the way to the top; it was just a matter of how quickly and by which route. Unfortunately for Ihaka, Charlton's chosen route ran slap-bang through his career.

Charlton had been given his nickname by an Aussie cop over on secondment. "Boy" Charlton was an Australian folk hero of the 1920s, a swimmer who set world records and won an Olympic gold medal. The famous public swimming pool in the Sydney Domain overlooking the Woolloomooloo Finger Wharf was named after him.

Ihaka was thrilled to learn, in the course of a moan to a contact in the New South Wales Police Service, that the Boy

Charlton Pool was a renowned homosexual hangout and pick-up spot. He'd disseminated this information far and wide but the take-up was disappointing, perhaps because Charlton's wife was as good-looking as he was. The fact that Charlton was a lust object for some female officers and administrative staff might also have had something to do with it.

One step behind Charlton came Detective Sergeant Ron "Igor" Firkitt, a shaven-headed hulk with a chain-smoker's poisoned well of a mouth. Some likened their bond to that between McGrail and Ihaka, but there was no comparison. Charlton and Firkitt were rusted onto each other, hence Firkitt's nickname referring to the shambling monster who does his master's dirty work in Gothic horror stories.

Given that Ihaka regarded Charlton as personifying the police force's transformation into an organization in which he didn't fit, he might have been expected to find common cause with Firkitt, who was even more old-school than he was. It didn't work out that way. Perhaps there was an element of two bulls in one paddock, of Auckland Central not being big enough for both, but from day one Firkitt made it clear he wasn't interested in cooperation. Whereas Charlton treated Ihaka with studied politeness, Firkitt never missed an opportunity to remind him that there had been a power shift and now he was on the outer. Ihaka assumed the aim was to isolate him, and that Firkitt, as always, was doing his master's bidding.

"That's got nothing to do with it," said Ihaka. "I just forgot."

"What a load of shit," said Van Roon crisply. "So are you coming?"

Ihaka turned around. The floor space previously occupied by the woman had been taken over by a couple of young Asian guys who smiled shyly at him.

"Yeah," he said. "Friday night in Ponsonby, though. It might take a while to get a cab."

"If you have any trouble, give us a ring and I'll come and get you," said Van Roon. "I'm on OJ tonight."

Ihaka looked around. The woman was over in the far corner, talking animatedly to a handsome Polynesian who had the pale glow of minor celebrity.

He drained his beer and headed for the exit.

When Ihaka walked into the inner-city pub bar where the farewell function was beginning to wind down, Firkitt sucked even more fiercely on the unlit cigarette he'd been toying with for several minutes. "Well, fuck me," he said. "Look what the cat dragged in."

Behind him, Charlton was taking his turn to butter up Worsp. He paused in mid-sentence, glancing over his shoulder to see what Firkitt was talking about. "Must be a mighty big cat," he said.

Worsp, who had a backside that wobbled in the wind, broke into a silent, heaving chuckle. "Bloody typical," he said. "Still, better late than never, I suppose."

"That's one way of looking at it," said Charlton. "Another would be: better never than late."

He was so pleased with his witticism that he shook Worsp's hand for the fourth time that day. "I really have to hit the road, Ted, but don't be a stranger. It'd be a crime to let all that wisdom and experience go to waste."

Even though he'd been lapping up free drinks and flattery all night, Worsp hadn't had his fill of either. "Just quietly," he purred, "I suspect life after Ted will come as a rude shock to some of these chaps. But you know me, sir, the old warhorse. When the bugle sounds, I start pawing the ground."

"You've been a good soldier, mate," said Charlton, his voice husky with camaraderie. "All the very best."

Firkitt dropped a rough hand on Worsp's shoulder. "Good on you, champ. Take it easy now."

They watched Worsp lumber off in search of someone who hadn't shouted him a drink. "Don't be a stranger?" said Firkitt incredulously. "A good soldier? Give me a fucking break."

Charlton shrugged. "Sometimes it doesn't hurt to sprinkle a little sugar. Needless to say, I rely on you to make life hell for anyone who encourages that old fraud to come within five kilometres of Central."

"You bet."

"Right, I'm off. Are you sticking around?"

"Not for long," said Firkitt. "Looks like she's running out of steam."

"Well," said Charlton, "should you happen to find yourself *tête-à-tête* with our brown bro…"

"What the fuck does that mean?"

"If you talk to him."

"Oh, I'll be talking to him all right," said Firkitt. "And I'll tell you what, I won't be sprinkling any fucking sugar."

"Glad to hear it," said Charlton. "The man's overweight. A little sugar is the last thing he needs."

Ihaka was beginning to relax. Maybe this wouldn't be a complete horror show after all. He'd done the decent thing by Worsp, biting his tongue when the old prong greeted him with, "Let me guess – your mother had another fall?" He'd bought Worsp a Scotch and dry and let him crap on about how the troops at Auckland Central would soon discover the meaning of the word "indispensable". He'd remained calm when Worsp suggested – "Just putting it out there" – that maybe they hadn't seen the last of him because Boy seemed reluctant to let him "ride into the sunset". And he'd shaken hands and said all the right things as if he meant it.

Yes, he felt a little nauseous but, at the same time, quietly proud of himself, like someone who has eaten something disgusting to win a dare.

Charlton had left so that was another plus, and Firkitt had either taken off with him or was outside having a smoke. McGrail, of course, was long gone which was also a relief: now that they didn't have a day-to-day working relationship, he wasn't all that comfortable around the Ulsterman. It was like a self-fulfilling prophecy: Ihaka was keeping his distance from McGrail on the assumption that McGrail, now that he was district commander, would want to keep his distance from him.

In fact, leaning on the bar with his sixth beer of the evening chatting to Van Roon and Beth Greendale, who'd left the force a few years earlier to have kids, Ihaka was in danger of enjoying himself.

Firkitt entered the conversation like a home invasion. "Well, well, fucking well," he said. "Look who's here."

Ihaka sighed. "Igor."

"You can knock that shit off for a start," said Firkitt.

Ihaka asked Greendale, "Do you two know each other?"

"We've met," said Greendale, giving Firkitt a tight smile. "How are you finding Central?"

"Since you ask, it's Fred Karno's fucking circus," he said. "But we'll sort it out."

"We being you and Charlton, I assume," said Greendale, "and the circus being everybody else?"

Firkitt grinned, a sight that resembled an artist's impression of a black hole. "Got it in one, darling."

"If there's one thing on God's green earth I'm not," said Greendale, "it's your darling."

"Is that right?" said Firkitt. "Well, when you're back in the suburbs changing nappies and wiping arses, it won't matter a damn either way, will it?" He turned to Ihaka.

"Fucking class act you are, showing up three and a half hours late."

"What do you care?"

"I couldn't give a shit," said Firkitt. "I'm just pointing it out. That's why you never had a dog's show of making DI – you've got no fucking idea."

"Whereas you, on the other hand —" said Van Roon.

Firkitt eyed up Van Roon. "The difference is I know my limitations. Or, to put it another way, I don't have my head up my big, fat, brown arse."

"There's no room," said Ihaka. "You'd have to ask Boy to remove his cock first."

"Well, you'd know all about that," said Firkitt. "How many years did you bend over for Creeping Jesus?"

"Listen, guys," said Greendale, "it's been great to catch up, but I think I'll be running along. When you've been out in the suburbs changing nappies for a few years, this sort of gay banter doesn't do it for you any more."

"See you," said Firkitt without looking at her.

"Hang on, Beth," said Ihaka, "me and Igor have run out of things to talk about."

"Like fuck we have," said Firkitt. "I'm just getting started."

"Give it a rest, Firkitt," said Van Roon. "This isn't the time or the place."

Firkitt pulled a cry-baby face. "This isn't the time or the place," he whined. "I'll be the judge of that. It so happens I've got some stuff I want to share with big boy here, so feel free to bugger off."

"You might as well," Ihaka told the others. "This is like therapy for him. It'll get worse before it gets better."

Having had a brief but vivid reminder of why she didn't miss being a cop one little bit, Greendale couldn't wait to get out of there. Van Roon offered to see her to her car.

Firkitt was in full, toxic flow before they were even out of earshot: "Do you ever think about what a fucking loser you are? I mean, mate, you had everything in your favour: you were the man on the spot, you'd put in the hard yards, you had the new DC on your side. On top of all that you're a Maori and, as we all know, it's not a level playing field these days. Three capable white blokes and a deadshit Maori go for a job, Hori gets it every time. That's what the fucking world's come to. So you have to ask the question: what sort of a cunt would you have to be to have all that going for you and still blow it?"

Firkitt rocked back on his heels, hands in pockets, awaiting Ihaka's response with an expectant half-smile. He's had a few, thought Ihaka, but he's not pissed. He knows what he's doing: he's seeing how far he can push me.

"I've got to take a piss," said Ihaka.

"Me too."

Firkitt followed Ihaka into the toilet, hovering on his shoulder. "You know what really fucked you, right? Harassing that poor bastard whose missus got cleaned up by a boy racer. Christ, that would have to be the dumbest fucking thing I've ever heard of. Even you brownies can't get away with that sort of shit. I mean, you can have your little sluts on tap, bone them up the arse with a baton if you want. That's fine; we understand you people like that sort of thing. But deciding you don't need a scrap of evidence to know some eastern suburbs big shot took out his wife, following him around, barging in on him at some ungodly hour, fuck me." The diatribe ended in a jarring cackle.

Ihaka registered that none of the stalls were occupied. He stepped up to the weeping wall. Firkitt followed suit, still snorting with amusement. As Firkitt unzipped, Ihaka threw a hard, fast elbow, spearing it into the side of his jaw, just below the ear. Firkitt bounced off the wall, his knees gave way, and he slid face first into the trough of the urinal. Ihaka unbuttoned his jeans and took a long, leisurely piss. The drainage flow encountered an obstacle, but the obstacle didn't seem to notice.

Ihaka washed and dried his hands and walked out of the toilet. Firkitt still hadn't moved.

He left the bar without looking left or right and got a taxi home. Home was an Edwardian bungalow in a quiet cul-de-sac near Eden Park, one of a number of houses in the streets between Dominion and Sandringham Roads which were built for troops returning from the Turkish campaign. He went into his shed, found a hammer, and pulverized his cellphone, partly because he wanted to be incommunicado, partly because he blamed the cellphone for the way the evening had turned out. He had a ham and cheese sandwich, made a thermos of coffee, and threw a few items into an overnight bag. Forty minutes after leaving Worsp's farewell, he reversed his car out of the drive and headed for the harbour bridge. He was almost certainly over the limit but his head was clear. Besides, he firmly believed that he drove better with a few beers under his belt than most civilians did stone-cold sober.

Ihaka went north to his family's bach, an authentically dilapidated pole house at Tauranga Bay on the south head of Whangaroa Harbour, where he spent the next thirty-six hours sleeping, fishing and sitting in the sun. He didn't think about the Firkitt incident or the likely consequences because he was a fatalist and it wasn't in his nature to fret over things that couldn't be undone or potential developments that he couldn't control. On Sunday afternoon he drove back to Auckland. The checkout girl at the Victoria Park supermarket was the first person he'd spoken to since getting out of the taxi.

There were twenty-three messages on his answerphone. If there'd been three or four he might have listened to them. He showered and had a couple of beers while he marinated some chicken thighs, scrubbed new potatoes and prepared a salad. When he was ready to barbecue, he switched to red wine.

Ihaka was a latecomer to wine, as he was to cooking. Wine had been something other people drank and their rituals and palaver stirred up the dormant class warrior in him.

Recently, though, he'd begun jettisoning some of his fixed ideas, particularly the ones he'd carted around since his state-house childhood. What was the point of trying to improve your lot in life if you wouldn't let go of the habits and prejudices that epitomized everything you were trying to outgrow – fast food, slop beer, bad attitudes, wilful ignorance? A bloke just had to keep in mind that wine wasn't meant to be drunk quite as fast or in quite the same quantity as beer.

He ate dinner on the veranda with family noises floating over the back fence. Lately, he'd also revised his attitude to other people's kids. They used to be bratty little attention-seekers; now they were a reminder that the normal world was a very different place from the war zone he worked in. In the normal world people did an honest day's work and watched their kids grow up and died of natural causes.

He'd just finished cleaning up when the doorbell rang. As a rule he ignored the doorbell on the basis that the few people he didn't mind turning up unannounced would just let themselves in, while the rest could fuck off. Sensing this caller wouldn't be easily discouraged, he went to the door. His visitor was the Auckland Police District Commander, Superintendent Finbar McGrail.

They contemplated each other for a few seconds. "The fact you're not wearing a tie tells me this is a social call," said Ihaka. "But since when did you make social calls?"

"It's not a social call."

Ihaka stood aside to allow McGrail into his house for the very first time. They went down the corridor to the kitchen/dining room. McGrail's eyebrows arched as he took in the house-proud orderliness, the spotless bench, the fresh basil on the windowsill above the sink, and the wine glass and open bottle of Pinot Noir on the table.

"If you weren't here, Sergeant, I'd assume I was in the wrong house. I was warned to expect squalor."

"You've been talking to Van Roon, right? The day he made DS, he swore he wouldn't set foot in here again until I'd had the place steam-cleaned."

"That was two years ago."

"Shit, so it was," said Ihaka. "I must get him around some time."

"What brought about the change?"

Ihaka shrugged. "Personal growth and development. Either that or a mid-life crisis."

"A bit early for that, isn't it?"

"Could be a bit late. My old man dropped dead at fifty-one." He pulled a chair out from the kitchen table. "Take a seat. Can I get you something – a juice or a cup of tea? Or a wine?"

McGrail, who was virtually teetotal, sat down. "I'm fine, thank you. You obviously know why I'm here."

Ihaka sat opposite him and poured himself another glass of wine. "Well, yes and no. I know why someone's here. I'm surprised it's you."

"Firstly," said McGrail, "Charlton can't deal with this because of his relationship with Firkitt. Secondly, it reflects the seriousness with which we're treating this matter.

Thirdly… Well, frankly, Sergeant, this isn't going to go well for you, and I wanted you to hear that from me. Charlton wants you charged with assault."

"He'd have a hard time making that stick," said Ihaka. "No witnesses, Firkitt's word against mine."

"What's your version?"

"He followed me into the dunny mouthing off, had a bit of a turn, fell over, and clonked his head on the way down."

"Really?" said McGrail. "So why didn't you go to his aid?"

"Because he's a cunt. I wouldn't piss on him if his hair was on fire."

"Funny you should say that," said McGrail. "He claims that's exactly what you did do."

Ihaka took a gulp of wine to stop himself laughing. "Well, he's wrong. But next time he finds himself face-down in the pisser, he might want to be upstream rather than downstream."

A pained expression rippled across McGrail's face. "I'd have to say, Sergeant, that's a somewhat threadbare account. Fortunately for you, however, a witness for the defence has come forward."

"And who might that be?"

"Ms Greendale. According to her, Firkitt was going out of his way to be provocative…"

"What's new?"

"An element of racism, by the sound of it. Not for the first time, you're fortunate that your friends look out for you more than you look out for yourself. Ms Greendale would be a very credible witness, should it come to that. But it won't come to that. No one emerges from this sorry affair with any credit, so it's in all our interests to put it quietly to rest."

"But? There is a but, isn't there?"

McGrail nodded. "Charlton's fallback was to put you through a full disciplinary process with a view to demotion or dismissal. I pointed out that such a process could hardly ignore Firkitt's conduct or Ms Greendale's evidence, so he might very well end up killing two birds with that stone, one of them being his pet raptor. His final, non-negotiable position was that you leave the Auckland district, with immediate effect." McGrail looked at his watch and stood up.

"So that's that, eh?" said Ihaka. "I'm gone?"

"Well," said McGrail, "one of you has got to go, and I don't mean either you or Firkitt. I mean either you or Charlton. That's the way he's framing it, and I'm afraid you don't even have a starter's chance in that contest." He looked down at Ihaka, who was staring into his glass, swirling the wine. "You know what's so galling about this: Charlton and Firkitt have won. This is precisely the outcome they wanted."

"Yeah," said Ihaka. "I worked that out a while ago."

"So why the devil play into their hands?"

Ihaka looked up. "Maybe I've had enough. Maybe I also wanted this outcome – or something like it."

"Good God, man," spluttered McGrail, "you could've just put in a request for a transfer."

Ihaka smiled. "Where's the fun in that? Besides, just more paperwork."

McGrail shook his head in wonderment. "The Lord's not the only one who moves in mysterious ways. So do you have somewhere in mind?"

Ihaka picked up the wine bottle and studied the label. "Where exactly is Martinborough?"

2

It didn't occur to Ihaka to wonder if promotion and the passing of time would have changed Finbar McGrail. Why would it? During the years they'd worked together, McGrail had changed so little that you had to wonder if he'd discovered the secret of eternal early middle age. Apart from crow's feet at the corners of his eyes and the odd grey hair, he looked pretty much the same the night he came to Ihaka's house to cut him loose as he did the day they met.

There was no magic formula. McGrail stayed trim thanks to relentless jogging and an austere lifestyle. And while some sneered, behind his back, at his drab attire – he had half a dozen cheap suits in various shades of grey, and wore short-sleeved white polyester shirts all year round, donning a cardigan knitted by his wife when it got cold – Ihaka had a sneaking (and undeclared) admiration for his boss's lack of vanity. Although Ihaka despised meanness and operated on the principle that if you spend more than you earn, someone will eventually bring it to your attention, he soon realized that McGrail wasn't averse to spending money per se. He was just averse to spending it on himself.

So when Ihaka was shown into McGrail's office he couldn't help gawking at the sleek, elegant figure who emerged from behind the desk with a smile and an outstretched hand.

No two ways about it: McGrail had had a makeover. He'd gone management.

Not a trace remained of the public-service clerk look – the geek specs, the blind man's haircut, the man-made fibres and pastel shoes from Asian sweatshops. His hair had been cut by someone who didn't think the object of the exercise was to remove as much as possible as quickly as possible. He was wearing Armani glasses, a white linen shirt with French cuffs, greenstone cufflinks, a navy-blue suit with a delicate pinstripe which fitted so perfectly it had to be tailor-made, and a plush, rich-red silk tie. Ihaka was no expert but he was pretty sure the watch on McGrail's left wrist was the same one Leonardo DiCaprio had been endorsing in the in-flight magazine. In his former life McGrail had been perfectly happy with cheap digital sports watches that looked as though they were designed by the people who make the plastic junk which falls out of Christmas crackers.

Equally amazingly, he'd put on weight. The beautifully cut suit couldn't hide the swell of paunch, and a fold of throat flab bulged over his collar. His previously chalky complexion now had the pink tinge common among self-indulgent men of a certain age.

Seemingly oblivious to the scrutiny, McGrail shook hands, led his visitor to a sofa, and evinced close interest in life in Wairarapa.

"Well, it certainly looks as if it agrees with you, Sergeant," said McGrail, almost jovially. "Would I be correct in thinking you've lost weight?"

"A bit. I ate like a horse when I first got down there because there was nothing else to do. After a while I found other ways to fill in the time."

"Such as?"

"Tramping, fishing, hunting, cricket – you know, manly outdoor stuff."

56

"Good for you. I, on the other hand…"

"Well, I wasn't going to mention it…"

McGrail sighed. "My knees went wonky and the doctors banned me from jogging. I also have to do a fair amount of networking, most of which seems to take place in restaurants. I've discovered that things which supposedly aren't good for us are rather more enjoyable than some of the things which supposedly are."

"Welcome to the human race. Is it also a job requirement to dress like Lord Muck?"

McGrail leaned back, smiling thinly. "Lord Muck, eh? I haven't heard of him for a while. Does my get-up offend you, Sergeant?"

Ihaka shook his head. "I just thought you didn't have a vain bone in your body."

"Don't dwell on the externals," said McGrail. "The fundamentals haven't changed. But I'm in this job to make a difference, and if wearing a nice suit and lunching with politicians helps me do that, so be it. I didn't invent this world, but I have to function in it."

"I don't," said Ihaka.

"You're not pleased to be back in the big city?"

"Well, it's an okay place to visit…"

"But you wouldn't want to work here? One would almost think you've undergone a Damascene conversion."

"Sounds painful."

"Well, it certainly can be for others. But I get the message: you're wondering why on earth, given the resources of the Auckland district, you've had to rush up here at such short notice. Remember Hamish Bartley?"

"The QC, right?" said Ihaka. "He represented that prick whose wife got run down."

McGrail nodded. "Last Friday Bartley took me to lunch at his club. The Northern Club."

"I didn't think it would be the Panmure RSA."

"I'm pleased to see the heartland hasn't softened your sense of humour," said McGrail. "Anyway, we had a pleasant lunch and talked about everything except what we were there for, as you tend to do when a third party is paying. When the coffee arrived, he finally got to the point: Christopher Lilywhite wants to see you."

"The guy whose wife…"

"Got run down. Yes, that Christopher Lilywhite."

Ihaka sat back, staring at McGrail. "Why the fuck would he, of all people, want to see me, of all people?"

"Because he's dying."

The doorbell was answered by a thirtyish woman, shapeless in baggy track pants and an oversized T-shirt. Her hair was clipped into an untidy holding pattern, and red-rimmed eyes and nostrils glowed angrily amidst the pallor. Before he could introduce himself, she said accusingly, "You're Ihaka."

He nodded.

"You're the last person who should be here."

"It wasn't my idea."

Her head vibrated with pent-up anger. "He's got this weird idea about making peace with you. I tried to talk him out of it, but he wouldn't even discuss it. I suppose that's his privilege, but he's dreaming if he thinks I'm going to be polite to you." Her voice rose. "How you can still be a police officer is beyond me – you behaved like an absolute fucking Nazi. You hounded a man who was at the end of his tether, and what you put him through is the reason he's back there dying right in front of my eyes."

"Are you a doctor?" asked Ihaka politely.

"No," she snapped. "I'm a daughter." She turned and walked away. "The room at the end of the corridor," she said over her shoulder. "You can let yourself out."

Ihaka walked down the corridor into a sunny living room. There was a well-stocked cocktail cabinet, a wall-mounted television, a sideboard stacked with framed family photographs, and several paintings including the inevitable Central Otago landscape. The flat surfaces were abloom.

Christopher Lilywhite lay on one of two long black leather sofas, his head sunk in a bank of pillows. Although the room was warm, almost stuffy, he wore an old-fashioned heavy dressing gown and had a cashmere blanket pulled up to his chest. He wasn't as gaunt as Ihaka had expected, but the year-round playboy tan had faded, exposing skin the colour of office equipment.

Lilywhite put a bookmark in a slim paperback and found a space for it among the bottles and glasses and pill containers on the coffee table beside him.

"*The Outsider* by Albert Camus," he said in a smaller voice than the smug honk Ihaka remembered. "I'm trying to work my way through the books I always meant to read, but never got around to. I do find myself drawn to the short ones, though."

"That's understandable," said Ihaka. "How long have you got?"

"Put it this way: we're counting in weeks now. I hope Sandy – my daughter – didn't give you too hard a time. I asked her to be civil, but got the distinct impression that that was one dying man's request which wasn't going to be granted."

Ihaka shrugged. "I've had worse."

"Would you care for a drink?" asked Lilywhite. "That cabinet over there contains most alcoholic beverages known to man. I also nagged Sandy into making a pot of coffee."

"Well, seeing you both went to the trouble."

Ihaka poured himself a cup of plunger coffee, added sugar, and sat down in the visitor's chair pulled up in front of Lilywhite's sofa.

"I'm sorry you got run out of town," said Lilywhite. "Of course, at the time I was delighted."

"I wasn't unhappy with how it panned out," said Ihaka. "And if that's the worst thing you've got on your conscience, you should be at peace with yourself."

Lilywhite managed a weak smile. "Good point. We'll come to my conscience shortly. I don't think you'll leave here feeling you've wasted an afternoon, but could you do me a favour before we get down to business: why were you so sure I killed my wife?"

"Instinct, experience, process of elimination. Once you take away the baby bashers and the psychos and the dumb-fuck trash out of their tiny minds on drugs or booze, most murders boil down to sex or money. If a marriage is made in heaven, neither of those things comes into it. If it isn't, one or the other or both generally do." He paused. "Okay, a man who's used to getting away with things has a rich wife. He likes the rich part, but she doesn't do it for him any more. So he gets rid of her making it look like an accident, gets the money all to himself and, after a decent interval, moves the girlfriend into the master bedroom. That's pretty much how it went down, right?"

"But the outcome doesn't prove the theory," said Lilywhite. "If Joyce had died of natural causes, I still would've got all the money and ended up with someone else."

"Who said anything about proof? I didn't have any proof; that's why the investigation got canned. Come back to the key question: were you happily married? Your wife's friends thought so because that's how your wife saw it – or chose to see it – and they got her version. Your mates said all the right things, but I've been lied to by experts. A couple of them who tried to tell me it was all sweetness and light sounded like they'd learned the lines off by heart. Why would they have to do that? The truth should speak for itself. I've also had to deal with people who've had someone precious just vanish from their lives. Grief is a hard act, and you didn't ring true. And then there were those fucking boy racers. Boy racers race, they don't steal cars to go and see where the rich folks live. If they steal a car, they thrash the shit out of it for a few hours, then dump it. There were street races all over town that night, but no one saw the Subaru. Boy racers aren't master criminals, either. Most of them are fucking dimwits who've sucked up too many petrol fumes. They couldn't keep a hit-and-run secret if their lives depended on it. The bottom line is that if boy racers mowed down your wife, we would've found them inside a week."

"When you put it like that, it seems obvious. Why weren't you able to persuade your colleagues?"

"In one corner you've got a well-connected, white, middle-aged businessman, in the other a couple of phantom boy racers. For some people that's a pretty easy call."

Lilywhite nodded slowly. "I could say that's a rather cynical point of view, but I suppose you'd come right back and call me naïve – or disingenuous. So you still think I got away with murder?"

"I wouldn't be here otherwise. You tell me something. What did your friends, particularly your wife's friends, think when you hooked up with her PA?"

"Well, some of them were a bit stiff-necked about it but a decent interval, to use your phrase, had elapsed."

"Bullshit," said Ihaka. "You were sneaking her in here long before you went public." Lilywhite blinked in surprise. Ihaka gave him a quizzical look. "You think I stopped watching you just because the minister threw a wobbly?"

"Did you report that?"

"Jesus, that would've got *me* in the shit, not you. By that stage the investigation was on the back-burner and I was under strict orders to stay away from you. Just mentioning your name was enough to get me in strife. No, it was just for my benefit."

"The quiet, private satisfaction of knowing you were right and your critics were wrong?"

Ihaka shook his head. "No, more the relief of knowing I hadn't fucked up my career over nothing."

Lilywhite subsided into the pillows, closing his eyes. A minute went by, then another. Finally, his eyes opened and locked onto Ihaka: "There's one condition attached to what I'm about to tell you: that you keep it from my children until I'm gone. Beyond that, well, anything you can do would be much appreciated. Agreed?"

"Agreed."

"You're right, of course. I had Joyce killed." He tapped his chest. "In a funny sort of way, the guilt has helped me come to terms with this. Why should I have what I took from her?"

"So who killed her?"

"Well, there's the catch. I don't know."

3

Christopher Lilywhite made his confession as if he had all the time in the world. He began at the beginning.

In 1972 Joyce Herbertson came down from Dargaville, where her father dug holes for the Ministry of Works, to attend Auckland Teachers' Training College. She lived in Royal Oak with her aunt and uncle, who mowed sports fields for the city council.

A friend of her aunt's worked at Smith and Caughey's in Queen Street, where one got to fawn over a better class of person. She took a shine to shy little Joyce, who'd been brought up to be respectful of her elders no matter how ghastly they were, and wangled her a part-time job in the Manchester department.

Joyce studied hard, she played competitive netball, she went to church every Sunday, even paying attention to the sermons. Her aunt soon gave up stealing peeks at the diary which Joyce wrote up in bed each night and kept under her pillow. Although she rationalized this invasion of privacy as *in loco parentis* concern for her niece's welfare, it was nothing more than prurience, and in that regard Joyce was a disappointment. After two anticlimactic months her aunt decided she got more of a tweak from a Mills and Boon.

Now and again Joyce permitted herself to dream, but what she expected to do was go back to Dargaville, teach at the primary school she'd attended, and couple up with a nice young man with reasonable prospects, a steady sort who'd go on to be a deputy this or assistant that or a sub-branch manager. Her parents would want him to be a churchgoer, but that wasn't a sticking point for her. After all, if you took out the miracles – the virgin birth, and take up thy bed and walk, and on the third day he rose again (all the slightly hard to believe stuff) – and the ritual – the prayers and psalms, the stale wafers and communion wine – it really boiled down to being a good person and treating people the way you'd like to be treated. She would never have voiced this thought, but it often occurred to her as she slid to her knees to drone along with the rest of the congregation: wouldn't it have pretty much the same effect if they dispensed with the Father, Son, and Holy Ghost and just drummed the Golden Rule into everyone?

She got a job at Remuera Primary School and moved out of her aunt and uncle's place into a flat in Meadowbank, sharing with a couple of girls from her netball team. One of them was in her second year of a Bachelor of Education at Auckland University. People were always telling Joyce she had a good brain, so she enrolled at university and paid her flatmate's rent for a fortnight in return for her notes and essays from the year before. She worked even harder, played social netball, and went to church every second or third Sunday. She gave up keeping a diary. There just didn't seem much point in depriving herself of fifteen minutes' sleep to record the fact that today had been pretty much the same as yesterday and the day before.

She went out with Stuart, an arts student she met in the university library. Stuart wrote hectoring poems about the downtrodden masses and having to get by on a B bursary, and studied her minutely as she read them. She developed a routine of ambiguous sighs and shakes of the head which seemed to satisfy him. They went to gloomy films with subtitles and had long pashing sessions back in his room at the hostel that left her with bruised lips and an aching jaw. The pashing escalated to fondling through clothes, then to hand-jobs for him and less than reciprocal ferreting between the legs for her. Even though Stuart was the one getting his rocks off, he pressed her to go all the way and dumped her when she said not yet. A fortnight later she drank too much sparkling wine at a party at her place, and gifted her cherry to a gatecrasher who made her laugh.

She awoke with the worst hangover ever and upset with herself, not so much for losing her virginity but for giving it away to someone who wouldn't appreciate it. She went to church, which made her hangover worse. Maybe her other flatmate, who'd quit teaching and got a sales job with Air New Zealand which enabled her to lead parallel sex lives in Auckland and Sydney, was right: there was going out with a guy, up to and including having sex with him, which actually wasn't that big a deal; and there was falling in love and getting married, which was. That was the bit you only wanted to do once.

She got back on with Stuart, who pretended not to notice that something had happened to her virginity. She'd thought that sleeping with her boyfriend, as opposed to an amusing gatecrasher, would feel better in both senses, but it didn't seem to work like that. It was good having a boyfriend, though. One-night stands were like Chinese takeaways: quick and convenient. One moment you were laughing at a corny joke, next thing you were on your back. When you woke up, the guy was gone and you could get on with things, as if it was a day like any other. She knew people who pretty much lived on Chinese takeaways. She didn't want to do that. She'd heard guys talk about girls who did.

By the time Joyce was into the third and final year of her degree, her expectations had changed. Back in Dargaville for Christmas and New Year, she understood why being in prison was called doing time. Nothing much happened, the hours crawled by, then you turned on the TV. She got her flatmate's boyfriend to ring up pretending to be the principal, and told her parents she had to go back to work early to help him sort out some unspecified problems. They were quietly proud – not surprised, mind you, but proud – that he'd called on their Joyce in his hour of need. She drove south in her Morris 1100 with the certain knowledge that she would not go back to teach at her old primary school, and would not marry a local boy, whatever his prospects.

One Friday night Joyce and Stuart met Penny, the flatmate who worked for Air New Zealand, at a cheap and cheerful Italian in Parnell. She arrived with a guy she'd picked up at the pub. Christopher worked for a company that exported kiwi fruit; he travelled overseas on business and drove a company car. He was different from the guys she knew: Stuart, the bleeding poet, and her friends' sporty, self-satisfied boyfriends, and the various goofs who took pride in aspiring to being nothing more than a bit of a lad.

By upbringing and instinct Joyce was a National Party supporter, but she kept her views to herself, partly because she wasn't an ideologue and partly to avoid upsetting Stuart, who was an anarcho-communist. As far as Joyce could make out, that meant he'd quite like to eliminate every political figure who wasn't an anarcho-communist, starting with the prime minister, Rob Muldoon, whom he wanted to eliminate even more than Augusto Pinochet and all the whites in South Africa. Christopher turned out to be a Muldoon admirer but, unlike Joyce, wasn't inclined to soft-pedal his views to keep the peace. Unlike Stuart, he could argue about politics without losing his temper.

Stuart got flushed and sweaty; he raised his voice and jabbed his finger; he called Christopher "a fucking Nazi". Christopher told him to grow up. Joyce didn't know where to look. Penny asked if they could please change the subject. A waiter came over to remind Stuart that he was in a restaurant.

Stuart told Joyce they were out of there. Without even thinking about it, she said, "See you later."

"People couldn't believe it when I started going out with Joyce," said Lilywhite. "Understandable, really. My previous girlfriends had been either private-school princesses or party girls like Joyce's flatmate. Suddenly here was this small-town girl, this rather earnest primary schoolteacher, not bad-looking by any means but not someone who stopped the conversation when she walked into a room. Put it this way: my mates weren't green with envy.

"What they didn't get was that her difference was the big attraction. I went to a private school. I'd been going out with precious, empty-headed little bitches since I was fifteen. Joyce might have been unworldly, in the sense of not being sophisticated, but she came from the real world. She wasn't stupid; she read newspapers as opposed to glossy magazines; you could have a conversation with her that wasn't about things that don't matter. The party girls were fun but, let's face it, you don't take them home to meet your parents. Well, I certainly didn't. My father was one of the Canterbury Lilywhites – first four ships, Christ's College, all that stuff. He gave me two pieces of advice about women: the most important quality in a prospective wife is loyalty; and while you don't want a prude, if you marry a sexual animal, she'll end up humiliating you. That's a direct quote.

"Joyce and my parents got on well. She was polite to the point of being deferential. They liked that, and they liked the fact that she obviously adored me. Of course, they weren't too thrilled about her background, but I guess it was a case of two out of three ain't bad. And while appearances can be deceptive in this regard, she didn't come across as someone who couldn't get enough sex.

"The idea was that Joyce would keep working till she got pregnant, but the Lilywhite juice is high-octane stuff. Once we put our minds to it impregnation ensues like night follows day. By the time we got back from the honeymoon she was pregnant. Six months after Matthew was born she was pregnant again. Our marriage was very much like my parents' – I was the breadwinner; I went off to work, Joyce stayed home to look after the kids, keep the house immaculate, and have dinner waiting for me when I returned from slaying dragons. Everything revolved around me, and that was that. We'd go to dinner parties where wives got cross-eyed drunk and made bloody fools of themselves or played footsie under the table or picked fights with their husbands, and I'd thank God I'd had the good sense to marry Joyce. It wasn't long before my mates, who'd been a bit patronizing about her, were telling me what a lucky man I was.

"Without over-egging the pudding, we chugged along very happily for twenty-odd years. With the benefit of hindsight you could question whether a woman as able and energetic as Joyce could be truly happy in that arrangement but, as I'm sure you know, Sergeant, lots of able and energetic women are. Bright, healthy kids, a good provider, a nice home, security – plenty of women have been content with that package. As the kids got older she did some relief teaching, and threw herself into supporting their extra-curricular stuff – coaching Sandy's netball teams, scoring for Matthew's cricket teams, sewing outfits for their stage productions, chauffeuring them all over the show.

"I was quite content with my lot too. I might've played up once or twice when I was away on business but that was just the old male ego, proving to yourself that you've still got it. Afterwards you feel bloody ashamed, and go and buy the wife something expensive. The plan was basically to retire at sixty having made more than enough money, get a decent-sized boat, play a lot of golf, and watch the grandkids grow up – all, of course, predicated on the assumption of a long twilight.

"Then in 1999 a couple of things happened. Sandy left home so we were empty nesters, and I got in the financial shit. The old story – taking your eye off the ball, trusting people because they're members of Royal Middlemore, delegating too much because work keeps getting in the way of a good time. Joyce was entitled to say 'I told you so' because she had. She'd always taken an interest in my various projects. I'd ignored her, of course. 'Don't worry your little head about it, darling, I'll come out smelling of roses as I always do.' But she didn't say 'I told you so.' She must've thought it – she would've had to be a saint not to – but that wasn't Joyce. Well, not yet anyway.

"One night, when I was on my third or fourth nightcap and blaming everyone except myself, Joyce announced that she was going to start cleaning houses – other people's houses. Well, I went fucking ballistic. No wife of mine was going to be a charlady, I'd rather live under a bloody bridge, my parents would be spinning in their graves, the whole nine yards. And, you know, it was really the first time in our marriage that she just dug her toes in and basically said go ahead, squawk till you're blue in the face, it won't make a scrap of difference.

"The way she looked at it, we simply had to generate some income. With the kids gone she had time on her hands, and there was a demand out there. People were always complaining that they either couldn't find anyone to clean for them, or the cleaners they had were useless. That set me off again: bad enough that she was going to clean houses, but doing it for people we knew and socialized with! She wouldn't budge on that either. 'Our doctor and lawyer are friends of ours,' she said. 'What's the difference? They don't work for mate's rates and neither will I.' I should've realized I was bashing my head against a brick wall, but I was so used to having my own way. I yapped away till she hit me with a question I couldn't answer, or maybe I didn't want to: why was I far less troubled by what people thought of me going bust than of her being a cleaner?

"She had it all worked out. After three months she'd hire someone to give her a hand, and someone else three months after that, and so on. After a year she'd quit doing cleaning work and focus on building the client base and managing her staff. She'd hire recent immigrants because they'd work their arses off and wouldn't have hang-ups about doing menial work. I said, 'You really think it'll be that easy?' You know what she said? 'If you haven't got anything constructive to say, I'd prefer you didn't say anything at all.' As it turned out, her business plan erred on the side of caution: after six months she had a crew of Eastern European women working for her. Dumpy, hairy little boots they were, like something out of that *Borat* movie, but I'll tell you what: they weren't frightened of hard work. Before the year was out she'd sold her first franchise."

Joyce started cleaning houses and Lilywhite went underground. When the money started coming in, though, it dawned on him that he'd fallen on his feet.

Like every other borderline charlatan in the property game, he'd taken steps to ensure that one bum project wouldn't put him in the poorhouse: their house was in Joyce's name, and he'd set up a maze of shell companies and trusts designed to drive creditors to distraction. Even so, he was reconciled to having to sell the house, trade down, and pull his horns in. But with Joyce reinventing herself as a human ATM, none of that was necessary. In fact, he was actually better off: he had the same standard of living without having to work for it.

He took on a couple of consultancies to keep his hand in, but otherwise devoted himself to the agreeable pastimes of the idle rich – skiing, boating, golf, lunch. He rewrote history, turning the trainwreck which had put him out of business into the necessary second act adversity in a drama that would end happily ever after.

But it didn't take him long to realize that while he'd gained an enviable lifestyle, he'd lost something he'd taken for granted and which was central to his self-image: the upper hand. He was no longer the dominant partner. Not that Joyce expected him to be a house husband. Far from it: it was a point of honour for her that no matter how busy she was, she didn't let things slip on the home front. Their friends developed a line of banter around the housewife superstar who built a business empire by day, then rushed home to cook her husband a gourmet meal and remove the wine stain from his favourite golf shirt.

It was hardly surprising that Joyce became more confident and assertive: everything she touched seemed to turn to gold. She opened a café in Remuera catering to young mothers. There was a play area and kiddies' programmes ran non-stop on a big-screen TV. She hired students who were good with small children; they'd bring the mothers a latte and read the kids a story. She helped a friend get a similar operation off the ground in Takapuna, taking a twenty-five per cent stake. She took over a little family business that made strollers and pushchairs. Lilywhite thought she was mad, but he had no idea how much research she'd done. Like all her ventures, it was a winner.

For twenty years Lilywhite's opinions had carried a decisive weight, whether they were discussing war in the Gulf, how much to spend on recarpeting the lounge or whether Sandy's party outfit was appropriate. When he held forth at dinner parties, as he tended to do, he was used to having Joyce back him up or, if she happened to disagree with him, keep her opinion to herself. At first her dissent was so mild it barely registered, but slowly the pushback became less diffident.

When a relationship is undergoing such a transformation, there comes a moment when you simply can't go on pretending that nothing has really changed. Lilywhite announced he was seriously thinking about getting back into property development; Joyce flatly vetoed it. They argued on and off for a week, but she was implacable. When he finally played the "if I don't do something, I'll become an alcoholic" card, she said she could do with some help on the marketing side.

He stared at her. "You mean work for you?"

"Why not?" she said. "I'm a very good boss."

He said he'd think about it.

Joyce still did wifely things, but the housewife superstar carry-on began to grate. She would get home; they'd sit out by the pool with a glass of wine; her cellphone would ring. It would be work-related, and that would be the end of their catch-up, the window supposedly set aside to talk about them. He'd hire a movie she'd expressed interest in but she'd half-watch it with a computer on her lap, or not watch it at all because she couldn't afford the time. He'd complain that he never used to bring work home, but she'd just shrug. One night he made the mistake of asking what the shrug was meant to mean. She said, "Perhaps you should have."

While she didn't become overtly resentful of his foibles and self-indulgence or dwell on the disparity between her workload and his life of expensive leisure, he deciphered the code and felt the chilly draughts of unarticulated disapproval. Time was if she didn't want any more wine, she'd just say so; if he wanted to open another bottle, that was up to him. Now her moderation had to be elaborated on: as much as she'd like a second glass, it wouldn't be a good idea because she had a diary like Helen Clark's. When he got irritated, she told him he was being oversensitive – they were statements of fact, not digs at him. Lilywhite found this hard to believe. He thought she was becoming self-important, entranced with the notion of herself as a self-made, workaholic high-achiever.

She became a fitness fiend. She'd always kept herself in reasonable shape by walking the dog and irregular jogs, but now the early-morning run was as entrenched in her routine as the bedtime cup of peppermint tea. Her hair appointments now swallowed whole afternoons and cost more than a gold tooth. She would emerge from her walk-in wardrobe in outfits he hadn't seen before, and for which his seal of approval wasn't sought. It crossed Lilywhite's mind that she might be having an affair with one of the lawyers or accountants or financial advisers she was always in meetings with. After all, she hadn't been half as particular about her appearance during the twenty years that her life had revolved around him. Now that it no longer did, she spent twice as much time in front of the mirror.

So it was suspicion and curiosity, rather than a desire to make himself useful or reinvigorate their relationship, that led him to take up her offer. Two or three times a week he'd go into the open-plan office in a tinted-glass, low-rise box on Great South Road which was the nerve centre of Joyce's mini-empire. He'd sit in on meetings with the bullshit artists – as he regarded them – from the advertising agency, or liaise with retailers. No one, least of all Joyce, treated him as just another employee. He was the boss's husband, which made him, in the eyes of some of the people he dealt with, the boss's boss. He played along with this misapprehension, but the knowledge that it was an inversion of reality and believed only by rubes, people of alarming ignorance, burned his insides like peasant firewater.

Once he was satisfied that Joyce wasn't having an affair, and had seen enough to know that her success was no happy accident (she was more alert to opportunity, harder-working and better at managing people than he'd ever been), he maintained his involvement for one reason and one reason only: his wife's personal assistant, Denise Hadlow.

Denise was a single mother in her mid-thirties. She was clued-up and competent, even though the job was really her third priority after her little boy and the ongoing dirty war with her ex over child support. She had one of those faces most people would call pretty and some would wonder what all the fuss is about but no one, least of all Lilywhite, a leg man from way back, could quibble with what lay south of the jawline. He reckoned she could have made a fortune in Hollywood as a body double.

The other thing Lilywhite noticed about Denise was that she was the only employee who didn't take their cue from Joyce and adopt a demeanour of bulldozing cheerfulness. He put her detachment down to the fact that she was sexier than the other women and smarter than the men and wielded a certain amount of obstructive power by virtue of her position. But there was another dimension to it: she was the only person who worked for or with Joyce who didn't think she was wonderful. In fact, he was pretty sure Denise didn't actually like his wife very much at all. Joyce wasn't entirely oblivious to this, but typically it just made her more determined to draw Denise into the fold. Lilywhite thought she was wasting her time. Denise's alienation went deep; it wouldn't be charmed away by lunch at the French Café or bribed away by a bonus and an extravagant birthday present for her son.

And when Denise began making protracted, almost brazen eye contact, he realized, with a jolt of lust and a vengeful thrill whose intensity surprised him, that he'd found someone who would willingly join him in ensuring that Joyce's ascendancy came at a cost. Or maybe it was the other way around, and she'd found him.

Lilywhite's daughter Sandy made an unheralded entrance.

"All right, Dad?" she asked. "Maybe you should get some rest. You've been at it for ages."

"I'm fine, thank you, my dear," said Lilywhite. "How about you, Sergeant? Something to eat, perhaps?"

Before Ihaka could reply, Sandy said, "Okay, I'll leave you to it." She exited, closing the door behind her with a pointed thud.

Lilywhite raised his eyebrows. "Looks like room service isn't available just at the moment."

"I'm right," said Ihaka.

"You've been very patient," said Lilywhite.

Ihaka shrugged. "I'm not in any rush to get to the serviced apartment."

"Where is home these days, if I may ask?"

"Wairarapa. A cottage down a country road."

"Sounds delightful. Do you share it with anyone?"

"Don't worry about me," said Ihaka neutrally.

Lilywhite nodded. "No, you didn't come here to exchange chit-chat, did you? If you're wondering why I'm being so long-winded, it's because I'm only doing this once." He paused. "And I want you to understand what happened to me, as well as to Joyce."

"I got that."

"Ah, but do you realize what it means? It means you're my de facto father confessor."

"You're in the shit, then," said Ihaka. "I can't help you there."

"On the contrary, you're perfect. I don't want absolution; I don't deserve it. What I want is to make amends. You can help me do that."

Lilywhite was aware there was another dimension to sex. He'd heard the stories, although you obviously had to take some with a grain of salt. Being aware was one thing; experiencing it was something else. Denise Hadlow was the closest thing he'd ever come across to the wanton angels splayed across the centrefold. If her body wasn't proof enough, her casual sensuality was emphatic confirmation that he'd somehow stumbled into the hot zone.

Why had Denise latched onto him rather than a man in her own image, a hard body she could thrash under all night long? Lilywhite assumed she saw their affair as psychic sabotage: she could watch Joyce being the Woman Who Had It All and think, look at her – she thinks she's so onto it, but she can't even see her husband's left the building. He further assumed that since Joyce was oblivious, Denise's private satisfaction would soon wane. But an illicit affair suited Denise. Her little boy was the man in her life, and she didn't want a would-be partner competing for her time and attention.

She went along with his subterfuges because she didn't want to wreck his marriage or lose her job. He would have spoiled her, even kept her, if she'd let him, but she wouldn't have it. "What would that make me?" she'd ask. She often asked if he'd thought it through. Did it really make sense to risk so much upheaval for a once- or twice-weekly blast of high-end sex? There was no false modesty on that score. Occasionally she taunted him, suggesting that when the affair had run its course, he should quit while he was ahead and retire from sex altogether.

He wondered if the idea was to get him hooked, to ruin him for Joyce. If so, it was working. He stopped fretting about being found out and began inventing scenarios in which Joyce didn't figure, imagining an existence from which she'd been purged. Then he would be free to have as much of Denise as she'd allow him. He'd be so rich she might let him have all of her.

His craving for Denise took away his appetite and made his stomach flutter with nausea. He could barely bring himself to be civil to Joyce. She assumed his brusque disengagement was payback for her vetoing a return to property development, and softened her position, agreeing to consider any reasonable proposal. But Lilywhite had reached the point of twisting everything she said or did, however placatory or well-intentioned, to stoke his obsessions. Thus this olive branch was actually a trap: she was pretending to be open to persuasion, getting his hopes up so that the inevitable knock-back would be even more deflating.

The annual boys' weekend couldn't have been better timed, although Lilywhite found himself in a strange position. When the conversation turned to wives and girlfriends, as it always did because two of the group had effectively given up marriage and taken up adultery, he was still cast as one of the lucky buggers – great wife, dream marriage. But later on, when the unlucky buggers began talking up the invigorating thrill of spontaneous fellatio or desktop fornication, he became poor old Chris, missing out on the fun because he was too married for his own good.

Lilywhite was tempted to trump them with the Denise card. Maybe next year? Next year, my arse, he thought. I'll be struggling to hold it together till the end of the month. But he held his tongue and stayed in character, restricting himself to a cryptic grumble and a throwaway line about finding a hitman in the Yellow Pages.

The following week a man rang him up offering to kill Joyce for $25,000.

"What did he say?" said Ihaka. "Exactly."

"He said, 'A little bird tells me you might be interested in changing your domestic arrangements. I can make that happen.' I said, 'Who is this? What the hell are you talking about?' He said, 'Listen, I'm not fucking around here. It'll cost twenty-five grand and no one will be any the wiser – it'll look like an accident.' I was so stunned I don't think I said another word. He told me to think about it and he'd call back in a couple of days. If I said no, that would be the end of it, he wouldn't ask a third time. That's it, pretty much word for word."

"You didn't recognize the voice?"

Lilywhite shook his head. "It wasn't his normal voice. I don't know if he had a handkerchief over his mouth or something, but it was a bit distorted. Regardless of that, it didn't have a familiar ring, if you know what I mean."

"Then what?"

"He rang back three days later…"

"Definitely the same guy?"

"Yes."

"By which time you'd had a chance to think about it?"

"I'd thought of little else. I took the 'just out of curiosity' tack. It was very simple, he said: it would happen within thirty days of me paying a ten-grand deposit. I'd then have two or three months to pay the balance. The time frame was to enable me to get the money together in dribs and drabs, thereby avoiding suspicious transactions. There'd be no face-to-face meetings; communication would be restricted to arranging the handovers. As long as I kept my end of the deal, I'd never hear from him again."

"So you agreed?"

"No, I asked for more time. He said maybe, maybe not, and hung up. A fortnight later he rang again: 'This is it,' he said. 'No ifs or buts or maybes.' I said yes. He told me to start getting the money together, he'd be in touch. The money wasn't an issue: I had some cash that Joyce didn't know about squirrelled away in a safety deposit box. It started out as a twenty-fifth wedding anniversary surprise fund."

Lilywhite grunted as if he'd been hit, and reached for his pills. Ihaka saw tears in his eyes and looked away. He wasn't sure why.

"A few weeks later I was at the Eastridge supermarket. When I got back to my car there was a typewritten note under the windscreen wiper instructing me to wrap the ten grand in newspaper, put it in a shopping bag, and take it to St Mark's Church in Remuera at five the following afternoon. I was to sit for a while in the third row from the back on the right-hand side of the aisle, then clear off, leaving the bag under the pew. Once I'd memorized the instructions, I was to rip up the note and throw it in a rubbish bin. I did what I was told and you know the rest."

"You never heard from him again?"

Lilywhite shook his head.

"And the balance?"

"Another note under the windscreen wiper. Different church this time, St Aidan's in Ascot Avenue."

"So you suspect one of your mates from the boys' weekend put him onto you?"

Lilywhite nodded. "For want of a better idea."

"On the basis of a joke about finding a hitman in the Yellow Pages?"

"That and the timing. It'd be a bit of a coincidence otherwise, wouldn't it. And maybe I wasn't as good an actor as I thought – bear in mind, those guys know me better than anyone."

"Except your wife, and she didn't see it coming."

"She wasn't looking."

"So do you have a theory on which one?"

"I don't," said Lilywhite. "Not for want of trying. I've given it a lot of thought, believe me. There's just nothing much to go on, and what there is doesn't point one way. For instance, one of them really loathes his wife but she's still alive. For that matter, she's still his wife. So what does that tell you?" He pointed to a manila folder on the sideboard. "The details are in there."

Lilywhite subsided into the pillows, closing his eyes. Ihaka watched the colour that had come back into his cheeks drain away. Without opening his eyes, Lilywhite said, "Does it seem likely to you that Joyce is his only victim?"

"No, that doesn't seem very likely at all."

Lilywhite gestured towards the folder. "That's what I thought. I actually became a bit obsessed with the subject – quite the amateur sleuth I was. I came across a couple of interesting ones. Might be worth a look."

4

Ihaka made two calls before he drove away from Lilywhite's house, the first to set up a meeting with Finbar McGrail, the second to see if Johan Van Roon had been able to do him a favour. He had. It came in the form of an address.

Ihaka drove east, past Panmure Basin, across the Tamaki Estuary, out through Pakuranga and Howick to Cockle Bay. It was rush hour, which meant a stop-start journey, the stops lasting longer than the starts. He thought of his drive home from work, a twenty-minute dawdle through countryside where man and nature had reached a pleasing accommodation. He station-surfed but the airwaves had been monopolized by jerk-offs with that oily radio voice which reminded him of perverts he'd arrested.

The address was a town house two blocks back from the water. It was 5.45 p.m.; the carport was empty. Ihaka parked on the other side of the road, tilted the seat back as far as it would go, and closed his eyes.

At 6.05 a Mitsubishi Pajero, the model before the model before last, swung into the carport. Ihaka got out of the car and crossed the road. The Pajero's driver's door opened. A balding middle-aged man swung his right leg out of the car and looked over his shoulder at Ihaka, keeping his hands out of sight. Ihaka stopped on the footpath, a few metres away. They examined one another.

"Is that a pistol in your pocket," said Ihaka, "or are you just pleased to see me?"

"Jesus, Chief," said the other man, "I was that close to giving myself permission to fire at will. Just as well I can tell you fucking Maoris apart."

"I was counting on that," said Ihaka. "How're you doing, Blair?"

The man was Blair Corvine, a former undercover policeman who'd been forced to retire after being shot five times at point-blank range. Last time Ihaka had seen him, he was quite a lot skinnier and had ear-studs, a ponytail and a wedge of fluff hanging off his lower lip. Back then his usual outfit was too-tight jeans, T-shirts with slogans intended to cause offence like 'So many Christians, so few lions', and cowboy boots. Now he looked like just another suburban joe who wore whatever his wife bought him at Farmers.

Corvine got out of the Pajero, slipping the semi-automatic pistol into a backpack. "Can't complain," he said. "It only hurts when I eat, drink, piss, shit, fart, root, sit down, stand up or water the plants. I take it you're still partial to a cold beer on a warm day?"

Ihaka shrugged. "I wouldn't want you to drink alone."

As they approached the front door, it was opened by a woman with short grey-blonde hair, dressed for the gym. She had the body of a forty-year-old but the face of a fifty-year-old. Ihaka wondered if exercise was penance for years of hard living. She stood in the doorway, hands on hips, her face clamped in a grim shape, itching for a fight. It was just a question of who she picked on.

"Hey, baby," said Corvine, bending down to kiss her on the thin white line where her lips used to be. "I know what you're thinking, but he's a cop. Tito, meet Sheree."

Ihaka put a lot of sincerity into his greeting. He might as well have spat on her cross-trainers.

"You want to take Tito out the back, babe?" said Corvine. "We're having a beer. Can I get you a glass of wine?"

"I'm going to Pilates," she said, making it sound like "I'm sleeping in the spare room."

The rear courtyard was a riot of colour: marigolds, petunias and pansies overflowed tubs and ceramic pots, and white and crimson roses swarmed over a trellis. Ihaka carefully lowered himself onto one of the flimsy-looking chairs around a metal café table.

Sheree remained standing, arms folded. "How did you find us?"

"A guy owed me one," said Ihaka as Corvine appeared with a couple of Peronis.

"Oh, cool." She trained her eyes on Corvine. "This place is supposed to be top fucking secret, right, and they're handing it out to anyone who's owed a favour?"

"Take it easy, Sheree," said Corvine. "Tito's not just anyone."

Her eyebrows arched. "Oh, really? So why's he here – to talk you into a comeback?" She snorted disgustedly. As she walked away, she tossed a "Fucking hell, Blair" over her shoulder.

Corvine sat down. "Sorry about that, mate."

"Not your fault," said Ihaka. "I have this effect on women."

"It was fucking hard on her, man, not knowing whether I was going to make it, then all that fucking rehab and a year down south when we just sort of sat around going slowly out of our minds. Now we're back here, which is great, but you live with the knowledge that there's some real bad bastards in this town who'd be round in a fucking flash if they knew where to find me."

Ihaka nodded. "I shouldn't have just turned up like that."

Corvine chuckled. "Run silent, run deep – that's always been the Ihaka way. Glad to see you haven't changed. Every other fucking thing has."

"What happened, Blair?"

"I got inside this Westie biker gang that was moving a ton of P. One night I got a call from the boss man, Jerry Spragg, to say he needed a hand. Standard stuff, didn't think anything of it. But when I turned up, they kicked the shit out of me, chucked me in the back of a ute, and took me into the bush where Spragg put five fucking rounds in me."

"Yeah, I heard all that," said Ihaka. "I meant, how did they know?"

Corvine shook his head slowly. "Beats me. I don't think I fucked up, though. When I first went under, I took that many risks and made that many fuck-ups, I could've been dealt to ten times over, but by then I knew what I was doing. You get a pretty good feel for when you're sweet, when you have to watch your step, and when it's time to get the fuck out of Dodge. Right up till the hammer came down, I was tight with these dudes. I'm telling you, man, it came out of nowhere."

"So if you didn't fuck up…"

Corvine shrugged. "Two possibilities: P paranoia – there's a lot of it about – or I was ratted out. But they kicked up an unholy shitstorm at Central, turned the place upside down, without finding anything that pointed to a leak. Sheree didn't buy it. Still doesn't. Hence the short fuse."

"What did Spragg have to say for himself?"

"Not a word – staunch as. Fat lot of good it did him. He's in Paremoremo for all of three weeks and whammo – they did him over, big-time. Now he's a fucking basketcase who sits in a wheelchair shitting his pants and singing 'Baa Baa Black Sheep'."

"Friends of yours?"

"Nothing to do with me, mate," said Corvine. "Routine gang shit slash prison madness, from what I heard. But yeah, I wasn't exactly inconsolable." He brightened up. "Hey, you know that scene in *Pulp Fiction* when the guy bursts out of the bathroom with a .44 Mag and unloads on Travolta and the black dude?"

"Vaguely. It was a while ago."

"Definition of a classic, Chief: it stands the test of time. He doesn't hit squat, remember? They don't have a fucking scratch, so the black guy's convinced it's a miracle and vows to renounce his evil ways. I always thought that scene was bullshit: how could you possibly fire six rounds at a couple of guys standing a few feet away and not even graze either of them?" Corvine threw up his hands, flashing the crazy grin Ihaka hadn't expected to see again. "Look what happened to me."

"Slight difference," said Ihaka. "Spragg didn't miss."

"He missed the vital organs, though – five times. I'm not saying it's a miracle, but it's certainly a freakish occurrence."

"You were just fucking lucky. A pro would've put one in your swede."

At 8.58 the following morning Superintendent McGrail got out of the lift on the eighth floor of a downtown serviced apartment building. He went down the corridor, stopping at apartment 8F. All being well, Detective Sergeant Ihaka would be on the other side of the door, in a presentable state and prepared for their 9 a.m. meeting.

But Ihaka hadn't responded to McGrail's secretary's voice messages and texts confirming the time of the meeting. And McGrail couldn't help but remember some of the disturbing sights and scenes witnessed by a young Johan Van Roon when he'd turned up to collect Ihaka from his place first thing in the morning. There was the blow-up sex doll in a deckchair on the front porch, with a cucumber in its mouth slot and a sign around its neck saying "I claim this house in the name of Satan". (An anti-Mormon device, apparently.) There were various distressed or angry women whose names Ihaka professed not to know and whose distress or anger he professed not to understand.

McGrail shook his head, as if deleting these unwelcome scenes from his memory bank. This wasn't Ihaka's house, it was a serviced apartment in which he'd spent a single night. Even the Ihaka of old at his oafish, anarchic worst couldn't wreak too much havoc in one night. And this wasn't the Ihaka of old. He'd changed during his years in exile. He'd matured.

Oh well, thought McGrail. If he's in a drunken stupor, at least I'll have the consolation of waking him up. He knocked. Ihaka opened the door. He was fully dressed, hair damp from the shower. He hadn't shaved, but then he often didn't. A box of cereal and a carton of orange juice sat on the counter separating the kitchenette from the living area.

"Good morning, Sergeant," said McGrail. "You got the message, then?"

"Yep."

"It didn't occur to you that a reply would've been helpful?"

"Silence means consent, doesn't it?"

"Ah, the Roman principle 'Qui tacet consentire videtur'."

"That's the bugger," said Ihaka. "Cup of tea?"

As Ihaka went through the cupboards looking for cups and saucers, McGrail mounted a bar stool. "Seeing you're still here," he said, "I'm assuming your session with Lilywhite was worthwhile."

Ihaka waited for the jug to boil. "He had his wife knocked off," he said eventually. When McGrail didn't respond, he added, "That's your cue to say 'Well, Sergeant, it looks like you were right and me and all those other fucking geniuses were wrong.'"

McGrail produced a small moleskin notebook and fountain pen. "Before I shower you with plaudits, perhaps you could brief me on it."

Ihaka delivered a highly condensed version of Lilywhite's confession.

"You obviously believe him?"

"Well, fuck," said Ihaka, "if anyone's entitled to think they can tell when this guy's lying and when he's not, it'd be me, wouldn't you say?"

"That's as may be, but to apply another of your Roman legal principles, 'Falsus in uno, falsus in omnibus'."

"Once a liar, always a liar?"

"Well done, Sergeant."

Ihaka shook his head. "Why would he?"

"I tend to agree. The only point of a false confession would be to protect someone else, but seeing the case was basically closed, there was no need to do that. I owe you an apology, Sergeant. You were right, and the rest of us were wrong. I should've had more faith in your instincts."

Ihaka shrugged. "What's one ruined career in the grand scheme of things?"

McGrail nodded. "You're entitled to feel aggrieved."

"I already did."

McGrail didn't take these remarks seriously. Ihaka had his weaknesses, but self-pity wasn't one of them.

"So what's in the folder?"

Ihaka passed it over. "Contact details for his three mates and some background on those two cases he reckons we should have another look at: a stabbing in Ponsonby and an old lady who fell down the stairs and broke her neck."

McGrail flipped the folder open. "Oh my goodness."

"What?"

"Jonathon Bell. That name didn't, well, ring a bell?"

"He's rich, isn't he?"

"That's like saying George Best was a fair footballer. He'll require careful handling."

"Why are you telling me?" asked Ihaka.

"Don't you want to follow this through?"

"Not if it means going back to square one. Fuck that."

"This would be a secondment, a special project. You'd report directly to me."

Ihaka stared. "Are you serious?"

McGrail gestured with the folder. "This is serious, don't you think? Serious matters demand a serious response."

"Charlton's not going to like it."

"He doesn't have to."

Ihaka's face creased happily. "Well, when you put it like that…"

McGrail nodded. "Good." He gestured with the folder. "I'm classifying this as a cold-case investigation. Apart from anything else, that should go some way towards appeasing our friend Charlton, but let's keep the hired killer element between ourselves for the time being. You're going to need some help." He waited for Ihaka's groan to peter out. "This could involve a lot of time on the computer and, as I recall, that wasn't your forte."

"I don't want one of Charlton's pet weasels spying on me."

"What about Beth Greendale?" said McGrail. "She's done a few part-time research projects for me."

"Beth'd be great."

"There, that wasn't so hard, was it? Now I've organized an office and a car, and I'll square your secondment with the Wellington district…"

"And I'll bet you've already got Beth teed up," said Ihaka accusingly. "You had it all worked out, didn't you?"

"I anticipated an outcome and put some arrangements in place accordingly. Don't look so suspicious, Sergeant: I do that sort of thing all the time. As a matter of fact, I did quite a lot of it when we worked together – you just didn't notice."

"But you were pretty bloody sure I'd fall into line."

McGrail resisted the temptation to break into one of his wintry smiles: if Ihaka decided he was being manipulated, all bets were off. "I thought that if Lilywhite turned out to be unfinished business, you'd want to be involved – providing we could put an acceptable structure in place." He stood up. "There's just the matter of your living arrangements."

"I'll sort that out," said Ihaka. "I've got some cousins living at my place. They'll be gone by lunchtime."

"Won't they expect some notice?"

Ihaka chuckled ominously. "I don't think they're that stupid, but who knows?"

He saw McGrail to the door. "I dropped in on Blair Corvine last night."

"Did you now? I won't bother asking how you managed to find him."

"The investigation: was it fair dinkum?"

McGrail cocked his head. "I'd say so. As you know, Corvine always operated perilously close to the edge. In the months before he was shot, his handlers expressed concern about his state of mind and health. His drug intake, in other words."

"So you're saying?"

"He probably gave himself away without even realizing it."

"Blame the victim, eh?" said Ihaka. "That's convenient."

There was a twitch of impatience at the corner of McGrail's mouth. "The fact that the conclusion was the desirable one from the organization's point of view doesn't *ipso facto* – as we classicists say – invalidate it."

5

The shoulder-length hair was silver and lifeless and the jawline had lost its battle with middle-aged sag, but not much else had changed. Same outfit: black Levi's, raucous Hawaiian shirt. Same back corner table in the same Herne Bay café. Same paraphernalia: the *Herald*, a highbrow paperback, a laptop computer, and the red soft-pack, made-in-the-US Marlboros he went through at the rate of one every half-hour. Same air of suppressed amusement, same contemptuous glint in the pale blue eyes, just in case you hadn't realized he was way smarter than you.

His name was Doug Yallop, but most people called him Prof. After doing a Ph.D. at Sydney's Macquarie University – the subject of his thesis was the life and works of the unfashionable English novelist Henry Green – he became a junior lecturer at the University of Auckland. It was the late seventies and, as was the case with a lot of university types at that time, Yallop's main priority was ensuring he never ran out of marijuana.

Like the man who admired the product so much he bought the company, Yallop went into the dope business. He quickly became the biggest weed dealer on campus, but while word of mouth was good for business, it was bad for security. As critics of incarceration often point out, prisons are where criminals go to meet like-minded people, swap ideas and become better criminals. During his seven years in Mount Eden, Yallop got to know a lot of career criminals. He was struck by how many of them possessed all the attributes needed to be successful in their chosen field bar one: intelligence.

When he got out of jail, Yallop set himself up as a consultant in and facilitator of crime. He advised crooks how to carry out specific crimes and organize their ongoing operations; he put together crews; he acted as a go-between and mediator when competition escalated into conflict, or when rival groups could see the benefits of cooperation but didn't know how to go about it. He even researched and planned jobs and sold the blueprints to the highest bidder. Because he was careful and smart and had a good lawyer, it proved so difficult to convict him of anything that eventually the police stopped trying very hard.

Ihaka sat down at his table. "Hey, Prof. How's it going?"

Yallop looked up from his book, removing his reading glasses. "Well, I'll be fucked," he said in an accent as dinky-di as the day he crossed the Tasman. "I thought you'd been put out to pasture."

"Think of it as a journey of self-discovery."

Yallop snorted, shoulders shaking. "I could've saved you the trouble."

"How's that?"

Yallop bookmarked the paperback and put it aside. "Why are you a cop, Ihaka? We both know it's not for the money."

Ihaka shrugged. "A bloke's got to do something."

"That's it?"

"And I'm good at it."

"Yeah, but you'd be just as good playing for the other team – and much better rewarded."

"Well, Prof, I'm not a materialistic person. And let's face it, the other team are a bunch of cunts, present company excepted."

Even though he knew Ihaka didn't mean it, Yallop ducked his head as if acknowledging a compliment. "Whereas your mob are top blokes, to a man?"

"I wouldn't say that, but the cunt count's definitely lower. Now a brainbox like you doesn't ask a question without knowing the answer, so you tell me: why am I a cop?"

Yallop leaned back, pink with admiration for his own perceptiveness. "Becoming a cop was the only way to stop yourself becoming a crim. As you're well aware, you've got deep-seated antisocial tendencies. If you weren't a cop, sooner or later they would've come to the fore. So the answer to the question is: self-awareness."

"It's one thing to be aware you've got antisocial tendencies, it's another to want to keep a lid on them."

"Ah, that always goes back to the same thing: upbringing; family background; parental example."

"Is that your excuse?"

"Shit, no, my folks were the salt of the earth. They scrimped and saved so that little Dougie, the apple of their four eyes, could go to a private school. No, mate, I'm the exception that proves the rule. So what brings you back?"

"Just tidying up a few loose ends."

"None of my fucking business, in other words. Fair enough. But seeing you obviously want something from me, a little give-and-take wouldn't go amiss."

"I don't see it that way, Prof. You've had a pretty good run."

Yallop reopened his paperback. "Thank you linesmen, thank you ball boys, fuck you."

Ihaka frowned like someone stuck on a crossword clue. "You know, I could lean over and smack you in the mouth, or I could pretend I didn't hear that. You have a preference?"

Yallop held Ihaka's stare, stretching it out, although they both knew how it was going to end.

"What the hell," said Yallop eventually. "I'm sixty-five next month, I'm virtually retired. I just want to be everyone's mate. Of course, sometimes being matey with one bloke means being very un-fucking-matey with another, but we'll cross that bridge when we come to it. What's up?"

"Three cases spread over six years. A woman run over in Kohimarama, a bloke stabbed on his way home from the pub just around here, and an old lady in Remuera who went arse over elbow down the stairs. Current status is unsolved hit-and-run, unsolved robbery-murder and accident, but we've picked up a whisper there's a hitman out there."

Yallop's expression gave nothing away. "Well, we can both think of a few guys who'd take out their grannies in a heartbeat if the price was right, but this doesn't sound like them. First off, they're shooters. They don't fuck around trying to make it look like an accident. Secondly, apart from the odd grudge, hits are usually a tactical measure or countermeasure in an ongoing blue between professional criminals over territory or supply or market share. What we have here, if I'm not mistaken, is a bunch of dead people with no connection to what's melodramatically referred to as the underworld."

"As far as we know."

"This is amateur hour, Sergeant – I'm assuming that's still your rank." Ihaka nodded, noting the sparkle of malice in Yallop's eyes. "Something rotten in the leafy suburbs, fear and loathing in Labrador land. Not my scene – I'm fussy about the company I keep. Can't help you, I'm afraid."

Yallop was a skilled liar, but Ihaka tended to believe him. The reason he didn't know anything was the reason he might have coughed up if he did: it wasn't his world, therefore no skin off his nose.

"So someone walks in here tomorrow wanting a hitter, what would you tell them?"

"If I didn't know them," said Yallop slowly, "or know of them, I'd tell them to fuck off. If I did know them or they came with a reference, I'd tell them two things: one, don't say another word to me; two, go and see the heavy mob. You know who they are as well as I do. You also know bloody well that the stuff you're talking about – clipping eastern suburbs dowagers – isn't their bag. They'd regard that sort of shit as beneath them."

Ihaka nodded gloomily. "Changing the subject, what about Blair Corvine?"

Yallop's guffaw sounded forced. "You're asking me? Your lot were all over that like a cheap suit."

Ihaka shrugged. "No harm in getting a second opinion."

Yallop scooped up his cigarettes and lighter. "Smoko." They went out to the courtyard. Before they'd even sat down, Yallop had lit up and was exhaling with the gratified, drawn-out sigh of a man who counted the minutes till his next cigarette.

"We were talking about Corvine."

"So we were. I haven't heard anything to suggest he was ratted out, if that's where you're coming from. Word on the street was he got careless with his cellphone – used it to ring the wrong people then left it lying around for someone to have a nosey through call history."

"That doesn't sound very likely," said Ihaka.

Yallop looked away, concentrating on his cigarette. "You asked, I told you what I heard. It's a matter of complete fucking indifference to me whether you believe it or not. How's he doing, by the way?"

It came out smoothly, a casual enquiry about a mutual acquaintance. "I wouldn't know," said Ihaka, a reasonably accomplished liar himself. "Haven't seen him for years. But I'm touched by your concern."

"Actually, I couldn't give a shit," said Yallop with a crooked grin. "I just have a vague professional curiosity. How many new holes did they give him?"

"Well, one's too many, isn't it."

"I seem to remember it was quite a few too many. But, hey, he lived to tell the tale."

"Which apparently is more than you can say for Jerry Spragg."

"Eh? He's still around."

"But not telling too many tales, I hear."

"Oh, I see what you mean. Yeah, it seems the post-prison career as an after-dinner speaker isn't a goer."

"What happened there?"

Yallop sat up straighter, drumming his fingers on the tabletop. "Let's see, you asked me about a hitter and your boy Corvine, and now you want to know about Tom the Turnip or whatever the fuck Spragg answers to these days. You running a tab here, Sergeant?"

"I'd say I'm still in credit," said Ihaka with a faint smile. "This could make us all square."

"I'll hold you to that. I thought Spragg would be okay inside because he had protection, but I guess when you're used to being the big dog, it's hard to get your head around the concept of vulnerability. I heard he made two mistakes: he treated people like shit and he didn't listen to his minders. First rule of maximum, Sergeant: the price of staying in one piece is eternal vigilance."

"I thought it was: if you drop the soap in the shower, let someone else pick it up."

"No, mate, you don't get to choose. Some guys drop the soap, some guys have to bend over and pick it up. Pure social Darwinism."

"So who dealt to him?"

Yallop stood up, stubbing out his cigarette. "Random hard-arses. It was standard recreational violence, so what fucking difference does it make? I think we're done here."

Back inside Yallop slipped into his seat and jabbed his laptop into life. "Have to say, Sergeant, that's a lot of loose ends."

"I've got a bit of catching up to do."

"You around for a while?"

"Not if I can help it."

"Let's not do this again. I've got a reputation to protect."

"That works both ways."

Yallop snickered. "You sure about that? You've been gone a while, digger. Your reputation ain't what it used to be."

Ihaka gave him a long, unfriendly stare. "Watch this space."

Ihaka's house wasn't immaculate, but it was a lot cleaner and tidier than when he'd arrived there unannounced that morning to give his nephew and cousins a life lesson: all good things must come to an end. It was a short visit and an even shorter conversation, culminating with his promise that if the place wasn't spick and span when he returned he'd hunt them down and confiscate their scrotums. After Uncle Tito had got back in his car and driven off, the boys had a bit of a laugh about that. Then they got down to work.

Ihaka's sister and one of his aunts had left messages on the answerphone, complaining about the suddenness of the eviction. He couldn't be bothered ringing them back to point out that lack of notice was the downside of a peppercorn rent.

He made a pile of sandwiches from the rotisserie chicken and salad ingredients he'd picked up at the supermarket and ate supper on the veranda. He wasn't really sure what he felt about the turn of events. On the one hand it was nice to be back in his own home; on the other he'd grown quite attached to the rented cottage on a country lane that snaked through farmland between State Highway 2 and the edge of the Tararua Forest. He was a born and bred Aucklander, in tune with the erratic rhythm of the city, unfazed by its mass and sprawl. He enjoyed the buzz of striving, restless humanity. And unsentimental and solitary though he was, the blue lure of the harbour or the diamond-studded silhouette of the city at night still gave him a sense of belonging.

But in Auckland he was always a cop, and therefore always on a war footing. In Wairarapa he left the job behind when he turned off State Highway 2. Being a loner in the city seemed to cause others aggravation: they called him bloody-minded, told him he had an attitude problem, interpreted solitariness as alienation, if not hostility. Country folk respected solitude. They understood the oppressiveness of other people.

He would enjoy working with McGrail again and was tickled by the prospect of enraging Charlton and Firkitt, but there was every chance the investigation would be a dead-end street, and a short one at that. Lilywhite had incriminated himself at length but hadn't provided a lead to the killer. There was just the coincidence of the approach coming straight after the boys' weekend. No doubt his three mates would trumpet their innocence and outrage, then take cover behind QCs. After that, all he and Beth Greendale could do was trawl through their pasts looking for a hint that they might know or know of a killer.

Yallop was right: professional hitmen didn't do this sort of stuff. Apart from anything else, if people like Lilywhite and his friends went looking for a professional hitter, they'd leave a trail a pimple-arsed thicko straight out of Police College could follow. He didn't have a view one way or the other on the rest of what he'd got from Yallop, not that it amounted to much. If, in Yallop's complicated calculations, he could see a potential benefit to himself somewhere down the line, he might tell the truth. If not, he'd recycle the conventional wisdom, or give you a bum steer just for the hell of it. That exercise was more about poking a stick into a hole and seeing what, if anything, crawled out.

Then there were those two cases Lilywhite had picked out. What made him think the TV guy and the old girl were contract hits? Had guilt and torment driven him around the bend so that every time he checked the death notices, he saw sinister happenings, men like him turning their twisted fantasies into reality by hiring an invisible killer who could somehow anticipate when daydreams would harden into murderous intent?

Lilywhite didn't seem lost in a maze of conspiracy where there was no such thing as an accident or random, opportunistic crime. On the other hand, all he'd provided was a few newspaper clippings. Maybe he knew more than he'd let on. He'd described himself as obsessive, quite the amateur sleuth: it wasn't out of the question that he'd looked so hard, he'd seen something no one else noticed. Maybe he'd wanted to say more, but had run out of steam. By the end of their session he'd looked incapable of blowing out a match.

Ihaka cursed himself for not having pressed Lilywhite on the other deaths. He'd been unprofessional on two counts, letting himself feel some sympathy for a man who'd cold-bloodedly gone about the elimination of his wife, and giving in to the urge to get the hell out of there. So it was a lot of grief and guilt for one day? Tough shit: that was the job, pal. He used to be renowned for his ability to plough through that stuff, to function in the presence of death and heartbreak when more sensitive officers had to duck outside to throw up or shed tears. But as Yallop had enjoyed reminding him, it was a while since anyone had clapped eyes on that Tito Ihaka.

There was an ambulance outside Lilywhite's house and the front door was open. Ihaka walked quickly down the corridor towards the sound of anguish.

The paramedics were young, no more than twenty-five. One was over by the long leather couch setting up a mobile stretcher. The other, a woman, was comforting Sandy, who glanced up, her face a blur of misery. Ihaka saw a flash of recognition and anger in her eyes, then another wave of grief rolled in and she dropped her head back onto the paramedic's shoulder. Ihaka had heard those shuddering sobs many times. He didn't need to look at Lilywhite to know he was dead.

He looked anyway. Lilywhite lay on his back, his hands dug into the cashmere blanket. His head was tilted back and his eyes and mouth were wide open, like a backstroker on the last length. He looked like the oldest man on earth.

Ihaka showed the male paramedic his ID, herding him out through the open French doors onto the bowling green lawn. "What happened?"

The paramedic was tall and slim with a dark fringe he had to keep brushing out of his eyes and a five o'clock shadow that had fallen early. He stared at Ihaka through guileless eyes. "He seemed okay, so she nipped out to the supermarket. When she got back, he was gone."

"I saw him yesterday," said Ihaka. "He seemed pretty good considering. He thought he had weeks left."

"It's not an exact science."

"So this is within what you'd call the normal time frame?"

The paramedic shrugged. "Usually it's more a steady decline. I would've expected him to pass away in a hospice."

"Maybe he decided to hurry it up?"

The clear eyes widened. "That hadn't occurred to me. Someone who's terminally ill, you don't tend to think about the whys and wherefores."

"Do you know his specialist?"

"I've got the name in there somewhere."

"Do me a favour, give him a ring and get his take on it. And let's leave Lilywhite where he is for now."

The paramedic gulped. He was used to death being low-key and uncomplicated. Call-outs to the living were much more fraught. "You think there's something not quite right here?"

"I'm just saying, under the circumstances…"

"What circumstances?"

"Has it crossed your mind to wonder why I'm here?" It obviously hadn't, but now he was making up for it. "Don't say anything to the daughter, okay? Not a fucking word." The paramedic gulped again, nodding rapidly. "What's happening with her?"

"Some friends are coming over."

"Get them to take her to their place," said Ihaka. "Don't take no for an answer."

He rang McGrail, who was in a meeting. Ihaka told him to get out of it. He heard McGrail's muffled apology and the click-clack of his leather soles on a wooden floor.

"Well?"

"Lilywhite's dead."

"That's somewhat earlier than expected?"

"Yep."

"But hardly unexpected?"

"His daughter came back from a quick trip to the supermarket to find him dead. She'd left the place wide open. And for what it's worth, this time yesterday he didn't seem like a man who was going to croak inside twenty-four hours."

There was a long pause. "I take it you're there now?"

"Yeah."

"Why? Because you thought he had more to say?"

"Maybe." The paramedic was hovering. "Hang on."

"I got hold of the specialist," said the paramedic. "He would've expected Mr Lilywhite to have stayed pretty much the same for a few weeks, then to decline significantly, plateau for a week or so, then go quite quickly. But he did stress that…"

"It's not an exact science. Got it. Thanks, mate." The paramedic went back inside. Ihaka asked McGrail, "You hear that?"

"I did."

"We should get a crime scene team out here."

"I suppose that would be prudent."

"What should I tell them?"

"About your involvement?" McGrail thought about it for a few seconds. "Well, if I was you, I'd tell them you had nothing to do with it."

6

As agreed, Ihaka arrived early to receive his instructions: don't provoke, don't react, leave the talking to McGrail.

"So why do I have to be here?" he grumbled. "Talk about a spare prick at a wedding."

"What a revolting expression," said McGrail.

McGrail put his nose in a thick draft report. A few minutes went by in frosty silence, broken only by McGrail's long-suffering exhalations as he corrected the author's grammar. Ihaka wondered why McGrail had taken exception to that particular remark given the torrent of filth he'd chosen to ignore in the past. The only explanation which came to mind was that he was a bit on edge over the imminent meeting with Detective Inspector Tony Charlton and Detective Sergeant Ron Firkitt.

They were punctual, and as wary as forest animals. Charlton looked exactly as Ihaka remembered, only with a deeper suntan, but time had landed a few hammer-blows on Firkitt's flushed, lumpy face. He reminded Ihaka of the limping, putty-nosed, sponge-eared ex-players you see in rugby clubs, famous brutes in their time, snarling into their beer about coloured boots and hair gel and how the game's gone soft.

Ihaka gave them a mock salute. "Inspector," he said affably. "Ron. Jesus, mate, what's your secret? You don't look a day over seventy-five."

High on Firkitt's shaven scalp a thick vein squirmed alarmingly. He took a deep breath through his nose, fixing Ihaka with a lizard stare.

"Nothing's changed, eh, Sergeant?" said Charlton, herding Firkitt to the far end of the boardroom table.

Ihaka kept smiling. "You tell me."

McGrail sat at the head of the table. "I don't want to have to say this twice," he said. "We're dealing with at least one murder. The preliminary report on Lilywhite indicates he was asphyxiated, which makes two. Assuming we're dealing with a professional killer, there's likely to be more. It should go without saying that this is not a situation in which senior police officers should be squabbling like spoilt children."

"With all due respect, sir," said Charlton, "that's easy for you to say. You weren't the one who was assaulted and urinated on."

Ihaka gave Firkitt a deadpan wink.

"I don't need a history lesson, thank you, Inspector," said McGrail crisply. "The incident happened five years ago and was dealt with at the time. You obtained the outcome you sought, once it was pointed out to you that neither party would've fared well under a more formal and transparent process. Our duty now is to put it behind us and move on."

"That would be a lot easier," said Charlton, "if there was some evidence of contrition in the form of an apology."

"I don't want a fucking apology," said Firkitt, his voice rumbling like an idling hot rod. "Look at him. He's not sorry so even if he said so, it wouldn't mean a bloody thing."

"Well, what do you propose, gentlemen?" said McGrail. "That we put this investigation on hold until you resolve your differences?"

"No need for that," said Charlton. "Once Ihaka has briefed the investigating team, he can go back to Wairarapa, where I'm sure he's sorely missed."

McGrail leaned back in his chair, head cocked. "Really? So you're planning to dispense with the services of the only person in the organization who was right about this case all along?"

Charlton shrugged. "Point one, Sergeant Ihaka's no longer part of the organization. Point two, if Lilywhite was still alive I could see an argument for Ihaka's continued involvement, but he's not, so I can't. To all intents and purposes he's a witness in this case, so we'll treat him like any other witness – we'll take his statement and let him go home. Frankly, sir, the implication that we can't handle this without Ihaka is a bit of an insult to the rest of us."

"Oh, I think you're being a little thin-skinned there, Inspector," said McGrail, going back to his desk. "I thought Sergeant Ihaka's knowledge and insight would be useful, but clearly you have every confidence that your team can bring this case to a swift and satisfactory outcome. I look forward to your confidence being vindicated."

He put on his reading glasses and opened a folder. The meeting was over.

Charlton stood up, returning the mocking smile he'd had from Ihaka earlier. "Travel safely."

He left the room. Ihaka looked at Firkitt, who jerked his head towards the door.

Ihaka followed him out, wondering if he was crazy enough to start something right outside McGrail's office. They faced each other in the corridor. Firkitt's eyes were hooded and his arms hung loosely by his sides. He'd love to, thought Ihaka, he really would.

Firkitt read his mind. "Don't piss your pants, shithead – I'm not that dumb and you're not worth it. Doesn't mean I'm not going to get you one of these days, because I fucking well will. Second door on the right, my DC's waiting to take your statement. Then you can fuck off back to your sheep-shaggers and battered babies."

"You don't want to hear it first-hand?"

Firkitt was already walking away. He looked over his shoulder, his face twitching. "You wouldn't want me in there," he said. "You wouldn't come out in one piece."

As Ihaka was giving his statement, he got a text from McGrail's secretary: 'Pls c ADC wen yr dun.'

McGrail looked up, peeling off his spectacles when his secretary brought Ihaka in.

"Well, that went well," said Ihaka, as the door closed behind him. "Did you really think Charlton would welcome me with open arms?"

"I didn't think for one minute he'd welcome you," said McGrail. "I thought he might tolerate you, but it seems the faithful Firkitt has the power of veto where you're concerned. Whoever said time heals all wounds – I believe it was Chaucer – obviously never suffered the psychological scarring that accompanies being laid out in a latrine. But it's Charlton's baby now, and seeing he's claimed it, he's obliged to give it high priority. And to get it right."

"Which was really the whole point of the exercise?"

McGrail smiled his miniature smile. "Let's say that was plan B. So what are you going to do now?"

"Probably stick around for the rest of the week – see a few people, do some chores around home."

"I understand Lilywhite's funeral is on Friday, at the cathedral in Parnell. You might want to attend."

"Wouldn't that be a bit provocative?"

"For whom?"

"Charlton."

"It's a funeral, Sergeant. I know the inspector has empire-building tendencies, but for the time being church services fall outside his bailiwick."

"His what?"

"It's really none of his business if you choose to attend the man's funeral."

"What about Lilywhite's kids?" said Ihaka. "I'm pretty sure they'd think it was their business."

"I dare say. But he did choose you as his father confessor."

"That's exactly what he called me."

"Well, there you are then. Ask yourself this: if Lilywhite himself had a say in the matter, would he want you there?"

Ihaka couldn't remember the last time he'd been in church.

As a child, he'd wondered if his parents were devoted to each other in spite of their political and philosophical differences, or because of them. His father was a Marxist, but his heretical streak and relish for rocking the boat often put him at odds with comrades who toed the party line and took direction from a foreign capital. When it came to religion, though, he was a card-carrying atheist. Not only was his mother a believer, but her denomination of choice was the Anglican Church, aka the National Party at prayer. Although compromise didn't come easily or naturally to Jimmy Ihaka, he and wife Barbara made a deal over little Tito's spiritual upbringing: he would attend Sunday school, then go to church once a month until he turned sixteen. After that it was up to him.

Now Ihaka remembered: the last time he'd been in church was a week before his sixteenth birthday.

After he'd heard his father declare for the hundredth or so time that religion was the opium of the people, twelve-year-old Tito asked him what it meant.

"Religion and opium both get people hooked and take away their spirit," said Jimmy. "That makes them easy to control. You can't change the world when you spend half your life on your knees."

Barbara chipped in, "So why do people keep falling for it?"

"Because they're ignorant," said Jimmy. "Once the masses are properly educated, they'll see religion for what it is, a tool used by the establishment to control them."

"Going to university didn't stop me believing in God," said Barbara.

"Yeah, but you're high-caste. It goes with the territory."

"Why did you marry her, then?" asked Tito.

"That's a stupid question," said Jimmy. "Have a look at your mother."

Tito did as he was told. "Okay, I get it," he said. "But why did Mum marry you?"

Barbara laughed, a sound her husband and son never tired of. Jimmy chased Tito outside, roaring, "Cheeky little bugger. If I get my hands on you, you won't sit down for a week."

Ihaka smiled at the memory, thinking, maybe I should come to church more often.

The service began. He was surprised to find himself mouthing the words of a long-forgotten hymn – "Time like an ever-rolling stream bears all its sons away; they fly forgotten, as a dream dies at the opening day" – and that his wandering mind could seize on a couple of sentences from the priest's soporific incantation: "I held my tongue and spake nothing: I kept silence, yea, even from good words, but it was pain and grief to me. My heart was hot within me, and while I was thus musing the fire kindled, and at the last I spake with my tongue."

During the prayers Ihaka surveyed the expanse of bowed heads, wondering how many of the murmuring suppliants actually believed that God was all ears. He wasn't the only one who couldn't be bothered pretending to pray. Across the aisle a woman sat and fidgeted as if she was waiting for a well-overdue bus.

There was something familiar about her, but her face was obscured by a swoop of dark hair. Perhaps sensing Ihaka's scrutiny, she turned her head, her gaze tracking across the lowered heads and hunched backs to settle on him. He had seen her before, getting out of a car into the pale yellow beam of a street light and walking unhurriedly through the rain to Lilywhite's front door. After a few seconds Denise Hadlow's incurious gaze moved on, leaving no sign that she'd placed Ihaka as the persecutor of her former lover.

Businessman Jonathon Bell delivered the first eulogy, a numbingly thorough review of Lilywhite's life and times, from their meeting at Christ's College through to the most recent boys' weekend, a duck-hunting expedition. It was only when covering the final, inglorious phase of his late friend's career in property development that Bell discovered the virtue of brevity.

Then the children had their say. Matthew had a patrician air to go with the accent he'd acquired during his five years in London. He evoked a warm, caring father endowed with robust common sense and an unerring moral compass. While not a churchgoer, Lilywhite had drummed Christian principles into his children until knowing right from wrong came naturally to them.

Sandy declared that Lilywhite had never really recovered from the loss of his wife and the "ordeal" he'd been subjected to, her steely demeanour giving it the air of an official announcement. But the crackle of indignation soon gave way to a fragile tremor. After a few minutes she trailed off in choking sobs and had to be helped back to her seat.

The service concluded with the Twenty-third Psalm. The middle-aged mourners sang it with gusto, their raised voices swirling around the vaulted emptiness: "Though I walk through the valley of the shadow of death, I will fear no evil, for thou art with me."

Lilywhite wasn't counting on that, thought Ihaka. He took it for granted that God had washed His hands of him.

Hand in hand Sandy and Matthew followed the pall-bearers down the aisle and out into grey heat that throbbed with the threat of rain. The congregation swept after them. Having sat through the ceremony designed to reduce death's sting, the friends of Christopher Lilywhite were now eager to emote. Ihaka went with them. He didn't want to do this, didn't think it would be well received or do any good, but it felt like the right thing to do.

Sandy saw him coming over the shoulder of the woman she was hugging. Her expression went blank. She must have said something because the other woman made a clean break from the clinch and moved aside.

Ihaka pushed in front of another sympathizer, a woman wearing a hat from the era of royal tours and cigarette holders. "I'm sorry for your loss," he said.

Sandy shook her head weakly, like a pummelled fighter signalling he'd had enough. "I don't believe this," she said. "What are you doing here? I don't want your fake sympathy, so just go away."

The crowd buzz hushed. People stared. As Ihaka turned away, he heard Matthew call out, his acquired accent faltering under the strain, "Is that him? Is that the guy you were telling me about? Hey, you, hold it right there. I want a word with you."

The crowd shrank back, creating a clearing. Sandy wanted nothing to do with it. She plucked at her brother's sleeve, reminding him that they were due at the crematorium.

Matthew freed himself, giving her hand a squeeze. He got up close to Ihaka, his shiny eyes bulging. "I want to know what the hell's going on."

"I'm not involved," said Ihaka. "You should speak to Detective Inspector Charlton."

Matthew's jabbing finger stopped just short of Ihaka's chest. "I want to hear it from you."

Ihaka shook his head. "No you don't."

Matthew grabbed his arm, but Ihaka shook him off and shouldered his way through the crowd, ignoring the complaints, just wanting to get the hell out of there. When someone yanked on his sleeve, he whirled around to give them a good look at what they were messing with. It was Denise Hadlow.

"You're Ihaka, right?"

He put his expression in neutral. "Yeah."

"Well, you've got a nerve," she said. "I'll give you that."

"I could say the same about you."

"No, they all pretend I don't exist," she said. "I just have to keep a low profile and not talk to anyone."

"Have you got a minute?"

Before she could answer, Firkitt materialized at her elbow, flourishing ID. "We'll take it from here. Detective Sergeant Firkitt, Ms Hadlow. We'd like a word."

She raised her eyebrows at Ihaka, mimicking his resigned shrug. As a DC led her away, Firkitt lit a cigarette and blew smoke in Ihaka's face, forcing him to take a step back.

"You never learn, do you, fat boy?" said Firkitt.

"I'm on leave."

"Well, go fucking fishing. If you don't back off, Charlton's going to come after you with a fucking flame-thrower. And don't think Creeping Jesus will protect you. He'll be too busy covering his own arse."

"Is it okay with you if I go and get a cup of coffee? See, the thing is the fancy stuff, your skinny decaf lattes and what not, are a bit hard to come by down my way."

"Do it and get the fuck out of town. Last warning."

Ihaka sat in the car arguing with himself. It wasn't his case, wasn't his problem. He could spend the weekend with the whanau, then go home. Yeah, Wairarapa was home now. He'd been perfectly content with his life before this interruption and would be again. Well, perfectly was a bit strong: he'd been content. Yes, the fact that Lilywhite had confessed to him made it personal, but there was no way back in; Charlton would make sure of that. It was over.

But less than forty-eight hours after Lilywhite had opened up, he was murdered. That was quite a coincidence. Why would you kill a dying man? Maybe whoever knocked off the wife had got wind that his client was talking to the cops and had shut him up.

There was another way of looking at it: less than twenty-four hours after Ihaka had spoken to Yallop, Lilywhite was murdered. Was that how the killer had got wind that Lilywhite was telling all? Yallop's view that murder in the eastern suburbs didn't have a professional criminal feel to it made a certain amount of sense, but go back to the starting premise: the Prof would tell the truth only if he had nothing to gain from lying and if he calculated that by playing along he could bank a favour to be called in down the track. But Yallop had made it clear he saw Ihaka as yesterday's man, an Auckland nobody. Why would he help a cop who couldn't return the favour?

It started to rain as Ihaka drove over to Ponsonby. By the time he parked on a bus stop across the road from the café, rain was hissing from a milk-white sky, emptying the pavement tables. Yallop's table was occupied: a couple of real estate agents, guessed Ihaka, and two plump sitting ducks from the secretarial pool, fifteen years younger and depressingly eager to live down to expectations.

He asked the guy behind the counter what time Yallop had left. Yallop hadn't been in that day. He'd probably popped over to Sydney for a few days.

Ihaka rang Central to get Yallop's address. Yallop lived in a short street on the south side of Jervois Road, behind Three Lamps village. As Ihaka expected, the restored villa was neither more nor less twee than the neighbours'. Yallop knew how to blend in, whatever the setting.

He climbed the steps to the veranda. Six jabs on the buzzer got no response. The front door was locked and the curtains were drawn.

The gate at the side of house opened to Ihaka's push, although there was a deadbolt on the inside. He would have picked Yallop as a stickler for basic security. He went down the side of the villa to the back porch. Yallop had been out there having a beer while he barbecued a steak. The beer was on the outdoor table, half-finished. The steak was on the grill, half-cooked. Yallop lay on his back with a neat hole in his forehead.

Ihaka sighed. "You didn't see that coming, did you, Prof?" he said. "Guess you weren't so fucking smart after all."

7

On the last day of her life Lorna Bell had a $375 haircut and lunch at the Viaduct Basin. She drank a champagne cocktail while she studied the menu, another with her pan-fried snapper, and a $200 half-bottle of Chateau Rieussec with her two desserts – summer berry compote and crème brûlée. While a regular luncher, she wasn't in the habit of eating alone and rarely drank more than a glass of innocuous white wine or gave the dessert menu more than a lingering, regretful glance. Equally out of character, given that she was a responsible citizen whose husband was in the public eye, she drove home to Paritai Drive knowing full well that she wasn't entirely sober.

She got changed into a pair of baggy track pants – the sort her daughters called "fat pants" – and wandered around the house just looking at things: the art (a recent magazine profile of her husband had called it "undoubtedly one the finest private collections of New Zealand modern art"), her favourite pieces of furniture, photo albums. Several times she picked up a phone and started to make a call, but thought better of it.

She went into what used to be the girls' bedrooms. They were guest rooms now, as immaculate as the rest of the house, stripped of all trace of girlishness or teenage posturing. She didn't regret doing that: her daughters were young women now, one foot in the present, the other in the future, and unsentimental about the trappings of their indulgent childhoods. Some of her friends had kept their children's bedrooms intact, as if they had some historical significance, like the royal bedchamber in a French chateau: this room has been preserved exactly as it was when Samantha was in her last year at St Cuthbert's; note the poster of Madonna in her Jean Harlow phase. It seemed like a slightly tragic form of denial, empty nesters not wanting to accept that the chicks had got too big for the nest and wouldn't be back. Still, she wished she'd kept the books she used to read the girls at bedtime, sitting on their narrow little beds, watching their faces sag and their eyelids flutter as they slid into sleep. Thank God they were adults now, too far into their own lives to turn back.

Lorna stood on the terrace looking out at the harbour and the gulf beyond, as still as a photo in the breathless humidity. How many hours of her life had she spent captivated by that shimmering vista? Not enough. There was a faint growl of distant thunder. Another wild night was on the way; it had been that kind of summer.

She roamed the garden, the self-contained world where the hours meandered by like bumblebees. Their garden guru had been through a few days earlier, otherwise she might have been tempted to get down on her knees with a trowel.

She reminded herself that she was working to a timetable. She could probably afford to spend another hour dwelling on what she'd leave behind, but what was the point? She went inside and washed her hands, taking care not to look in the mirror.

She poured vodka into a cut-glass tumbler and added orange juice, hurrying now, almost in a rush to retrieve the sleeping pills from the bottom of the drawer, under layers of winter cashmere.

She climbed the stairs, the drink sloshing in the glass, not noticing the art now, just concentrating on placing one foot in front of the other.

She went into her bedroom – she and her husband no longer slept together; his snoring had been the catalyst, or perhaps the excuse – and shut the door behind her.

Her husband, meanwhile, had spent a not atypical day in the life of a corporate titan: five and a half hours in an aircraft, two and a half hours in airports, two and a half hours in cars travelling to and from airports, forty-five minutes in a meeting, and three and a half hours in one of Sydney's most expensive restaurants. He got home at 1.15 a.m.

On discovering his wife's body, Jonathon Bell did what he always did when things hadn't gone according to plan: he rang his lawyer.

When Tito Ihaka arrived slightly late for the Sunday morning meeting in the Auckland District Commander's office, at which he would have to explain why and how he came to discover Doug Yallop's body and then be interrogated and abused by Charlton and Firkitt, he was surprised to find it unoccupied.

"They're going to be late," said McGrail's secretary. "Something's come up."

"Oh yeah," he said. "What's that?"

She smirked, telegraphing the lie. "No idea."

He nodded. "How long are they going to be?"

"No idea."

"It didn't occur to you to let me know?" he asked. "Seeing as I am on holiday."

"I've been flat out," she said, paying more attention to her computer screen.

Ihaka thought about making her wish she'd called in sick, but he was in enough trouble as it was. Besides, scaring silly bitches out of their frillies was something else he was trying to give up. He walked away. She was still bleating that the ADC could be there any minute as the lift doors closed.

He was finishing his short black when he got the text to say the meeting had convened. He hailed the waitress to order another coffee.

It wasn't the confrontation Ihaka had expected. McGrail and Charlton were preoccupied with Lorna Bell's suicide, and Firkitt was on visible police presence duty in Paritai Drive.

Ihaka went through why he'd gone to see Yallop in the first place, what the Prof had to say on the subject of hitmen, and why he'd gone back for another go.

Charlton leaned back in his chair, examining the ceiling. "Do I detect a pattern here?" he said. "You talk to someone. Some time later you think of all the things you should have asked them and realize you'll have to go back for another bite at the cherry. Except by the time you get around to it, they're dead and therefore unable to answer the questions you should've put to them in the first place. I know Lilywhite asked to see you, but you sought Yallop out – which probably means your inability to follow orders got him killed."

"Yallop was a piece of shit that we've been trying to nail for fucking years," said Ihaka, "so excuse me if I don't have a cry. And if he was killed because someone saw me talking to him, then the question is: why me and why now? Because as you know bloody well, Inspector, over the years plenty of blokes around here have talked to him. I'd bet a month's pay Firkitt's been up to that café for a few chats. Who knows? You might've even been up there yourself. I

116

mean, that's what we do, isn't it – talk to people who might be able to provide useful information."

McGrail swivelled in his chair, awaiting Charlton's response with an expectant expression.

Charlton decided the best form of defence was to pretend he hadn't been attacked. "Who knew you'd talked to him?"

"It was after four on a Tuesday afternoon," said Ihaka. "The only other people there were a couple of young women, student types, and the guy making coffee."

"You didn't tell anyone?"

"I understood the question the first time. Maybe you should focus on who Yallop discussed it with."

Charlton shook his head. "Jesus, you've got a lot of attitude for someone who's been busted doing precisely what he was ordered not to do." He turned to McGrail. "Sir, seeing Sergeant Ihaka seems incapable of letting this go, I'm going to have to ask you for an assurance that when I get to work tomorrow he won't be in this city, let alone in this building."

McGrail nodded thoughtfully.

Charlton waited for verbal confirmation, but none was forthcoming. He got to his feet. "If I can make a suggestion, sir, you might want to personally escort Ihaka onto the plane and secure the doors. Now if you'll excuse me, we're pretty busy right now."

"Never rains but it pours, eh?" said Ihaka.

Charlton eyed Ihaka coldly from the doorway. "Until we meet again. Let's see if we can make it a nice, round decade this time."

"Busy's an understatement," said McGrail when the door closed. "They're stretched to breaking point."

"Boo hoo. What's the story with this suicide?"

McGrail told him what they'd learned so far: how Lorna Bell had spent her last few hours; that her distraught husband wasn't aware of any reason why she'd take her own life; that there were no medical issues, although she'd recently undergone minor cosmetic surgery and had more planned; that she didn't leave a note.

"Pretty fucking weird, wouldn't you say?" said Ihaka.

"Which particular aspect?"

"Well, the haircut for a start."

"I wouldn't attach too much significance to that," said McGrail. "Think of it as a variation on clean-underwear syndrome."

"She'd had cosmetic surgery and there was more in the pipeline, right? Are you really going to book yourself in for a nose job or arse suction or whatever if you're planning to pull the plug?"

"People are contrary," said McGrail. "They think one thing one minute, and the exact opposite the next. I don't see it myself, but I've heard it said that the ability to hold contradictory views simultaneously is evidence of a sophisticated mind. Secondly, money wasn't an object, and when money's no object people find all sorts of daft things to spend it on. Thirdly, I dare say we wouldn't have to look too far to find a psychiatrist who'd tell us that cosmetic surgery is a manifestation of low self-esteem."

"She didn't leave a note."

"You've seen the studies, Sergeant. The percentages vary, but they all make the point that quite a few suicides don't."

"Okay," said Ihaka. "A guy gets the sack. His wife shoots through with the kids – turns out she's screwing his best mate. She convinces some dickhead social worker that he's a potential child molester, so he's denied access. If that bloke sticks a shotgun in his mouth, it's pretty fucking obvious what was on his mind, so who needs a note? This woman, her life's a bed of roses, yet suddenly she's out of here without a word of explanation." He shook his head.

"If you ask me, she hadn't been building up to this: something came at her out of the blue, something she couldn't handle. So why didn't she tell her nearest and dearest?"

"The studies also conclude that the nearest and dearest sometimes withhold or destroy the note, whether to protect the victim's reputation or their own."

"Doesn't that possibility worry you?"

"We're policemen," said McGrail. "We like to know everything. The poor woman killed herself, and there's an end to the matter. If she did so because her husband was a swine, then he'll have to answer to a higher power than the law."

"Some of us don't buy that."

McGrail nodded. "Oh, I'm well aware of that. One thing about being a believer, it takes away the temptation to play God."

At six o'clock that night Ihaka was at the airport swearing at an automatic ticketing machine. If he hadn't been wearing jandals, he might have been kicking it as well. His cellphone rang.

"Where are you?" asked McGrail.

"The airport."

"Which one?"

"I haven't left yet," said Ihaka. "And if these fucking machines don't give me a break, I probably never will."

"Well, they are designed so that any fool can use them but, as we know, Sergeant, you're not just any fool." McGrail waited for a reaction, but his little joke fell on stony ground. "Doesn't matter, though. You're not going."

"I'm not?"

"There's been another murder," said McGrail. "This time I was able to persuade Charlton that he could do with another pair of hands, even if they're yours."

"Christ, how did you do that?"

"I simply pointed out that his people are overwhelmed and you're an experienced homicide detective who knows this city like the back of his hand. Besides, this has nothing to do with the Lilywhite case, so there's no reason why you and Firkitt should bump heads."

"You still had to pull rank, right?"

"Charlton's too canny to let it get to that," said McGrail. "But I may well have given the impression that I would've if I had to."

"Do I have a say in this?"

"Of course."

"The reason I ask is it seems to be taken for granted that I'll put my hand up for this gig."

"Yes, I can see how it might look that way," said McGrail. "All I can say is, I had to move fast. Obviously you're entirely at liberty to say this isn't my patch, this isn't my problem, I'm going back to the Wairarapa. It would be somewhat embarrassing for me, but that's not your problem either."

"I'm normally immune to emotional blackmail," said Ihaka. "In fact, it brings out the worst in me. On the other hand, I'm flattered that you're prepared to resort to it. I'll be in first thing."

A jogger found the body, clad only in a pair of boxer shorts, in Cornwall Park. The deceased was a white male aged about thirty whose final hours had been as hellish as Lorna Bell's had been leisurely. Several of his fingers had been broken, there were cigarette burns all over his chest, and he'd been methodically beaten until his system couldn't take any more. It had "drugs" written all over it.

Ihaka was assigned a detective constable. Joel Pringle was twenty-five and had the look favoured by quite a few young city cops: gym-built, short, styled hair, moustache and beard set. Ihaka associated this look with guys who could sit all day at their desks with sunglasses perched on the tops of their heads, who'd rather be seen as cool than capable even though cool cops were a contradiction in terms, who weren't as tough as they looked and nowhere near as tough as they thought they were.

He rang Van Roon. "Joel Pringle. What's the story?"

"He's a good enough soldier," said Van Roon. "No Sherlock Holmes, obviously, but give him a job to do and he'll do it."

"Okay, now let's have the bad news."

"He's one of Firkitt's boys."

"So he's a plant? Fucking great. Every move I make's going straight back to Firkitt and Charlton."

"For Christ's sake, Tito, what did you expect?"

"At least I've got Beth Greendale. McGrail jacked that up when we were going to run the Lilywhite thing as a cold case."

"Maybe she's McGrail's eyes and ears," said Van Roon.

"Are you serious?"

"Look, mate, all I know is McGrail's a bit of a political animal these days," said Van Roon. "It goes with the territory. I'm sure he's pleased to have you back because he knows you get the job done, but don't assume it's you and him against the rest. McGrail didn't get where he is today by not putting his own interests first."

"I worked with the guy for thirteen years," said Ihaka. "I think I can trust him."

"Mate, you're not listening – he wasn't ADC then. Look, I don't know what's going on up there, but it sure as hell isn't business as usual. If I was in your shoes, I wouldn't trust anyone."

Ihaka laughed. "Jesus, you should hear yourself. And to think you used to call *me* cynical."

"You know what?" said Van Roon. "You were right to be."

*

121

In the first twenty-four hours Ihaka and his team made zero progress towards identifying the dead man. On Tuesday morning a young Kiwi Asian woman came into Central with a photograph of her boyfriend, who'd uncharacteristically stood her up on Saturday night and wasn't answering his intercom or his phones. Because the boyfriend, whose name was Arden Black, was a white male aged thirty-one, Tiffany Wong soon found herself face to face with Ihaka.

The photo wasn't much help: Arden Black was extremely good-looking, as the dead man might well have been before his face was pulped. The extent of the damage and disfigurement meant there was little point in putting Tiffany through the ordeal of looking at the body.

She and Arden had been an item for almost two years, but living together wasn't on the agenda because her parents didn't hold with it and Arden liked his space. He had fingers in a few pies: he part-owned a café, did some modelling and photography, dabbled in scriptwriting, and had a meet-and-greet gig at a bar cum late-night supper club, which basically involved setting a benchmark of attractiveness and cool that discouraged unattractive, uncool people from trying to gain entry. Ihaka thought Arden had "drugs" written all over him.

Tiffany had heard about the Cornwall Park corpse on the radio. She was sure it wasn't Arden, but she just couldn't keep those dark thoughts out of her head. This was so unlike him: he was well-organized, punctual, and hated putting people out – you wouldn't meet a more considerate person. In fact, her father had paid him the ultimate compliment, saying that if it wasn't for his round eyes, Arden could have been Chinese.

Ihaka said, "Lots of drugs around that nightclub scene."

Tiffany snorted, but with amusement rather than indignation. "I guess," she said, "but it wouldn't matter to Arden

– he's way too health-conscious. I mean, he's got this look he gives me if I have a second glass of wine, like 'What the hell, Tiff? Do you have any idea what you're doing to yourself?' Here's another thing: his Sunday morning workout was like non-negotiable. Didn't matter what was going on, if I was sick as a dog. Shit, it didn't matter if *he* was sick as a dog, he did a big weights workout on Sunday morning. I checked with his gym: he didn't show."

She was obviously telling the truth, not that it proved much either way. Men were good at compartmentalizing and some women didn't force the issue, preferring to stay away from the sealed-off areas on the basis that what they didn't know couldn't hurt them. Besides, there were drug dealers who wouldn't dream of using their own product and despised those who did. On the other hand, the medics had said that if the dead man hadn't been in such good physical shape, his torment wouldn't have lasted as long.

"What sort of underpants does Arden wear?"

Tiffany looked almost affronted. "What's that got to do with anything?"

"Every little bit helps," said Ihaka, gesturing vaguely. "These things are just a process of elimination."

"Actually, he's got a bit of a thing about jocks," she said, as if Ihaka could relate to that. "He only wears plain white pure cotton boxers. Moschinos. He's got like fifteen pairs."

Ihaka restricted his reaction to an expressionless nod, resisting the temptation to glance at the open folder in front of him. He was 99 per cent sure that the dead man shared Arden's thing about jocks.

Pringle knocked and entered. "Quick word, Sarge?"

Ihaka followed him out into the corridor. Pringle's face was tight with excitement or perhaps alarm.

"What's up?"

"There's been another one. A woman dumped in a quarry in Mount Wellington." Pringle paused for effect. "Wearing nothing but a pair of knickers. Same thing: cigarette burns, broken fingers, smashed to shit."

Ihaka dragged a meaty hand across his face. "Fuck."

"You reckon we've got a serial killer on our hands, Sarge?"

"Slow down, son."

Maybe Auckland really did have a serial killer whose monstrous thrill was to strip his victims down to their briefs and club them to death after some low-tech torture, but Ihaka's money was still on drugs. Just as Jonathon Bell rang his lawyer when he had a problem, the maniacs in the dope business reached for their baseball bats.

They'd know one way or the other soon enough. If there was a psycho out there, two strikes in forty-eight hours suggested he was way gone, totally in thrall to the voice inside his head telling him that he was a higher being, unbound by law, convention or morality, and ordinary humans were fair game, to be hunted down and annihilated for sport and pleasure.

And if that was the case, it wouldn't be long before another near-naked, pulverized corpse turned up.

8

The murdered woman was in her mid-thirties, medium height, with dark hair and a trim figure. So was a guest who'd checked into an Ellerslie motel over the weekend and promptly disappeared. Ihaka sent Detective Constable Joel Pringle out there.

He rang in an hour later. "Sarge, her name's Eve Diack. She's from Wellington. She checked in early Sunday afternoon, dumped her bag in the room, and called a cab. That was the last anyone here saw of her. The bed wasn't slept in either night. She told the manager she was on a flight home first thing this morning, so when she didn't check out, they knocked on her door. Her gear's still in the room, but it doesn't look like she's been in there since Sunday."

"The motel's got her details – address, cellphone, credit card?"

"Yep. They tried ringing her, but there was no answer."

"Okay," said Ihaka. "I'll send a team out. You get back in here. Wellington cops, phone records, cab company – in that order."

Arden Black's dental records made it official. Now the dead white male had a name. Soon he'd have a home with drawers and cupboards and locked filing cabinets; he'd have a background, a routine, a lifestyle, a call history, a social circle. And maybe bad habits, dubious friends, murky dealings with people who needed to be handled with extreme care.

Home was on the top floor of a low-rise apartment block on the harbour side of Parnell Rise. One look told you two things: Black was fanatically tidy, and he liked his toys. The kitchen was a design magazine cliché right down to the bowl of lemons: wall-to-wall stainless steel, Italian bar stools, state-of-the-art German appliances. The living room had a Bose sound system and a flat-screen television that occupied most of one wall. Arden stared moodily out of several framed studio portraits. There was a shot of him on a beach, pearly grin splitting a lean, tanned face and abs like brickwork. It made Ihaka feel like a sumo wrestler.

There were no photos of Mum and Dad or freckled, gap-toothed nephews and nieces, no mates-for-life scenes from his twenty-first birthday party or big brother's wedding, no high-school first fifteen, no OE shots of him in front of the Eiffel Tower or trying to get a rise out of a sentry at Buckingham Palace. It was as if the road that led to Cornwall Park began right there, in an apartment that looked and felt like a display home.

Also conspicuous by their absence were the usual trappings of hedonistic bachelorhood: drugs, pornography, a little black book. Having as jaundiced a view of human nature as the next cop, Ihaka took the fact that Tiffany's photo was out of sight in the bedside table drawer to mean that she hadn't been the last woman to enter Arden's bedroom.

Hypothesis: Arden had another woman in his life. Question: why hadn't she come forward?

According to Tiffany, Arden never left home without his iPad. Seeing he hadn't been killed at home, it followed that it had been taken or disposed of by the killer. Ditto his Alfa

Romeo. He backed up the information on his iPad onto his laptop, which he kept in the bedroom in case he woke up during the night with a script idea that was bigger than *Ben-Hur*. The laptop was gone.

Hypothesis: whoever killed Arden used his keys to get into the apartment and remove the laptop. Question: why?

Tiffany's parents lived in Epsom, in a two-storey house, whitewashed stone with a grey slate roof, down a long drive.

The doorbell was answered by a middle-aged Asian man with a military crew cut. Ihaka identified himself and was taken through to the kitchen, where Tiffany was perched on a bar stool watching an older woman, presumably her mother, chop vegetables.

They looked at Ihaka expectantly, too unworldly to assume the worst. He'd seen this done and done it himself often enough to know there was no point in trying to break it gently. Only fools believed their hushed euphemisms or watery-eyed empathy made a scrap of difference.

"I'm really sorry, Tiffany," he said. "Arden's dead. That was him in Cornwall Park."

Tiffany stared at him, knotting her eyebrows, unable to believe that all the scenarios with happy endings which she'd constructed to account for her boyfriend's disappearance had turned out to be wrong, and the one which she'd persuaded herself was too far-fetched for words had turned out to be right. Her mother dropped the chopping knife with a clatter and hurried to the other side of the bench. Tiffany placed her forehead on her mother's chest and howled like an abandoned puppy.

Her father touched Ihaka's arm. "Thank you for coming," he said. "We'll take care of Tiffany now."

At the door Ihaka said, "I'm afraid we're going to have to talk to her again."

"I'll tell her."

"She might find out things about Arden she'd rather not know." The father looked at him unblinkingly. "You understand what I'm saying?"

"You mean he was different to what she thought?"

Ihaka shrugged. "Part of him."

"Was he a criminal?"

"We don't know yet," said Ihaka. "We don't know why he was killed – he might have been an innocent victim, or a guy who got out of his depth. But the chances are Tiffany's going to get hurt all over again."

The father nodded. "Poor Tiffany. I always hoped she would never find out how hard the world can be."

Danny Howard, the owner/manager of the Departure Lounge, the nightclub where Arden had worked, was a fortyish knockabout who made no bones about the fact that he'd lost an asset as well as a mate.

"He was worth his weight in gold, that bloke," he told Ihaka. "A very classy, professional dude – and, just quietly, an absolute chick magnet. I've seen a chick scrawl her phone number on the back of his hand while her boyfriend was a metre away buying her a fifty-buck cocktail. I've seen another one complain she was feeling crook, get the poor bastard she was with to take her home, then bowl in here solo an hour later sexed up to the max. That sort of shit happened all the time, but he never let it become a situation, you know what I mean? He could handle himself, he could handle these feral women, and if their boyfriends or husbands twigged what was going on, he could handle them too."

"What was his secret?"

Howard threw up his hands. "He just had a way about him. He'd smile that smile of his and come out with some line that let the chick know it wasn't a happening thing, but without making her feel like a silly little slut for coming on so strong and getting the big fend. Sometimes he'd say thanks but no thanks and do a swift fade, and they'd be standing there thinking, did that really happen or did I imagine it?"

"Or maybe, is that coke I did in the shithouse fucking with my head?"

"Hey, come on, man," protested Howard. "I run a clean house."

"Sure you do," said Ihaka.

"Damn right," said Howard, apparently under the impression that Ihaka was being sincere. "And for the record, if there was anyone more anti-drugs than me, it was Arden. He could have a motherfucker of a headache, but he wouldn't even take a Panadol."

"How did he handle the guys, especially the ones who saw it as him hitting on their girlfriends rather than vice versa?"

"You're not wrong there, mate," said Howard. "That's how it usually works. He'd just laugh it off, as if they were making a mountain out of a molehill. Put them off balance and walk away. Make them think, if I want to go on with this, I stand a pretty good chance of looking like a real fucking jerk. His fallback, when they just wouldn't let it go, guy or girl, was to tell them he was gay." He shrugged. "Let's face it, he was pretty enough."

"So it was his professionalism that stopped him taking up these offers, as opposed to the fact he had a girlfriend?"

"Oh shit no, it was both. Like, Arden was a pro, as I say. He understood you can't have staff hitting on the clientele, even the singles, because that just pisses off other singles who are on the prowl. But Tiffany had a bit to do with it – he was pretty keen on her. He was just a classy dude, and not screwing around was all part of it."

*

The last confirmed sighting of Arden Black was at around four on Saturday afternoon when he met his business partner at their Newmarket café.

Beth Greendale went out to Newmarket to meet the partner, a sleek young gay named Lucas Smythe. As he sniffled his way through a pack of tissues, Smythe told her that he and Arden had discussed cash flow and their increasingly temperamental barista and how, if it came to that, they'd spin his sacking at an Employment Relations Service hearing. Arden was his usual chilled-out self, looking forward to dinner with Tiffany at a new Vietnamese restaurant in K Road.

"Was he a good guy to be in business with?" asked Greendale.

"Oh, absolutely. The best. But he was just a good guy, full stop. He didn't deserve this. He wasn't a hard person, you know? He treated people well. My only peeve with him was that he didn't spend enough time here because he could pull a crowd, that boy – both sexes. My gay friends were always ringing up wanting to know when Arden was coming in. It was usually after lunch, so he gave a few queens sleepless nights in more ways than one."

"How close were you?" asked Greendale. "I mean, did you socialize?"

"No, not at all," said Smythe. "I'm a single gay, he was a coupled-up straight. Plus he had his nightclub gig, so he wasn't into clubbing on his nights off. I can relate to that: I only ever go into a café to work or to check out the competition. Plus Arden was kind of obsessive about keeping the different parts of his life separate. Like, I've spoken to Tiffany on the phone heaps of times, but I've never actually met her. He wouldn't even show me a photo. He had this saying, 'That's why they call it a private life'."

"Really? So you didn't know Tiffany was Asian?"

"Nooooo! You're kidding me."

"Does that seem out of character?"

"Oh, God no. Arden was a cool guy, he didn't have any hang-ups or prejudices. I just assumed she'd be some drop-dead gorgeous model girl. Not that Asian girls can't be drop-dead gorgeous – we get them in here all the time. Oh my God, I'm tying myself in knots here. You know what I'm trying to say." Smythe paused. "I did find out one of his secrets, although I never let on. You people must know this."

"What?"

"His name. You obviously know about his name?"

"Why don't you tell me about his name?" said Greendale.

The thought of being one step ahead of the police did wonders for Smythe's mood. "When we started up this place and set up the partnership, we used Arden's lawyer. Because I was always here and Arden often wouldn't answer his cellphone – he was quote too busy unquote, although he wouldn't tell you what it was that kept him so busy – the lawyer usually dealt with me, so I got to know him quite well.

"Anyway, one night I ran into him in a bar in Ponsonby. He turned out to be one of those people who get a bit indiscreet when they've had a few. 'I could tell you a secret about your partner,' he said. 'Really?' I said. 'You bet,' he said. 'You want to hear it?' And I said, 'Should you be telling me this?' He said it wasn't a big deal, it was just funny, so I said, 'Okay, let's hear it.' He said, 'Arden Black isn't his real name. He went through the process to get it changed legally.' 'Is that right?' I said, thinking, wow, some secret. He said, 'You've got to promise not to let on to Arden that you know. When I tell you what his real name is, you'll understand why our friend Mister Cool would be absolutely mortified.' That sounded a bit more like it, so I crossed my

131

heart and hoped to die. He lowered his voice as if he was about to reveal some hideous scandal: 'His real name,' he said, 'is Warren Duckmanton.'"

Smythe shook his head in wonderment. "I mean, really, Warren Duckmanton? My dear, in my entire life I've never met anyone who was less of a Warren Duckmanton than Arden."

Wellington sent up Eve Diack's dental records, which gave the dead white female a name. Where would we be without dentists, wondered Ihaka. Even though her divorce had been finalized more than a year earlier, she'd understandably opted not to revert to her maiden name, which was Duckmanton.

Ihaka was on the phone to Van Roon when Beth Greendale passed him a note. It said: "Arden Black wasn't his real name. He changed it from Warren Duckmanton."

Ihaka stared at the note, hardly hearing the sensational information concerning a prominent politician, a transvestite and a rude awakening which Van Roon was sharing with him in the reasonable expectation that it would make Ihaka's day.

Ihaka ended the expectant silence that followed the punchline by asking, "Did Eve have any brothers and sisters?"

"Did you hear what I just said?"

"Sorry, mate, my mind was somewhere else."

"Where?"

"On the job, as a matter of fact."

"You need a holiday," said Van Roon. "You're losing your sense of perspective."

"A couple of brutal murders can do that to you. Brothers and sisters, yes or no?"

"Keep your hair on," said Van Roon. "Okay, let's have a look here. Yep, she had a younger brother."

"Called?"

"Warren."

"Where's he these days?" asked Ihaka, already knowing the answer: Warren Duckmanton was downstairs on a cold slab.

"Interesting," said Van Roon. "Warren shot through years ago – hasn't been heard from since."

There was no serial killer. Serial killers either had a specific gender/age/physical type victim profile, or exploited target-rich locales opportunistically. A brother and sister sadistically murdered felt like a vendetta. It felt deeply, savagely personal.

After the break-up of their marriage, Eve's ex-husband Ray Diack had moved to Auckland to become head of PE at a North Shore high school. He lived in Mairangi Bay, in a weatherboard cottage whose peeling paint and tragic flowerbeds reminded Ihaka of a former life.

Diack had long silvery hair, a gold earring hanging from his left lobe, and was slightly browner than Ihaka despite being Pakeha. His brief shorts and singlet showed off densely muscled thighs and arms. Ihaka guessed he was into bodybuilding and nudism, both of which he associated with sexual deviance.

After examining Ihaka's ID minutely, Diack took him out to the backyard. His outdoor furniture consisted of a well-padded recliner and a couple of wonky plastic chairs. When Diack was reclining comfortably, he said, "You look like you could use a beer."

It was a warm afternoon. There was a film of sweat on Ihaka's face and damp patches under his arms. "I'm on duty," he said.

"You want a juice or something?"

"She's right," said Ihaka. "I don't want to take the edge off my thirst. I've got big plans for it."

Diack chuckled. "Know what you mean, mate. I'll be lining up a few frosties when the sun goes down."

"You seem to be bearing up."

Diack fiddled with his earring. "Yeah, well, it was a hell of a shock, obviously. Bloody terrible business." He stopped fiddling and looked Ihaka in the eye. "Look, I'm not going to pretend I've been bawling my eyes out. Eve and me, we had some good times, but it didn't last and she hasn't been part of my life for a couple of years now."

Ihaka's eyebrows twitched inscrutably. "So you weren't in touch with her?"

"There was the odd loose end, but that was it. Put it this way, we didn't ring each other to say happy birthday."

"When was the last time you spoke to her?"

Diack decided it was time to deploy his sunglasses. "About a month ago, I suppose. She was coming up here and wanted to know a good restaurant. I'm a bit of a foodie, you see."

He made being a foodie sound like an achievement, akin to doing the Coast to Coast or adopting a little Chechen.

"So she was up here a month ago?"

"Something like that."

"It'd be useful to know exactly when."

Diack shrugged. "Mate, it was like a two-minute call. I didn't make a note of it."

"Did she say why she was coming up?"

"We didn't have those sorts of conversations. She asked about restaurants, I made a couple of suggestions, she said thanks and hung up. It was short but not particularly sweet."

"You ever meet Warren, her brother?"

"Not many people have," said Diack. "He disappeared well before I came on the scene."

"Did Eve ever talk about him?" said Ihaka. "What he was like, why he shot through, that sort of stuff?"

"Oh yeah, now and again, but she didn't have a clue why he buggered off. No one did, as far as I could make out."

"How did she feel about it?"

"She felt for her parents, I know that much. It was kind of hard to get a handle on what she really thought about it because she went through phases. She'd be pissed off, almost bitter, for a while, then she'd go, 'Oh, fuck him: he obviously doesn't give a shit about me, so why should I give a shit about him?' A few weeks later she'd be teary-eyed, saying how much she missed him and beating herself up for not doing more to track him down."

"So she did try?"

Diack's sigh drew a line from the pointlessness of Eve's attempts to trace her brother to the pointlessness of Ihaka's line of questioning. "Well, up to a point. She used to put ads in the personal columns on his birthday: 'Dear little bro, I miss you. Please get in touch.'"

"But he never did?"

"No."

"As time went on, would you say it was more or less of an issue for her?"

Diack tilted his head one way, then the other. "Shit, that's hard to say. See, the longer we were together, the less we communicated, so for all I know it could have been driving her nuts."

"What went wrong between you two?"

"We just weren't cut out for marriage." Diack's teeth gleamed. "That whole monogamy thing."

"When you say 'we'…"

"I mean 'we'."

"Well, at least you had something in common."

"That's one way of looking at it," said Diack. "Problem was, it got to the stage where we were both pretty much doing our own thing, so there didn't seem much point staying together."

"Sounds pretty amicable."

More teeth. "Well, I made the call and you know what women are like – they prefer to make that decision. And they don't like getting cut, whatever the circumstances."

"It's possible Eve and Warren were killed by the same person," said Ihaka. "Are you aware of the Duckmanton family or Eve herself having any enemies, or being involved in any sort of row or dispute?"

"I had bugger all to do with the family – by choice – but as far as I was aware, Eve didn't have an enemy in the world. And that includes me, by the way."

With the chesty strut of a man who felt he'd handled himself well, Diack walked Ihaka to his car. As he went to shake hands, Ihaka said, "Shit, I almost forgot to ask. Where were you on Saturday and Sunday night?"

The sun had almost gone and so had the sunglasses. Diack blinked as if he'd been slapped by a stranger and his mouth opened and closed. "Are you serious?"

"Two people have been murdered," said Ihaka. "Whoever did it went to some trouble to make it a lot more painful than it needed to be. You fucking bet I'm serious."

"I was here," blurted Diack. "Both nights."

"Who with?"

"No one."

"So you spent the whole weekend on your own?" said Ihaka, laying on the scepticism.

"Well, I was out during the day, of course. I'm just not in a relationship right now, okay?"

Ihaka nodded sympathetically. "Hey, brother, I'm a single man myself. Still, that does make you a suspect. Technically speaking."

9

Detective Constable Pringle traced the taxi driver who'd picked up Eve Diack from the motel. He took her to Mission Bay, but not to a specific address – anywhere around here, she'd said when they hit Tamaki Drive. He'd watched her in the rear-view mirror as he drove away. She stood on the footpath looking around, taking in the scene: Sunday afternoon on the waterfront, a sigh of breeze, a few ghost clouds out on the horizon, twenty-seven degrees of deep blue heat – there was a lot to take in.

She was quite chatty, he said, the usual taxi-ride small talk, stuck in a car with a stranger for fifteen minutes and not wanting to seem rude: now this is my idea of summer – in Wellington we'd call this a heatwave; I don't know why I put up with Wellington weather really, not that I could live here – the traffic would drive me nuts. Par for the course for visitors from the capital. They knock their weather to soften you up for the tourism-bureau spiel: having said that and on the other hand, Wellington's a real city, it's got a heart, it's got a soul, it's got cafés for Africa, it's got culture coming out its arse. Absolutely, positively bullshit, the taxi driver called it, and Eve Diack had it down pat.

They plastered Mission Bay with photographs of her, but no one came forward. She hadn't come up to Auckland twice in just over a month to go for a stroll along the waterfront:

she'd gone to Mission Bay to meet someone. Her long-lost brother? He was already dead, but she wouldn't have known that. Maybe they had re-established contact and her trips to Auckland were making up for lost time.

A lot of cruelty had gone into these murders. Maybe Warren was killed because he knew too much and the killer wanted to know if he'd shared that knowledge with anyone. In his pain and fear and desperation, Warren could have given up his sister and the time and place of their rendezvous. She went to Mission Bay to meet him, but the killer was waiting for her.

Then what? Did the killer go through the same savage routine to make absolutely sure he'd covered his tracks? Or did he just enjoy hearing a woman scream?

Ihaka stood in the domestic terminal at Auckland Airport, looking up at the departures board. Almost as if the gizmo could read his mind, it did that ripple thing. When the rippling stopped, his flight to Wellington had been delayed for an hour.

Ihaka sighed and swore. In the old days he reacted to this sort of inconvenience by proceeding directly to the nearest fast-food outlet. He'd had plenty of time to think in his Wairarapa exile and one of the things he'd figured out was that it made no sense to punish himself for other people's failings, such as being unable to make the planes fly on time.

As he turned to go and find a newspaper and a cup of coffee, he found himself face to face with Ron Firkitt.

"Sodding off back where you belong, eh?"

Ihaka shook his head. "Just a flying visit. Where are you off to?"

"Same as you." Firkitt's eyes narrowed. "You a member of the Koru Club?"

"No."

"Thank fuck for that."

Firkitt was already on board, in an aisle seat up the front. He didn't glance up from his magazine as Ihaka shuffled past, heading for the middle seat in the third row from the back. The aisle seat was unoccupied. The kid in the window seat was lost in the music coming through his earphones. He didn't even open his eyes when Ihaka sat down.

The cabin crew went through, closing the overhead lockers, but Ihaka knew better than to entertain the hope that he wasn't going to be sandwiched. Sure enough, there was movement up the front: an enormously fat man was coming down the aisle like a slow-motion avalanche, trailed by an attractive blonde woman. The other vacant seat was in the very back row, but Ihaka knew he was going to have this fat bastard's arse coming over the armrest all the way to Wellington. Whenever he flew he played a morbid game, watching people come down the aisle and trying to guess which one would end up beside him. His system was simple but reliable: rule out the presentable women, then pick the most obvious freak from the rest.

Every fucking time, he thought. Why me? What the fuck have I done?

The fat man stopped at Ihaka's row. He gazed longingly at the empty seat. He glanced at Ihaka, who thought he detected malicious amusement in his eyes, black dots in a doughy expanse, like sultanas in a bun. This is his idea of fun, thought Ihaka: squashing people on aeroplanes.

The behemoth drew a long, rattling breath and plodded onwards. The blonde woman checked her boarding pass, slipped off her shoulder bag and sat down.

"Welcome to row twenty-five," said Ihaka, his voice husky with sincerity. "We saved you a seat."

The woman smiled enigmatically. She kicked her bag under the seat in front, buckled up, leaned back and closed her eyes, as if trying to block out the safety announcement.

She was in her late thirties, guessed Ihaka, with slightly wild shoulder-length dark blonde hair and the slim, firm body of someone for whom exercise was a duty, done willingly but a duty nonetheless. If she missed her yoga class she'd fret all day and have a bad night's sleep. She had long, elegant fingers with chipped, unpainted nails. A gardener, he thought, maybe a vego who only eats what she grows. She was wearing blue jeans tucked into ankle boots and an oversized white shirt with a wide brown leather belt. There was a greenstone tiki around her neck, a stack of bangles and clasps on either wrist and rings on every finger except the wedding ring finger. He didn't read anything into that. She was obviously a bit counterculture, so a wedding ring would be against her principles. In fact, marriage would be against her principles. She'd probably been shacked up with a fellow bohemian for twenty years.

She was sitting dead still, head back, eyes closed, giving off a strong "do not disturb" vibe. First time I'm sat next to an attractive woman, he thought, she goes into a trance. Still, it was better than having to fight off Hippo-Man.

The plane took off. Ihaka tilted his seat back and closed his eyes. Next thing, he felt a prod on his bicep. The woman had twisted around in her seat to stare at him.

"You were snoring," she said.

"What?"

"I said," she said deliberately, "you were snoring."

"I couldn't have been," said Ihaka. "I wasn't asleep."

"Excuse me?"

"I know I wasn't asleep because I was thinking."

"Really?" she said. "What were you thinking about?"

"I know this sounds lame," he said, "but I can't tell you – it's confidential."

"Lame," she said. "Excellent choice of word. But just as a matter of information, you don't have to be asleep to snore."

Ihaka sat up straight. "Do you know that for a fact, or did you read it in a magazine you flicked through at the supermarket but didn't buy?"

The woman paused, looking at nothing in particular, perhaps asking herself why she was having a debate about snoring with a perfect stranger. "My ex-partner used to do it. All the time."

"Which is why he's ex?"

She looked away again, grunting with bemusement. "There was a bit more to it than that. Getting back to the matter at hand…"

Ihaka made a placatory gesture. "Look, if I was snoring – and I'm sure you wouldn't have made it up just to initiate a conversation – I apologize. I'll try to keep my eyes open."

"Thank you," she said, getting a notebook out of her shoulder bag. "I hope I didn't break your concentration."

"No problem," said Ihaka. "Mind like a steel trap."

Suddenly Firkitt was looming over her. "Sorry to butt in," he said to her, "but would you mind swapping seats? I need to talk to this guy. We're police officers." He stood aside to let her out. "I'm in 2C."

She looked at Ihaka questioningly.

"I wasn't aware we had anything to talk about," he said, "but yeah, we're cops."

She shrugged and stood up. "Never let it be said I don't cooperate with the police."

Firkitt watched her all the way down the aisle. "Top sort," he said sliding into the vacated seat. "Nice face, nice arse. Don't look at me like that – you didn't have a shit's show."

"Maybe not," said Ihaka, "but getting knocked back by her beats talking to you any day. Since when did we have anything to discuss?"

"Oh shit, sorry, my mistake," said Firkitt. "For a moment there I had you mixed up with a police officer. I thought you might like an update on the Lilywhite case, but you're obviously more interested in passing crutch."

Ihaka stared at him. "You get me kicked me off the case, now you want to brief me on it. What is this shit?"

Firkitt returned the stare. "Am I happy you're back? No. Do I want to have anything to do with you? No. But the reality is you've got knowledge of this case so I'm being professional and putting the personal shit to one side for the time being."

"Very noble," said Ihaka, "but it's your case now. You pushed for it, you got it and you're fucking welcome to it. There's no point giving me an update because I'm not interested. I've got enough on my plate."

"Why did I expect anything different?" said Firkitt, shaking his head. "You don't give a shit, do you?"

"I know you and your boss don't do anything without a reason. Let me guess: Charlton's worried that if it ends up going nowhere, there'll be a review of how it was handled, so he's covering his arse? Fine, I'll play along. Just don't expect me to take it seriously."

Firkitt put his head on the headrest. "We've got nothing, basically. Bell's off-limits – he's still all broken up over his wife. I spoke to the dentist, Anderson. He pretty much accused me of making the whole thing up. I fucking set him straight on that, but he had nothing useful to contribute. I'm seeing Saunders, the MP, this morning."

"What about those other cases?"

"The bloke whose mother went for a gutser, he and his wife buggered off to Sydney as soon as the inheritance came through. The TV guy fired up big-time: 'How dare you imply that I might've had something to do with the murder of my best friend and partner, blah, blah, fucking blah.' He won't talk to us without his lawyer there."

"Did he ring true?"

Firkitt shrugged. "Everyone's a liar until proven otherwise. Problem is, the only way to make the case is to establish a connection between the perpetrator and the beneficiaries, but we don't have a clue who the perpetrator is. In fact, we've only got Lilywhite's word for it that there is one."

"You get anything from his ex-girlfriend?"

Firkitt shifted in his seat. "There's a different issue there."

"What's that?"

"She only wants to talk to you."

"Why the fuck didn't you say so in the first place?"

Firkitt ignored the question. "Well?"

"It's your case," said Ihaka. "If you want me to talk to her, I'll talk to her. What did you make of her?"

"You mean apart from thinking she could've done a hell of a lot better than Lilywhite?"

"Yeah, apart from that."

Firkitt thought about it. "You look at the facts and you think, oh yeah, she's just another dirty little gold-digger running on cunt-power, but I don't know. There might be a bit more to her than that."

"And you wouldn't say that lightly."

"No, I fucking would not." Firkitt stood up. "I'll see if Blondie wants to swap back. If she does, you could be in with a chance."

A minute later the woman was back.

"Wild horses couldn't keep you away, eh?" said Ihaka.

She rolled her eyes. "Actually, I always ask for a seat down the back – you've got a better chance of surviving a crash. So you work with that guy?"

"Well, yes and no. We're both currently working out of Auckland Central and there's some overlap on our cases, but that's it. We actually hate each other's guts."

"Good for you. What sort of police work do you do?"

"You might've noticed there've been a few murders lately."

"God, yes I have. What's going on?"

"That's what we're trying to find out."

"Have you caught many murderers? I mean you personally." He nodded.

"Will you catch this one?"

"Yeah, we'll get him all right."

"You're sure it's a he?"

"They usually are. This one definitely feels like a he."

"How come you're so confident?"

Ihaka gave her a look. "How would you feel if I wasn't?"

She nodded. "Good point. Well, best of luck. Now I don't mean to be rude, but I need to do some more prep for my appointment so…"

As the plane taxied to the terminal, Ihaka asked, "So what do you do?"

She rummaged in her handbag for a business card, which identified her as Miriam Lovell, freelance journalist. Seeing Ihaka's eyebrows lift, she said, "Don't worry, you didn't speak out of school."

"Actually," he said, "I was just wondering what would happen if I rang this number."

She shrugged. "Only one way to find out."

The seatbelt sign went off. "I'm going to have to go like the clappers," said Lovell. "Hope you get your man."

Then she was off, murmuring apologies as she pushed and manoeuvred her way up the congested aisle.

There was a driver waiting for him. Ihaka dropped him off in town and headed out along the foreshore motorway.

To Ihaka Wellington meant sagging skies the colour of birdshit and pedestrians leaning into the wind as if they were entering a ruck. People were always saying you can't beat Wellington on a good day, and this was obviously what they meant: a perfect sky, the harbour as flat and inviting as the crema on an espresso, dry warmth, crisp light. Too nice a day to be working, he thought. He should be in a restaurant down on the waterfront, or a little café out Eastbourne way, having lunch with Miriam Lovell instead of heading over the hill to see a mother whose kids had been clubbed to death like seals.

He liked the way Wellington branched out from the scraps of flat land between the hills and the sea, snaking up the gullies and along the ridges, pushing into the elements. It must have taken cussedness and vision to impose a city on this unruly geography. Auckland looked as if it just grew, like weeds.

He went past Petone and through the Hutt, following the river like the joggers and dog-walkers. A few years ago a woman went for a walk along this stretch of river. She had people coming for lunch so her family knew something was wrong when she wasn't back in good time. They found her under a tree, strangled – another pathetic sex crime. The guy who did it claimed he'd blacked out. It was amazing how many murders have been committed by people who claimed to have been unconscious at the time. In the midst of life, there is death. Even here, on the riverbank where mothers push their prams.

He drove over the Rimutakas to Greytown, aka Gaytown. It had been just another zombified little country town until a few gays from Wellington jazzed it up. Now people came up from Wellington for brunch at the cafés and restaurants along the main drag or a bed and breakfast stay-over.

145

Sheila Duckmanton ran a B and B in what used to be the family home, a pleasant villa in half an acre of lawn and flowerbeds backing onto a sports ground. It was business as usual, although to look at her you wouldn't have thought she'd pick herself up from one death blow, let alone a combination. She was petite and fine-featured – the children had inherited her looks – with prematurely white hair scraped back into a little old lady bun. It didn't take Ihaka long to realize that appearances were deceptive.

She offered him a cup of tea. He said he was fine, but she made him one anyway. They sat out on the veranda, him in a wicker chair that was more comfortable than it looked, her in a swing seat. Ihaka suspected she was going to spend a lot of time out there, swinging to and fro, tracking the disintegration of her simple dream of home and family.

"I've been crying for Eve," she said, resolutely dry-eyed, "but not for her brother. I've had plenty of time to get used to the fact he was never coming back."

"Why do you think he took off like that, Mrs Duckmanton? I know a lot of kids can't wait to leave home, but they don't just disappear."

"Why overlook the obvious? He didn't care. We didn't mean a thing to him. I kept telling Eve that, but she wouldn't accept it. And look where that got her."

"How do you mean?"

"Why do you think she was in Auckland? She was looking for him. I think she found him and got caught up in some dirty work he was up to his neck in."

"By the time she got to Auckland, he was already dead."

"You're the detective; I'm just a widow trying to make ends meet by letting strangers stay in my house. All I know is if she'd washed her hands of him, she'd still be alive."

"Why couldn't she let it go? From what I've heard, they weren't all that close."

She got the swing seat moving. "I don't know who you've been talking to. She doted on him, right from when they were toddlers. When I lost my husband three years ago, Eve got it into her head that finding her brother would somehow make up for that, make us a family again. I told her not to bother. Even if you find him, I said, he won't want to have anything to do with us. He said as much that one time he rang, right at the beginning. Don't look for me, he said. After that he never got in touch, not once. What does that tell you? But when Eve got a bee in her bonnet, she didn't take much notice of what anyone said. And now she's gone too."

"What made her think he was in Auckland?"

"She bumped into an old school friend who'd seen him in Sydney."

Ihaka waited for elaboration, but none came. He took it as the first sign of the disorientation he'd half-expected.

"You mean Auckland," he said gently. "The friend saw him in Auckland?"

"If I'd meant Auckland," she said with a snap, "I would've said so. I've still got my marbles, thank you very much." She talked over Ihaka's apologetic murmur: "He was with that Vanessa Kelly. She lives in Auckland, so that was good enough for Eve."

"You mean the Vanessa Kelly who's on TV?"

"Who did you think I meant?"

Vanessa Kelly had been on television as long as Ihaka could remember. She'd started out as one of those weather girls who make an anticyclone over the Tasman sound like "Your place or mine?" She became a reporter on the network news before finding her natural home on an infotainment current-affairs show. She could do it all: leak fat tears while brushing flies out of a starving African child's eyes, grill a Solomon Islands warlord with a yen for decapitation, and generate such chemistry with male celebrities that you wanted to tell them to get a room.

Her glamour and volatile private life made her a women's magazine fixture. She'd been through three marriages and, if the gossip was to be believed, there weren't many hale, male heterosexual New Zealanders of any note she hadn't pinned to a mattress. Like many celebrities, she sought to neutralize time by reinventing herself at regular intervals. Her latest stunt, according to a magazine article Ihaka had skimmed in a café, was claiming to have discovered the joys of celibacy.

"She'd be a bit old for him, wouldn't she?"

"She's famous," said Mrs Duckmanton, making it sound like a crime.

"When this friend said Warren was with her, did that mean…?"

"She said they were all over each other like a rash. That's clear enough, isn't it?"

"It'll do for now. Going by what you said earlier, Eve hadn't actually told you that she'd seen Warren?"

"No. She hadn't been up here for a month or so, which was unlike her, but she rang every few days. I could tell something was going on from the tone of her voice, but all she'd say was that she was getting warm. I knew what she had in mind. I knew my Eve better than she knew herself sometimes. She wanted it to be a surprise. She wanted to bring him back and for us all to live happily ever after. But that's the thing about life, Sergeant: there aren't enough happy endings to go round, so some families miss out."

Disobeying orders, Ihaka took his cup and plate – he'd eaten only one of the two Tim Tams, which pleased him as much as it displeased his hostess – through to the kitchen.

On the way out, he asked if there was anyone who might have held a grudge against Eve or the family.

"Her ex-husband." She spat the words out, as if trying to get rid of a bad taste in the mouth.

"Why?"

"She walked out on him; he swore he'd make her pay. He's just an animal."

Ihaka had been here many times. "What did he do to her?"

Mrs Duckmanton wasn't quite all cried out. Tears flooded her faded blue eyes. "He beat her up. My sweet little girl, he beat her black and blue."

10

Ihaka spent that afternoon and the following day, a Saturday, in Wellington interviewing Eve Diack's friends and neighbours and her colleagues at Land Information NZ, where she worked as an administrator.

Most of them were aware she had a brother but not even her close friends, the ones who thought of themselves as confidantes, knew the real story. In fact, the Eve who emerged from this process was, among other things, a prolific fabulist. She had a different version of where Warren was and what he was doing for every audience.

Some were under the impression he was an entrepreneur in Eastern Europe. Her best friend, who was sworn to secrecy, got the juicy details: he was in Budapest, running a porno mini-empire. She told the women in her social netball team that he managed an exclusive resort/detox facility in Hawaii, and was a personal friend of pretty much every fucked-up famous person you could think of. She told her book club he was earning big bucks working on an oil rig in the Gulf of Mexico. When they asked how he'd fared in the oil spill, she said he'd quit not long beforehand – the implication being that he'd seen where things were heading – and was now in Cuba, living like a king on his stack of greenbacks.

She was less creative with her colleagues, telling them her brother was in Hamilton, married with kids and selling cars.

After that, none of them took any further interest in him. She told her most recent boyfriend a similar story, except in this version he was in Waipukurau selling farm equipment. She had as little as possible to do with him because he'd found Jesus, joined some batshit religious outfit, and become a total pain in the arse.

None of them knew about her trips to Auckland. They thought she'd been in Greytown, seeing her mother.

Her friends never got the Ray Diack thing. They picked him as a dropkick from day one and were gobsmacked when the wedding invitation arrived. Within weeks of saying "I do", Eve started to come around to their way of thinking, and it was all downhill from there. As someone put it, it went from love-hate to tolerate-hate to hate-hate.

There were screaming matches and some violence, but it wasn't as clear-cut as her mother made out. Towards the end Eve sported a deep purple shiner which she wore as a badge of honour, telling people, "You should see the other guy." One friend did just that, bumping into Ray in town. He had angry scratches on his face caused, he said, by going over the handlebars of his mountain bike up on the town belt. When the friend mentioned it to Eve, she said "Yeah, right," and made claws with her hands.

They all said she'd walked out on him, not vice versa. In fact, even though the marriage had degenerated into an undeclared war, Ray took the break-up quite hard. No one remembered Eve saying he'd threatened her physically, but she did tell a couple of people that he'd vowed to post a sex video from their love-love period on the Internet. She claimed she'd called his bluff, warning it wouldn't do much for him but she'd be spoilt for choice.

She did tell a couple of guys she went out with that Ray had whacked her now and again. One of them wanted a piece of Ray but she talked him out of it. In the first place,

Ray was bigger than he was; secondly, she gave as good as she got; thirdly, she wouldn't go so far as to say she asked for it, but she did give him a lot of shit. "Put it this way," she said, "I wouldn't want to be married to me."

It wasn't as black and white as Sheila Duckmanton thought, or wanted Ihaka to think. In a way, thought Ihaka, the fact that Eve had treated Diack worse than he'd let on made him more of a suspect.

On the way to the airport to get the last flight to Auckland, Ihaka stopped off in town for a quick beer with Johan Van Roon.

They talked about the old days. Van Roon talked about life in Wellington and being a detective inspector and how well his kids were doing. When they'd got that out of the way, Ihaka asked about Blair Corvine.

"Come on, Tito," sighed Van Roon. "You've heard the story from people who were much closer to it than me."

"Yeah, but you'll tell me the truth."

Van Roon laughed. "I'd almost forgotten what an insidious bastard you can be."

"I keep hearing Blair was doing too many drugs," said Ihaka. "Christ, they were saying that ten years ago."

"Well, exactly," said Van Roon. "It's a cumulative process. You keep putting that crap in your system, it's going to catch up with you. The fact that people were saying 'Fucking Corvine, if he doesn't ease off, he's going to come unstuck' for a while before it actually happened doesn't mean their analysis was wrong. It just means they underestimated his capacity. As I heard it, he was taking too many drugs and too many risks and telling too many lies. Something had to give. I guess you could say the fact he got away with it for so long shows how good he was."

"So you don't believe there was a leak?"

"Mate, I'm saying you could see it coming," said Van Roon. "Shit, I can remember telling McGrail it was time to pull him out."

"What'd he say?"

"'Don't think I haven't tried.'"

"So basically he'd gone rogue?"

"Look, you know Corvine wasn't a team player. Okay, not many of those guys are, but the longer he was in, the less inclined he was to follow procedure. He pissed a lot of people off. Not to the point they were going to drop him in the shit or anything, but you know when it happened people just shrugged their shoulders."

As Ihaka's taxi pulled up, Van Roon grabbed his arm. "Mate, watch your step, all right? I know you think you can trust McGrail, but he's a different animal these days. And I know what you think of Charlton, but don't underestimate the bloke."

"Firkitt was on the plane coming down," said Ihaka. "He was almost civil. They want me to give them a hand."

Van Roon shrugged. "They've got something going on, Tito. Whatever they tell you it is, work on the assumption it's really something else."

Ihaka attached a fair amount of significance to a suspect's reaction to his unheralded appearance. They didn't have to shit themselves, but blithe unconcern was a downer.

Thus it was gratifying that Ray Diack, who answered the doorbell in a dressing gown even though the sun was squatting over the western ranges, gawked for a few seconds, then went red in the face, then started talking very fast.

"This is an incredibly inconvenient time," he babbled. "Besides, I've already told you what little I know. I really can't help you." He began to close the door. "So if you don't mind…"

Ihaka took a quick step and slammed the flat of his hand against the door, pushing back. "A word of advice, Mr Diack: if you're going to say bugger all, make sure it's true."

"What the hell are you talking about?"

With his other hand, Ihaka pulled the search warrant from his hip pocket and waved it in front of Diack, the signal to the search team in the unmarked van parked across the road. Diack's eyes bulged as the van door slid open and Detective Constable Joel Pringle and a couple of constables in plain clothes emerged.

"We're coming through," said Ihaka. "Just think of it as an open home. If we use the dunny, promise we won't do number twos."

Diack's face was a mask of nausea. He came out of the house, yanking the door shut behind him. "Listen, you can't do that."

Ihaka frowned at the warrant. "Really? That's not what the magistrate said."

"Jesus Christ, look, just hang on a minute." Diack's flush had drained away, taking his tan with it. "I've got someone here. She's married. To a mate of mine. They've got three little kids." He was jabbering like a racing commentator calling a photo finish. "This could cause no end of strife. Couldn't you just come back in half an hour? Please?"

"I'm afraid that would defeat the whole purpose of the exercise," said Ihaka urbanely. There was a murmur of assent from the search team, now poised at their boss's elbow and champing at the bit after hearing Diack's confession.

Having had his fun, Ihaka shifted gears. "Now are you going to get out of the way or do we have to go through you?"

"What's the basis for this?" demanded Diack, his tone veering from supplication to bluster. "I haven't done anything wrong. What the fuck gives you the right to barge into my house? I've got a right to privacy."

"You want reasons?" said Ihaka. "Okay. One, you belted Eve. Two, you lied about it. Three, she dumped you. Four, you lied about that too. Five, you don't have an alibi. Six, I've got a warrant. How many fucking reasons do you need?" Shouldering Diack aside, he threw the door open, hollering, "Coming, ready or not." He glanced over his shoulder at the search team, an appreciative audience. "I bet she's heard that before."

Diack's playmate had taken refuge in the bathroom. Maybe he'd told her to stay in there until she reached the age of consent. Diack had taken his last peek into the girls' changing rooms, but every cloud has a silver lining: in among the lurid detail of his pupil's statement was an alibi for the night his ex-wife was murdered.

Whenever a member of the public comes into a metropolitan police station like Auckland Central claiming to have vital information relating to a high-profile investigation but insisting they will only divulge it to the officer in charge, experienced cops exchange knowing looks. If said member of the public, on being advised that the officer in charge is currently unavailable, says he or she is prepared to wait and does so, uncomplainingly, for over an hour, that settles it: said member of the public is a crank. In this querulous day and age only cranks or perhaps saints don't resent being put on hold, and Ihaka knew full well how hard it was to be a saint in the City of Sails.

Not that the guy looked deranged. His outfit was smart casual – a style Ihaka had never quite got the hang of – and he had the solid, moulded build of a man who spent his lunch hours pumping iron. He would have been in his mid-thirties, although the receding hairline might have added a year or two.

But cranks – as opposed to out-and-out crazies – are cunning. They understand the importance of first impressions. They know that when it comes to gaining access, it's all about how you present. So Ihaka faced the prospect of having to listen to this fruitcake insist that Eve Diack was a human sacrifice in a satanic ritual attended by some of the most powerful people in the land. Or that she'd stumbled across a vast financial scam masterminded by the international Jewish conspiracy. Or that he'd seen her lifeless body tossed out of a flying saucer piloted by Elvis Presley.

Steeling himself, Ihaka went into the interview room. A minute later Pringle brought in the crank, who was stuffing a thousand-page paperback into his backpack. Ihaka would have put money on it being about UFOs or Stonehenge or the Third Reich. Grant Hayes had a crunching handshake, another sign of mania in Ihaka's book. He didn't like limp, sticky or ambiguous handshakes any more than the next man, but there was a happy medium, for Christ's sake.

"Thanks for your time, Detective Sergeant," said Hayes. Ihaka thought he detected a trace of an Australian accent. "Sorry for not coming in sooner. I've been down in the South Island tramping and only just caught up with the news. I'm a private investigator. Eve Diack was, briefly, a client of mine."

After his parents' divorce, Hayes's mother had taken him to Australia, hence the accent. He'd come back to Auckland and set himself up as a private investigator, positioning himself in the Yellow Pages as a people-finder specializing in tracking down Kiwis who'd crossed the Tasman and disappeared off the radar. He assumed that was why Eve had picked him.

"She came to see me about five weeks ago wanting me to find her brother. Someone had seen him in Sydney with Vanessa Kelly."

Ihaka nodded.

"You knew about that?"

"I went to see Eve's mother."

Hayes's eyebrows merged as it occurred to him that he might have spent an hour and a quarter in the waiting room for nothing. "Oh, well, then you probably know the rest of it?"

Ihaka shook his head. "Eve kept her mother in the dark."

Hayes's expression lifted. "I told Eve that if I managed to find her brother I'd ask him if he wanted to be reunited. If the answer was no, that would be the end of it as far as I was concerned. I learned pretty early on that sometimes the runaway has a bloody good reason for clearing off and the client has pretty dubious motives for wanting them found. If the runaway's safe and sound and capable of making the choice, I go with their call."

"What did she say to that?"

"She asked if everyone in the industry operates on that basis." Hayes smiled grimly. "I had to tell her that they don't."

"So you found him?"

Hayes shrugged. "It wasn't hard. I followed Kelly around and she led me right to him. I explained the situation and told him what I'd told Eve. He said his family hadn't been part of his life for umpteen years and that was the way he wanted it. When I reported back to Eve, she asked me to find out his address. I gave her the same speech. Well, started to anyway. She said if I wouldn't do it, she'd find someone who would, and hung up."

"How long did all that take?"

"From hired to fired, just under a week. She rang me a couple of times after that, trying to get me to change my mind, and when that didn't happen, wanting me to put her on to another private investigator. I told her I could only recommend people who operate on the same basis. You can imagine how that went down."

"Her mother warned Eve he wouldn't want to know," said Ihaka. "That's why Eve kept her in the dark. She didn't want to hear 'I told you so'. Then she came back up here to hire another finder."

"I'd be amazed if she didn't," said Hayes. "As you can imagine, I see quite a few obsessive people, but Eve was up there."

"I bet Warren wanted to know how you found him."

"They always do, but I never tell. We're like magicians – if the punters ever learn the tricks of the trade, we'll be out of business."

"Did you warn him Eve would get someone else?"

"Yeah, I thought it might persuade him to meet with her. He could say his piece and she'd get it from the horse's mouth. At least she would've set eyes on him and that might have got it out of her system. But he wasn't bothered, said he'd just have to be more careful."

"You can add them to your list of famous last words."

When Hayes left, Ihaka summoned Pringle. "We're going to have to check out every private investigator in town: the legit, the dubious, and the sleazy. That's the royal we, by the way."

Vanessa Kelly lived in one of the mock-brownstone apartment blocks which have sprouted along the harbour side of Remuera Road, providing views out to Rangitoto and down into the sleepy hollows populated by middle-class toilers who can afford the postcode but not the outlook. Ihaka turned up unannounced around dinner time. He pressed the buzzer and presented an unblinking stare to the security camera.

"Yes?" The familiar voice crackled with static and suspicion.

"Detective Sergeant Ihaka to see Vanessa Kelly." He held his ID up to the camera.

There was a silence lasting perhaps thirty seconds. "With regard to what?"

"Arden Black."

Another silence. "What about him?"

"Well, I thought we'd start with his murder and then just play it by ear."

There was a click which Ihaka interpreted as the sound of negotiations being broken off. He quite enjoyed it when people who, for whatever reason, thought they were special tried to treat him the way they invariably treated others. To put it another way, he enjoyed acquainting them with the reality that in a murder investigation people fell into one of two categories: cops and others. He was a cop; Vanessa Kelly was an other.

The lift door opened and Kelly strode into the foyer. She wore white capri pants, high heels and a tight black T-shirt with the words "Handle With Care". Her hair was pulled back into a ponytail and she had glasses with narrow black rectangular frames, a look Ihaka vaguely associated with dominatrix school mistresses in S&M magazines. Up close she verged on mutton dressed as lamb, and lacked the cloistered aura of someone who'd sworn off sex.

She examined Ihaka through the glass doors, tapping her chin with her cellphone. "You don't look like a policeman," she said.

"This isn't television, Ms Kelly. I didn't have to audition for the part."

"Who's your superior officer?"

"Superintendent McGrail." This was so predictable that Ihaka had memorized McGrail's direct line. Kelly turned her back and walked away, punching the numbers into her phone. The conversation lasted ninety seconds and, as Ihaka could have told her, didn't make her feel any better about the situation.

She pressed a button on the wall to open the glass doors. Ihaka went inside.

"I don't suppose you see many brown faces around here?"

"That's got nothing to do with it," she said with a toss of the head. "I'm just security-conscious. I would've thought you'd approve."

"Too right," he said. "Always assume the worst. You'll never be disappointed."

They rode the lift up to the penthouse apartment in silence and without eye contact.

Like Black, she had a lot of photos of herself on display, mostly standing very close to an international celebrity. Ihaka pointed at one. "Who's he?"

"Bono."

"Who?"

"Bono from U2. Don't tell me you haven't heard of U2? They're only the most famous rock band in the world."

Ihaka gave no indication that the most famous rock band in the world had ever come to his attention. "This was taken at night, right?"

"Yes."

"So why's he wearing sunglasses?"

"I don't know, he just does." Kelly seemed genuinely perplexed that this left-field irrelevance was all Ihaka could come up with. "I suppose it's kind of a trademark."

"Or maybe he's a tosser?"

"Gosh, that's profound," she said. "It might interest you to know Bono's probably done more for the cause of Third World debt than anyone on the planet."

"Good on him. I guess he can afford to."

She rolled her eyes. "What's that Oscar Wilde quote? A cynic is a man who knows the price of everything and the value of nothing."

"Remind me, what exactly is cynicism?"

"Always believing the worst of people."

"Well, seeing is believing, Ms Kelly, and I've been seeing the worst of people for quite a while now."

There was a bottle of wine in an ice bucket on the dining table. Kelly poured herself a glass.

"Tell me about your relationship with Black," said Ihaka to her back.

"What relationship? I met him once or twice, end of story."

"You never went out with him?"

"No."

"Never went on an overseas trip with him?" She made a face to indicate the question was absurd. "In case you need reminding, this is a murder investigation. These are basic yes-or-no-type questions, and you're obliged to cooperate."

"I never went anywhere with him, okay?"

Eyes front, she walked past him out onto the balcony. Ihaka followed. He stood at the balcony rail, admiring the view. "To summarize then, you met Black a couple of times. You never went out with him, never slept with him, never went away with him?"

There was no reply. Ihaka looked over his shoulder. Kelly was curled up in a chair, flicking through a magazine, slowly shaking her head.

"We have a witness who says she saw you and Black in Sydney, quote all over each other like a rash unquote. I guess she just made that up."

"Oh my God," said Kelly, not raising her eyes from the magazine. "Why don't these losers get a life?"

"You don't get it, do you?" he said. "You think this is just another 'he said, she said' twenty-four-hour wonder you can palm off to the PR flunkeys at the network."

She tossed the magazine aside and started jabbing at her cellphone. "What I really think is you should be talking to my lawyer."

Ihaka put his hands on the arms of her chair and bent down, his big head boring into her personal space. Her eyes widened and she put the phone down like a child told off for texting at the dinner table.

"Let me tell you what we're going to do," he said conversationally. "We're going to work this thing real hard. We're going to check your phone records, Arden's phone records, credit cards, airline reservations, hotel bookings. We're going to squeeze everyone who knew him and everyone who knows you. We're going to hit every bar and club and restaurant in this city with photos of the pair of you. And when we've established that you've lied and refused to cooperate, not only will I throw the book at you, I'll hang you out to dry in the media. I think you'll find there are a few journos out there who are only too happy to believe the worst of people."

11

Denise Hadlow lived in a stylish little townhouse in Point Chevalier. She led Ihaka inside and stood there, arms folded, looking amused, as he gave it the once-over.

"So how long have you been here?"

"Almost six years," she said. "I know what you're thinking."

"What's that?"

"You're thinking, how much of this did Lilywhite pay for?"

"And the answer is?"

Hadlow leaned against the kitchen bench, her long, tanned legs crossed at the ankle. "Have a guess."

"Not all of it, I assume."

"You assume right."

"And none would be a stretch."

She made a face: maybe, maybe not.

"I'd say he paid the deposit and bought you a new bed as a moving-in present, a great, big, knockshop-type bed."

She smiled sardonically. "Actually that's not a bad guess, but I already had a nice big bed. Personally, I wouldn't know what sort of beds they have in brothels, but I'd be surprised if they pay as much for them as I did. The way I look at it, we spend a third of our lives in bed, so you owe it to yourself to splash out on a decent one. No, he bought me that." She pointed to the biggest domestic espresso machine Ihaka had ever seen. "I'm also fussy about coffee, but I couldn't bring myself to spend three grand on a coffee machine."

"That's all?"

"Uh-huh."

"Jesus," said Ihaka. "I would've picked you to do better than that."

She walked past him into the living area, subsiding gracefully onto a sofa. The hem of her short skirt rode up to the tops of her thighs. Ihaka couldn't help himself. She casually pushed the hem down, and when his gaze tilted back up she was waiting for him, eyebrows raised. "Snap," she said.

Ihaka sat down opposite her. "So we're meant to believe you weren't in it for the money?"

"It was never about the money," she said. "It was about his wife."

"Lilywhite said you didn't like her much."

"That's not quite true. I didn't like her one little bit."

"Why not?"

"Way too bright and breezy for my taste. There's something wrong with people who are like that all day, every day; something askew in their DNA. Having an off day, being in a grump, getting out of bed on the wrong side – whatever you want to call it, it's natural, it's part of being human. You know what it was like working for her? It was like spending nine hours a day in an aerobics class with one of those fucking Energizer bunnies who keep telling you, 'Come on, you can do it,' with a big, cheesy, Colgate grin. Oh yeah, and she also didn't have a sense of humour. Literally none. She would've been blown away that anyone could even think that. She thought she had a wicked sense of humour – 'I mean, come on, I'm always having a giggle.' Which is the whole point. If you laugh at everything, including stuff that's not remotely funny, that doesn't mean you've got a great sense of humour. It means you're a pain in the arse and a borderline idiot."

"Would hate be too strong a word?"

Hadlow's expression turned thoughtful. "Possibly not. Whatever it was, the antidote was to screw her husband right under her nose. Once I started doing that, she didn't shit me nearly as much."

"I seem to remember she was very popular with her staff."

"Sure she was. But most of them were salespeople and, as I'm sure you know, salespeople tend to be suck-arses. And Joyce was the biggest one of all – she was the saleswoman of the century. She was always selling something, whether it was her crappy little strollers or her desperate housewives' cafés or herself. I used to say to Chris, 'She's a fucking machine, except there's no off-button.' She created this atmosphere, it was almost like a cult. You had to be upbeat and positive from the moment you arrived at work till you went home. And they all bought into it."

"Except you."

"Except me. I'm like that, a bit contrary. Always have been. I'm the one, everybody else thinks the movie or the restaurant or the club is awesome, I'm sitting there going 'Actually, it's not that good.' It pisses people off sometimes."

"Okay, the boss gives you the shits, so you get back at her by banging her husband. I can see that would've been a bit of a buzz for a while. But you carried on with it. Why?"

"Believe it or not, I quite liked him."

"That is hard to believe."

She cocked her head. "So your opinion of him hasn't changed?"

"We're talking about your opinion, not mine."

"My point is there was another side to Chris, and I bet you saw it."

"He made an effort," said Ihaka. "I'll give you that. But then he had a lot of ground to make up."

"True."

"Plus he was dying and remorseful. That always brings out the best in a cold-blooded killer." Hadlow's expression went blank. "So if he was such a charmer, why didn't you stick around and become Mrs Lilywhite the second? You'd be laughing all the way to the bank."

She smiled, but mirthlessly and not for Ihaka's benefit. "I'm not going to lie, the thought has occurred to me. What happened was I woke up one morning and knew it was time to move on. That's the way I roll. I mean, it was never going to be happily ever after. I doubt Chris believed that even in his wildest moments. Well, maybe in his wildest moments, but he certainly got no encouragement from me. I'm just not cut out to be a trophy wife – I get bored too easily.

"To start with, every time we did it, it was like sticking a pin in a Joyce voodoo doll, which was kind of fun. And Chris didn't have much of a clue about sex. Hard to believe you can reach that age and still be on L plates, don't you think? So it was also kind of fun teaching him how it should be done."

She smiled again. This one *was* for Ihaka's benefit. "He was very grateful, and it's nice to be appreciated. But as you said, the buzz or novelty or whatever only lasts so long, and then you start to notice the flab and the wrinkles. I mean, really notice them as opposed to being vaguely aware. And once you've really noticed them, you can't un-notice them. In fact, you can't put them out of your mind. That's when it hits you that you're selling yourself short. After that, the only way you can get through is by pretending, and I'm not into pretending."

"Who says romance is dead?"

166

"Get stuffed," she said good-naturedly. "And then what really sealed the deal, he started missing Joyce. At least that's what I thought at the time, anyway."

"Oh?"

"Look, I like a drink as much as the next girl, but I'm not big on drinking at home. I don't really get it. To me, drinking is something you do when you go out. But Chris liked a drink, full stop. Go out, stay in, it was all the same to him. So if he was settling down in front of the TV with a bottle of single malt, I'd just leave him to it. He'd complain, but as I kept telling him, getting shit-faced in front of CNN or some crappy old British comedy isn't my idea of fun. Anyway, this night I was sleeping over, but I couldn't get to sleep so I went back downstairs. He was out of it on the sofa, with this big wet patch down the front of his shirt. He'd obviously cried his eyes out."

"Or had a wet dream."

"No, I'm pretty sure he'd emptied the tank earlier."

"Some guys blub when they're pissed," said Ihaka. "It's just the way they are. Anything can set them off."

"I saw him pissed plenty of times; I never once saw him cry."

She eyed Ihaka curiously. "That other cop I talked to, or didn't talk to…"

"Firkitt."

"Yeah. He doesn't like you very much, does he? That's part of the reason I said I'd only talk to you: I knew it would piss him off."

"You like stirring things up, don't you?"

She crossed her legs unhurriedly. Ihaka's reward for maintaining eye contact was a teasing smile. "I just find it makes life more interesting. I would've thought you could relate to that. Why doesn't Firkitt like you?"

"I don't think there's too many people he does like."

"Maybe not," she said, "but there's not liking someone in the sense of not really giving a shit about them, and then there's active dislike. I got the strong impression he actively dislikes you."

"Call it professional rivalry."

"You call it that if you want. I'd say it's personal."

"I'd say it's irrelevant," said Ihaka. "Somebody knew or suspected that Lilywhite wanted to get rid of his wife. You'd have to be pretty intimate with someone to let that slip."

"Well, don't look at me. First of all, I had no idea he was contemplating it…"

"Even in his wildest moments?"

"Right."

"And you were the expert on his wildest moments."

"You'd better believe it," she said with another lazy lift of the eyebrows. "As I was saying before I was so crudely interrupted, secondly, I don't know any hitmen."

"I don't believe you."

Hadlow's eyes bulged and her mouth twisted. "What?"

"If anyone knew how Lilywhite really felt about Joyce, it would be his girlfriend. Common sense and a basic working knowledge of human nature tells you that."

Animation had flared and died like a match in the wind and now Hadlow was back to her default setting of cool detachment. "I knew he wanted to be with me, not her, and I'm sure there were times when he would've liked Joyce to just go away. But we all do that, close our eyes and count to a hundred hoping that when we open them the cloud that was hanging over us won't be there any more. Shit, I can think of a few guys I would've loved to have been able to snap my fingers and make them disappear. Doesn't mean I wanted them dead, I just wanted them out of my life. I never would've thought that of Chris, not in a million years. I still have trouble believing it. He was too fucking…

straight. And by the way, you might want to do a refresher course on human nature, because if anyone knew what was really going on in Chris's head it would've been the boys' club, Jonathon Bell and company."

"You're suggesting it was one of them?"

Hadlow shrugged. "I'm just making the point that if he told anyone, it would've been them, and look who they are – big shots, important people, people who know how to make problems go away. And from what Chris said, a couple of them, their marriages were completely shot."

"One big difference: their wives are still alive."

She shrugged again. "I'm just saying."

"You met them all?"

"Yeah."

"And?"

"Let's just say they're not my kind of people."

"I would've said that about Lilywhite," said Ihaka.

"Yeah, but he had one thing they didn't have: Joyce."

"What about Lorna Bell? Did you see that coming?"

"No way."

"And now, looking back on it?"

Hadlow shook her head. "She was the only one I liked. She was just a cool lady, none of that 'I'm rich and you're not' bullshit. Once or twice I might've got the feeling she was maybe a bit fragile, but most of the time she seemed pretty together."

"So you don't have a theory?"

Her gaze tilted upwards, as if she'd spotted an insect circling Ihaka's head. "No, I don't." She looked him in the eye again. "Are you investigating that as well?"

"No, just curious. Someone like that, it's strange, don't you think?"

"I wouldn't have swapped places with any of those women, including her. There was her husband, for a start."

"What about him?"

"I don't know, I just never really warmed to him. There was nothing specific – it's not like he ever did or said anything bad to me. And he was always lovey-dovey with Lorna."

"They say he's heartbroken."

"I can believe it."

"So what are you talking about?"

"I just found him… not cold exactly, but kind of sealed-off. As I said, he was always nice enough to me, but I never felt like it meant anything. Put it this way, I could've been Chris's dog, you know what I mean? Oh, you're a nice doggy, aren't you? Here's a little treat for you, now piss off. I wouldn't want to get on the wrong side of him. I don't think he'd be the forgiving kind."

"He's not the only one."

"Meaning?"

"You do realize this isn't my case?" She nodded. "Well, you know old Firkitt, he's not as nice as he looks. If it turns out you've lied or withheld evidence, he'll go out of his way to fuck you up."

Hadlow clapped her hands, radiant. "I love it – good cop, bad cop. So you guys really do that? I thought it was just in the movies."

"Don't say I didn't warn you."

She tilted her head coquettishly. "But if it came to that, you'd put in a good word for me, wouldn't you?"

Ihaka's expression didn't change. "That would depend on the question."

As Hadlow was showing Ihaka out, her little boy Billy arrived home from school. He was nine or so, a nice-looking kid with big dark eyes and long lashes. When his mother introduced them, Billy smiled shyly and put his miniature hand in Ihaka's big mitt.

"Sergeant Ihaka's a policeman, darling," she said.

170

His eyes grew even bigger. "Mum! What did you do?"

She turned to Ihaka. "I think that's a question for the sergeant."

Ihaka ruffled Billy's dark curls. "Don't worry, mate, I'm not going to take your mum away."

"I might hold you to that," she said.

"Mum, I'm starving," said Billy.

"Okay, sweetie," she said. "See what you can find, I'll be in in a sec. Say goodbye to Sergeant Ihaka."

"Bye-bye, Sergeant."

"See you, mate."

Billy went inside.

"You should be flattered," she said. "He's normally very wary with strangers, especially men."

"Been a few through here, have there?"

She rolled her head, feigning deep disappointment. "And you were doing so well. I'm talking about friends, people from work, tradesmen. There've been a lot fewer of the other sort of men than you obviously think." She paused. "And a damn sight fewer than there could've been."

"Where's his old man?"

"Long gone, thank God. It's amazing such a shitty relationship could produce such a sweet kid. So is this goodbye, or will we be seeing you again?"

"That's up to Firkitt. I'll put in a report. He'll either want me to have another go or he won't."

"I suppose I should hope he won't?"

"You might've seen the last of me," said Ihaka, "but I doubt you've seen the last of us. This thing's got a way to go yet."

"I might just have to put my foot down again, say I'll only talk to you."

"I doubt Firkitt will wear that a second time."

"Well, anyway, you know where we are now. Drop in for a coffee some time. I make a great cappuccino."

Hadlow watched Ihaka get into his car, gave him a little wave and another fathomless smile, and closed the door. Before he hit the first set of lights he'd come up with half a dozen reasons why he shouldn't even think about taking up her offer to drop in for a cappuccino. But he knew he would think about it. Quite a lot.

By the time he got back to Auckland Central, Ihaka had decided that the sensible course of action was to try his luck with Miriam Lovell.

He rang her cellphone; there was a message saying the number was no longer in service. It was a woman's privilege to change her mind, but that seemed a bit over the top. That left her email address, but asking a woman out via email, especially a woman who'd just changed her phone number, didn't feel right. Apart from anything else, it would make it easier for her to say no.

He briefly toyed with the idea of using the resources at his disposal to find out her home phone number, but decided against. If she worked out what he'd done – and he was pretty sure she would – that would be that.

For a few hours the next morning it seemed like they'd made a breakthrough. The Alfa Romeo that had belonged to Arden Black/Warren Duckmanton was clocked doing 157 kph on the North Western Motorway. The new owners, in the sense that possession is nine-tenths of the law, hadn't even bothered to change the plates. They were a couple of no-hopers from Te Atatu whose CVs included joyriding stolen cars and small-time welfare fraud. They were hoons who'd fight if cornered and double up on a guy just for being in the wrong place at the wrong time, but Ihaka doubted they had the stomach for the sustained, bludgeoning cruelty inflicted on Black.

The no-hopers claimed they'd snatched the Alfa from a supermarket car park in Western Springs two days after the murder. It was just sitting there begging to be taken for a spin: unlocked, keys under the driver's seat, gassed up and squeaky clean. There was nothing to connect them to Black, and their alibis for the nights he and Eve Diack were murdered were rock-solid – or as rock-solid as alibis get out west.

The Alfa gave up two sets of prints, no-hoper one and no-hoper two. Whoever cleaned it had done such a thorough job they'd erased all traces of Black, as well as of themselves.

Hamish Bartley QC, lawyer by appointment to the eastern suburbs, personally rang Ihaka to invite him to coffee and sandwiches in his firm's boardroom, where they would be joined by his client, Vanessa Kelly.

This was a rather different Vanessa Kelly, subdued in manner and appearance. She wore a dark business suit with a skirt that went all the way down to her knees, and celebrity hauteur had given way to alert unease. After a perfunctory reunion, she sat at the boardroom table scribbling notes on a legal pad while Bartley fussed over her like a trainee hairstylist. Ihaka sat opposite, helping himself to a wedge of mini-sandwiches.

Bartley embarked on proceedings with the stateliness of a large ship putting to sea. "Detective Sergeant, you should be aware that my client initiated this meeting. She's very conscious of her civic responsibilities and wishes to do everything in her power to assist your investigation." He paused, a signal to Ihaka that he should pay special attention to what came next. "Even to the extent of sharing information of a deeply intimate and sensitive nature."

Ihaka examined the plate of sandwiches, weighing up where to strike next. "Better late then never, I suppose."

Bartley gave Kelly an encouraging nod. She forced herself to look at Ihaka. "I apologize for not being more forthcoming," she said in a plaintive little voice. "It's rather embarrassing. I did have a relationship with Arden Black, but not in the usual sense. We spent time together because…" She bit her lower lip. Ihaka seemed to remember she'd done that a lot while covering the Christchurch earthquake. "I made it worth his while. He was an escort, or if you prefer the old-fashioned term, a gigolo."

After three marriages that soared, spluttered and nose-dived like cheap fireworks, too many messy affairs and too many headlines, Kelly had reached the stage of being happily single. Most of the time, anyway. It's not easy to kick the habits of a lifetime, and no matter how hard she tried to put it out of her mind, there were times when she missed having a man around. The problem was finding an attractive and interesting one who was prepared to accept her terms, which were basically that he should materialize when and only when it suited her. Err on the side of spontaneity, and you were in one-night-stand territory with its stab-in-the-dark randomness and demeaning mornings after. Go too far the other way and you were in a relationship, with all its logistics and compromises and squandered emotional capital.

She consulted some experienced singles, whose advice was varied and contradictory. One argued that the fact she was having this dilemma proved the futility of trying to be something other than her natural self: she was picking a fight with her own nature, and there could be only one winner in that contest. Another advised her to put herself about in cyberspace, which she felt was rather missing the point.

A third suggested a holiday in Jamaica. Why Jamaica? If I have to spell it out for you, girlfriend, she was told, you've got a bigger problem than you realize. Kelly thought this also missed the point. First, she didn't buy the idea that a ten-day binge would set her up for a year of serene celibacy. Second, there was something tawdry about flying halfway around the world for the company of strangers. Something hypocritical too, given that she'd made a programme that dealt scathingly with white male sex tourists pawing and grunting their way around Asia.

There was a birthday lunch in Parnell followed by some bar-hopping. As afternoon turned into evening, the celebrators peeled off or fell by the wayside until there were only two: Kelly and a friend of a friend, a woman whose name had escaped her five hours earlier. But when it's just the pair of you, juiced to the eyeballs in a spa pool sipping a cleansing pink champagne, you don't talk about other people's children or the seabed and foreshore ruckus. It seemed quite natural for her new bud – whose name was Helen Conroy – to confide that although her husband was her best friend and all that, they hadn't had sex for three years. Vanessa asked the obvious question, the answer to which was Arden Black.

Helen made him sound like the perfect solution: drop-dead gorgeous, hard-bodied, charming, value for money, discreet. For contact purposes, she became Penny from Goldman's Modelling Agency. She'd leave a message at his café saying he had a photoshoot at such-and-such a time on such-and-such a day. Seeing she was married with kids and averagely nosy neighbours, the transactions took place at his apartment.

It should have been simpler for Kelly, a single woman with a colourful reputation, but Arden had his system, so there were code names, message drops, precise arrangements and no public appearances. The long weekend in Sydney was just to get away from the cloak-and-dagger stuff. When she accused him of secretly enjoying it, he pointed out that not everyone was in her position: someone like Helen had an awful lot to lose. Apart from that little lecture, he never referred to other clients. She assumed it was part of the service to pretend it wasn't a commercial arrangement and she wasn't one of many.

The receptionist at Central smirked as she handed him the envelope. It was handwritten and addressed to Detective Ihaka. In her flamboyant scrawl Miriam Lovell had written:

Hi there,

I was being bugged by a guy I interviewed a while ago. Not quite enough to call it harassment, but enough to get a new number. It occurred to me afterwards that you might've tried to get in touch, and I wouldn't want you to think I'd changed my number to avoid that. If you didn't, please don't feel any obligation to do anything. I respond to emails.

Cheers,

Miriam L

Ihaka was about to call it a night when the phone rang.

"Hey, Sarge, I heard you were back in town." The words straggled from a throat sandpapered by decades of chain-smoking and bottom-shelf drinking. Whispering Willie was a career petty criminal. Because he wasn't much good at it on account of being a far-gone alcoholic, he spent more time in jail than out. Before Ihaka went south, Willie had been one of his informants. He wasn't much good at that either.

Ihaka was mildly surprised Willie was still alive. "Gidday, Willie," he said. "What are you up to these days?"

"Oh, you know, same old, same old. Bit late to change my ways, I reckon."

"They don't change by themselves, Willie. You ever thought of trying?"

"Don't be like that, Sarge. I didn't ring you up for a fucking lecture. I get enough of them from Father O'Homo down the church."

"You got something for me, Willie?"

"Maybe. You know how it works, Sarge. You scratch my back, I'll scratch yours. Tonight would be good. I'm as dry as a Pom's bathmat, me."

Ihaka sighed. Lovell had sent him her new number and he'd been looking forward to trying it out. "What is it, Willie? Give us a taste. I'm not traipsing out to some shithole to find out who's been knocking off garden gnomes."

"I'm offended, Sarge. As if I'd do that to you. Don't worry, this'll get you fizzing. It's about an Eyetie car. One owner, recently deceased."

12

Everything about Whispering Willie – the scorched complexion, the hair like dead weeds, the tics and twitches and hunched vagabond shuffle – supported the theory that alcoholism is suicide on the instalment plan.

They met in an illegal drinking club a stone's throw from the mangroves. Willie was wedged into a dark corner, making his pint of Henderson cask red last until Ihaka and his wallet showed up. Ihaka got him a beer and a neat gin chaser and pulled up a chair. By the time he'd settled in his seat, the gin had disappeared.

Willie lit a cigarette from the one he hadn't quite finished. "This is worth a shitload more than a couple of drinks, Sarge."

"I've heard that before. Turned out it wasn't worth a cup of rat's piss."

"Come on, Sarge, you know what happens. Sometimes people get the wrong end of the stick."

"That they fucking do," said Ihaka. "And sometimes people get the idea that I'll pay good money for any old crap if they talk it up enough." He slid three $20 notes across the table. "If it's the real thing, there's more where that came from. If it's who gives a fuck, I'll shut this place down. That should make you popular."

Willie squinted, not sure whether to take him seriously. His eyes looked like muscatels soaked in blood. "You wouldn't do that."

Ihaka smiled.

In his time, Willie had been on the receiving end of some genuinely disturbing smiles from some genuinely disturbed people, but Ihaka's was up there. He decided not to overplay his hand.

Arden Black's Alfa Romeo had been supplied to a West Auckland stolen-car ring specializing in late-model Europeans. Their lead-time from taking delivery to displaying the unit on a used car lot somewhere on the Australian eastern seaboard was a week to ten days. This time, though, someone in the organization had been keeping up with the news. Realizing they had a dangerously hot item on their hands, they cut their losses, gave the Alfa a deluxe clean and dumped it in a supermarket car park scouted by joyriders looking for a nifty set of wheels for the weekend.

"So far, so good," said Ihaka, furling another twenty like a roll-your-own. "But as you know bloody well, Willie, a story's only as good as the punchline. Who brought the Alfa in?"

Willie made a squeezed-lemon face. "Don't know, Sarge. No one's talking. Too many bad vibes, you know what I mean? But is that the good oil or what?"

Ihaka shook his head regretfully. "Right now it's just conversation, Willie, just a couple of shitheads sitting in a shithole talking shit. I need a name, someone who can finish the story for me."

"Jesus fucking Christ, Sarge, I'd be sticking my neck out big-time."

"Don't worry about it. I'll look after you."

Willie doubled up, coughing as if he was trying to eject his Adam's apple. His face went from salmon-pink to deep purple and his eyes frothed. For a moment or two Ihaka feared the worst, but it turned out to be Willie's version of a wry chuckle.

Wiping his eyes, he said, "You want to try again?"

"Not really."

Willie sucked resentfully on his cigarette. "I'd forgotten what a cunt you can be."

Ihaka didn't move, didn't speak, didn't blink.

"You're going to get me fucked up," groaned Willie, a picture of misery now. "You know that, don't you? Yeah, you know it all right, and you don't give a shit."

"What do you think I am, Willie, the Salvation Army?"

Willie withdrew deeper into the shadows. "They call this guy Jackie Vee, I don't know his real name. It's one of those fucking Dally names, sounds like a cat having a puke."

Ihaka started dealing from a thick wad of twenties. Addiction is a fire that never goes out. Addicts who lead a hand-to-mouth scrounger's existence live in dread of running out of fuel, knowing that if they don't feed the fire inside, it will feed on them. With each note that Ihaka flipped across the table, Willie's anxieties receded further into the distance until they were just a speck on his mental horizon.

"Something else I'd like your feedback on, Willie," said Ihaka, still holding a few notes. "What do you know about the undercover cop who got shot up and left for dead out this way a few years back?"

Willie's expression froze. If Ihaka hadn't seen it, he wouldn't have believed that someone so florid could go so pale so quickly. Willie scooped up the money and tried to stand up, but Ihaka put a clamp on his upper arm, a bone wrapped in loose skin, and forced him back down. "Hold your horses, pal. We're not done yet."

"I've got to go. I just remembered something."

"Like what? You promised to call your stockbroker back?"

"Give us a break, Sarge." Willie was whimpering, on the verge of tears. "I'm already in deep shit. Isn't that enough for you? I don't know fuck all."

"So why the panic?"

"All I can tell you is it's something you just don't talk about, not if you know what's good for you. It's like a fucking taboo subject."

"Who decided that? Who enforces it?"

"Honest to Christ, Sarge, I don't know and I don't want to know. A guy brings the subject up, right? Not that he knows anything the rest of us don't, he's just talking shit. Anyway, someone will give him this one" – Willie dragged his thumb across his throat – "and he'll just clam up. The word came down. I don't know who from, but it was loud and fucking clear."

Ihaka handed over the rest of the notes. "Okay, Willie, here's what you do. You find yourself a deep hole and stay down there. And I promise you this, if anyone fucks you up, I'll fuck them up like you wouldn't believe."

Blair Corvine rubbed his chin, puzzled. "You know what?" he said to Ihaka eventually. "There are only two people who haven't moved on here, and the victim's not one of them. There's Sheree, which is kind of understandable. If anyone's got the right to be all bitter and twisted – apart from me, of course – it's her. And there's you, Chief, and I don't get that."

"Two things, Blair," said Ihaka. "If everyone else has moved on, why is it still such a big deal out west? This old prick I talked to last night bloody near shat himself when I dropped you into the conversation. He says every lowlife out there knows it's a subject you avoid like the plague. Now why would that be?"

Corvine shrugged. "They probably haven't forgotten what happened to Jerry Spragg."

"Yeah, could be," said Ihaka. "I heard that was random prison shit but, given the source, chances are that was a lie. The other reason I'm curious is that there's a bloody big gap between your version and everybody else's. You say you didn't fuck up, you were on top of it; everyone else says the opposite. You fucked up, you got careless, you were off your face the whole time. Christ, I even heard you left your cellphone lying around, they checked call history and saw all these Blair-to-base calls."

"Fucking what?" They were in a little café in Panmure. Corvine muttered an apology to the pensioners at the next table and leaned forward, lowering his voice. "What the fuck do they take me for?"

"Well, now do you see where I'm coming from? If you'd said, 'Look, fuck it, okay, I was burnt out, I was losing it, I could've stuffed up without even knowing,' that would be one thing. And if everyone from McGrail down wasn't so keen to blame the victim and move on, as you put it, that would be another. I would've thought fair enough, shit happens, and gone back to worrying about global warming."

"You raised it with McGrail?"

Ihaka nodded.

"Did he tell you what I told him?"

"McGrail ran the party line," said Ihaka. "Coming from him it sounded good, but that's all it was."

Corvine's forehead was a grid of perplexity.

"What did you tell him, Blair?"

"This would've been two, maybe three weeks before it happened. The bikers were getting jumpy. There was a crew going round ripping off crims. Like guys would pull a job, they'd be divvying up, next thing these dudes in ski masks with sawn-off shotties would kick the door in and bag the lot. Or if it was a dope deal, they'd take the dope and next week it'd be on the street."

"That sort of stuff's been going on since the dawn of time. No honour among thieves and all that shit."

"True, but what I heard, and what I passed on to McGrail, was that there was a cop involved."

"Why the fuck," said Ihaka in his most reasonable tone, "didn't you tell me this last time?"

Corvine looked a bit bashful. "I assumed you were just being polite. You know, you pay a visit to the great survivor, what else do you talk about? I didn't expect you to give a shit. No one else did."

"Was anyone else there when you told him?"

"Mate, something like that, it's for the boss's ears only. What happens after that is his call. I went round to McGrail's place one night, told him face to face." Corvine paused. "I can understand why it wasn't in the report, but I would've thought McGrail might've mentioned it to you."

"I would've thought so too."

Ihaka took the softly, softly approach, sidling up to Helen Conroy at the supermarket, where she was stocking up on toilet paper as if she knew something the rest of Auckland didn't. He introduced himself in a murmur, holding his ID close to his chest.

"I'd like to talk to you about Arden Black," he said. "I can't give you any guarantees, but it mightn't have to go any further."

She stared at him, trying to blink away her fear and confusion. "But if you catch him, I'll have to testify in court, won't I?"

"Catch who?"

"The blackmailer." She mimicked Ihaka's frown. "Isn't that what this is all about?"

*

They went to a café deep in the adjoining mall. Helen Conroy had a round, pleasant face and was holding the line in the struggle with her weight. Ihaka imagined her, in happier times, as an eager social animal and energetic supporter of campaigns to make life in her part of the city even more agreeable. But she was pale and fretful now, distractedly fiddling with the cluster of gems on her wedding-ring finger as she contemplated the loss of her good name and enviable circumstances.

She'd been introduced to Arden by a woman with whom she'd lost touch, an acquaintance rather than a friend. She had an idea the woman was living in the South Island these days. Her account of her dealings with Arden coincided with what she'd told Vanessa Kelly. Like Kelly, she had no knowledge of his secret life beyond her own experience.

The blackmailer made contact on the morning Arden's body was IDed. She was home alone. The phone rang and a man speaking with a distorted voice told her to look in the letterbox. There was an A4 envelope containing photographs of her entering and leaving Arden's apartment building. The camera's automatic time and date function timed her visit at a fortnight earlier and an hour long. There was also a shot of her framed in the living-room window, eyes closed and head thrown back as Arden nuzzled her neck.

The phone rang again. The blackmailer told her she had till Friday afternoon to get her hands on $9500 in cash. She was to put it in a zip-up bag, go to the Langham Hotel on the corner of Symonds Street and Karangahape Road at 6 p.m. and have a drink in the lobby bar. At 6.15 she was to take the bag into the toilet off the lobby, go into the middle cubicle, wait there for five minutes, and then exit the toilet, leaving the bag in the cubicle, on the floor. If that cubicle was occupied, she was to go back to the bar, have another drink and try again at 6.30. When it was done, she was to go straight from the toilet to her car or a taxi and get the hell out of there. She was to burn the photos and envelope. She would be under surveillance: if she didn't follow instructions to the letter or departed from the script in any way, shape or form, her husband would get a set of even more damning photos. Sets of photos would also find their way to the *New Zealand Herald*'s gossip columnist and various individuals and organizations, including the Baradene College Old Girls' Association.

She did as she was told. The blackmailer called again to tell her she was a sensible woman, and as long as she carried on being sensible she had nothing to worry about. He wasn't greedy; he'd give her time to smooth out the finances before he came back for the second of five payments.

"Did you see anyone you knew or who looked familiar at the hotel?" asked Ihaka.

"No."

"Did you notice anyone looking at you?"

"Not that I can remember. I was so anxious not to do anything wrong that I really just kept my head down."

"Was there anyone in the toilet when you went in?"

She gestured, hands fluttering vaguely. "I think someone came out as I went in. I didn't really look at her, I just went straight to the cubicle."

"What about when you came out of the cubicle? Was there anyone in the toilets, or did anyone come in as you went out?"

"I think there was but, as I said, I wasn't making eye contact. I just wanted to get out of there as fast as I could." She was daring to hope, peering into Ihaka's face as if he was the saviour. "What happens now?"

He said he'd do his best to fix it.

*

Jackie Vlukovich, better known as Jackie Vee, had always been an early riser, but with each day he spent holed up in the bush, the longer he slept in. His business associates had decided it would be in everybody's best interests if he dropped out of sight for a while. They'd made it sound like a holiday, but it was more like doing time, just sitting around staring at the wall, so the longer he slept the less time there was to kill.

The cottage overlooked a west coast beach where the waves thundered in like a cavalry charge, petering out in a splatter of white foam on black sand. Urban to the tips of his crocodile-skin cowboy boots, Jackie had taken a few days to get used to the sound of the wilderness – waves, birdsong, insect buzz – and the sudden, ominous silences. Now that he could sleep through all that stuff, it had taken something else to wake him up: the sound of other people. There was someone in the kitchen. In fact, unless his hearing had gone haywire, there was someone in the kitchen making breakfast.

About bloody time. Some of his associates had thought about someone other than themselves for a change and dropped in to see how he was bearing up. Jackie rolled out of bed and pulled on tracksuit pants. Confident that his bladder could tough it out for a little longer, he padded down the corridor to the kitchen.

Neither of his visitors qualified as an associate. One of them was the guy who'd brought in the Alfa Romeo, the stiff's car, the reason he was stuck out there in hippy-dippy land sleeping in like a welfare bludger. Even if there hadn't been a pump-action shotgun on the table, Jackie would have surmised that he'd walked into a situation which had the potential to go very bad.

Like many rogues and fly-by-nighters, Jackie was a fantasist. He thought of himself as a tough guy, among other things, but his toughness was skin-deep, a flimsy veneer made of rough language and callous attitudes. The fact was that his career in violence had peaked around the time he was expelled from Kelston Boys' High. His uninvited visitors, on the other hand, looked like the real thing: graduates of the mean streets, professionals who measured their productivity in stitches and broken bones.

The guy standing at the bench pushing bacon around a frying pan, the guy who'd brought in the Alfa, was Greg "G-Force" Cropper. He was a ranking member of a criminal gang called The Firm, named after the outfit headed by the infamous Kray twins that operated out of the East End of London in the 1950s and 60s.

Although physically unremarkable, Cropper radiated malevolence. On meeting him Jackie's first thought had been, "I bet this dude owns a pit bull." Compared to his sidekick, though, G-Force was as intimidating as a door-to-door missionary. Spencer "Big Dog" Parks was gigantic, one-eyed and dreadlocked, with garish tattoos and a roadmap of ragged scars criss-crossing his wide, brown face.

Cropper put the bacon on a plate and began cracking eggs into the frying pan. "Here he is," he said. "Sleeping Beauty."

"What are you guys doing here?" said Vlukovich, his voice cracking as he forced words from a dry throat.

Cropper grinned wolfishly. "Have a guess."

"Hey, man, everything's cool," said Vlukovich. "It's just that we would've had a problem with our people in Aussie if we'd —"

"The fuck it is," said Cropper. "Everything's very fucking uncool, man. The cops are hunting high and low for you, and if we can find you, it's on the fucking cards they're going to."

"Okay then, I'll piss off. I'll go to Croatia, I've got family there."

"Is that right?" said Cropper. "Croatia, eh? The old country. Isn't that what you Dallies call it?"

Vlukovich nodded uncertainly, not sure whether Cropper saw merit in his suggestion.

"Breakfast's ready," said Cropper. He placed two heaped plates on the table, which at least gave Big Dog something other than Vlukovich to fix his harrowing monocular stare on.

"You know what?" said Cropper, projecting through a mouthful of churning protein. "You should be having a feed, not us. Like in the old days, when they chopped cunts' heads off or put them up against the wall or whatever, they always gave them a hearty breakfast. I reckon it'd be wasted on you, but one bite and you'd spew your ring out."

Cropper's point – that if they could find Vlukovich, so could the cops – was borne out sooner than he'd expected, or indeed allowed for. As he and Parks guffawed over the spreading stain centred on Vlukovich's crotch – the imminent prospect of having his face blown off proving a bridge too far for his bladder – the back door was smashed off its hinges as Ihaka and his team stormed the kitchen.

To make room for the plates of bacon and eggs, the toast, cups of tea, salt and pepper and the bottle of genuine Texas-style kick-ass barbecue sauce, Parks had moved the shotgun to the other side of the table, out of easy reach. He lunged for it, belly-flopping down on the table, which crumpled under his 140 kilos. As he wallowed among the wreckage, Ihaka took a couple of long strides and booted him concussively behind the ear.

Cropper didn't even think about trying for the shotgun. Notwithstanding Ihaka's exhibition of unarmed combat, it was pretty clear these guys wouldn't need much encouragement to use the semi-automatic pistols they were pointing at him. He sat back down and put his hands on his head.

Ihaka stood over Vlukovich, who'd crawled into a corner and assumed the foetal position. "I think you should come with us, Jackie. As safe houses go, this place leaves a lot to be desired."

The cops hit every known or suspected Firm hangout. They found drugs, drug-making equipment, unregistered firearms, implements designed or adapted to inflict grievous bodily harm, wanted persons, unwanted persons, missing persons, persons who were out way past their bedtimes, and a cornucopia of stolen goods. They didn't find Arden Black's laptop or personal organizer, but in the rat's nest that served as Cropper's bedroom they found the linen jacket which the late gigolo was wearing when last seen alive.

Parks had nothing to say, which was true to form. The total number of words he'd uttered in his various police interviews over the years was zero. For Big Dog, being staunch meant not saying anything to the pigs, ever. G-Force had plenty to say, but it was all foul-mouthed bravado which didn't shed any light on why Black, and presumably his sister, had got so far offside with The Firm.

Sensing he was on a roll, Ihaka asked Miriam Lovell out for a drink. She suggested a wine and tapas bar on Ponsonby Road.

Lovell arrived twenty minutes late in a gust of apologies and expensive perfume, both of which Ihaka interpreted as encouraging signs. Being a regular, she recommended that they shared a plate of tapas and a bottle of the house red. They swapped "how was your day" small talk, Ihaka hinting that she could sleep a little sounder as a result of his exertions.

"I've got to say, this is a first for me," said Lovell. "I've had a drink with cops in the line of duty, as it were, but never out of choice."

"You got something against cops?"

"Well, I used to be quite left-wing. Probably still am in most people's books."

"Say no more," said Ihaka. "My old man was a commie. When I told him I was joining the police force he bloody near disowned me on the spot."

Lovell's mouth fell open. "Don't tell me your father was Jimmy Ihaka."

Ihaka nodded.

"That's amazing."

"You wouldn't say that if you saw a photo of him."

"But that's just it: I have seen photos of him. God, how thick can you be? You're practically peas in a pod."

"Where did you see a photo of him?"

"When I was younger and definitely more foolish, I decided to do a Ph.D. The best part of a decade, a stalled career and a broken marriage later, I can just make out a pinpoint of light at the end of the tunnel, although knowing my luck it'll be a glow-worm. Anyway, my thesis is on communism in the trade union movement in the sixties and seventies. Your father cropped up quite a bit. He had this extraordinary appetite for confrontation. What was he like at home?"

Ihaka laughed. "I used to get asked that a lot as a kid. I remember a cousin whose old man was a bishop saying he got the same thing, people always asking what was it like to have a bishop for a father, as if he walked in the door in the evening and said, 'Let us pray.' I wouldn't say Dad left his politics at the door, but those labels they pinned on him – firebrand, maverick, class warrior, all that stuff – meant bugger all to me. He was just the old man."

Lovell nodded vigorously. "Yes, of course. We're all different people at home."

"Plus Mum had his number. Whenever he started going a bit Jimmy the Red on us, she knew how to bring him back to reality."

"What did she do?"

"Took the piss, mostly."

Ihaka's cellphone rang: Firkitt. Ihaka made his apologies and went out onto the footpath.

"Where are you?" said Firkitt.

"Off duty."

Firkitt grunted derisively. "No such fucking thing."

"In case you hadn't noticed, I've had a pretty big day."

"Bully for you, champ, but in case you haven't noticed, crime doesn't run to our clock. There's been another murder, so it's all hands to the pump. Charlton's giving a team-talk in half an hour. Be there."

"This murder. Would it have anything to do with all the other murders we've had lately?"

"You bet your arse it does. The deceased is Phil Malone, that TV guy whose partner got knifed. You know, one of the ones Lilywhite picked out."

"Jesus. What happened?"

"The cleaners found him in the bath, along with a plugged-in, switched-on hairdryer. The dryer belonged in the bedroom. According to his wife, he was so safety-conscious he wouldn't let her use it in the bathroom. He had headphones on, listening to his iPod. Probably didn't see or hear a fucking thing."

13

When Phil Malone sold his company to the Brits, over his partner's dead body, he built a McMansion on a lifestyle block in rural South Auckland. He was home alone there when the killer came. His wife and daughter were at a hockey tournament in New Plymouth; his son, a Monday-to-Friday boarder, was at school.

The Malones loved the privacy of their lifestyle block. So did the killer. No one had seen him or her come and go. There were a couple of sightings of unfamiliar cars in the area, but they were hopelessly vague. Someone remembered seeing a late-model dark grey sedan, a Nissan or a Honda. Or maybe a Mazda. Come to think of it, it might've been a Mitsubishi – it's hard to tell those Japanese cars apart. Someone else saw a late-model light-coloured SUV. He was pretty sure it was a SsangYong until he remembered a guy at work had been talking up his brother-in-law's new SsangYong and the name might have just stuck in his head.

Ihaka sat at the back of the room, half-listening to Boy Charlton's briefing. Charlton had the jargon down pat, and his slick presentation was testimony to a hundred Toast-masters breakfasts. When all was said and done, though, he'd dragged people into Central at eight o'clock at night or away from whatever they were doing to tell them what they already knew: there were no leads.

Now he was into the big rev-up, part motivational up and at 'em, part boot up the arse. Even before Malone, the media had been having a field day: the term "Murder City" was getting a workout on shock-jock radio, a columnist had actually used the phrase "the killing fields" and editorials dispensed advice in lofty generalizations. Down in Wellington the opposition was claiming that Aucklanders no longer felt safe in their own homes, and the Prime Minister had acknowledged that the public needed – and were entitled to – urgent reassurance that the police had the situation under control. The heat was on.

Ihaka glanced at his watch: 8.45. Miriam Lovell had told him to ring her if he got through before nine. If she wasn't soaking in a bath, they could reconvene at the tapas bar.

Charlton finished with a flourish. Ihaka was almost out the door when Charlton's voice cut through the hubbub: "Sergeant Ihaka, a word before you slip away."

Firkitt followed Ihaka into Charlton's office. Charlton dropped into the chair behind his desk with a grunt of fatigue. Up close he looked wound up and worn out.

"There's a press conference first thing in the morning to announce a breakthrough in the Arden Black case," said Charlton. "Your presence isn't required." He waited for Ihaka's response, which took the form of a non-committal shrug. "I suppose you're thinking, here we go: I do the work, Charlton takes the credit. I wouldn't particularly blame you, but the way I see it, if I have to take the heat, I get to deliver the good news. And, believe me, I've taken some heat lately, mostly from McGrail."

"He does have a way with words," said Ihaka.

"Tell me about it," said Charlton. "It's like being back at school. Having said that, I'm sure I'm getting less crap from him than he's getting from the Commissioner and the Minister. The higher you climb, the heavier it rains.

Still, I'm not asking for sympathy and no doubt I'd be crash out of luck if I was. I just wanted to say good job. You've earned the organization some breathing space, and we sure as hell needed it."

Ihaka acknowledged the compliment with a nod. Having dished out this carefully measured serving of praise, Charlton switched his attention to his computer. Without looking up he asked, "Any thoughts on Malone?"

Ihaka flicked a glance at Firkitt, who was looking straight ahead, stony-faced.

"Just this," said Ihaka. "I talked to Lilywhite, next thing he's dead. Ditto Yallop. Firkitt talked to Malone, now he's dead too."

Charlton gave him a sharp look. "You reckon Yallop's part of this?"

"I don't know," said Ihaka. "I'm just saying there's a pattern. Maybe the hitman's taking out everyone who can finger him."

"How could they?" said Firkitt. "If they're like Lilywhite, they've got no fucking idea who he is."

"Lilywhite called me his father confessor," said Ihaka. "I don't think he was finished with me."

"What are you saying?" said Charlton. "He wanted you to come back for another session, so he held something back?"

"Maybe."

"Like what?" said Firkitt.

"I don't know what Ihaka thinks," said Charlton, "but my guess would be that Lilywhite might've known more than he let on about those other cases, Malone's partner and the old girl."

They both looked at Ihaka. "Hitmen don't make cold calls just on the off chance," he said. "Someone put him on to Lilywhite and the others. Maybe Lilywhite had an idea who. He reckoned he'd done a lot of amateur sleuthing."

"The go-between," said Charlton. He got up and sat on the edge of his desk, clear-eyed and energized, as if he'd just had a power nap. "You're dead right. There's got to be a connection. All we have to do is find it. Find the connection, find the hitman, put five murder cases to bed in one go."

"And we'll all live happily ever after," said Firkitt.

Charlton showed his perfect teeth. "Steady on, Ron." To Ihaka: "Sergeant, you need to wrap up Eve Diack ASAP because we need you back on this. That shouldn't be too hard. They're not exactly criminal masterminds, Cropper and Parks."

"I thought you wanted me gone ASAP," said Ihaka.

"Circumstances have changed," said Charlton blandly.

"We still don't know why Cropper and Parks killed Black."

"True," said Charlton, "but if I was you, I'd assume it had something to do with drugs and proceed on that basis till you have reason to think otherwise. Now, gentlemen, if you'll excuse me, I'm going home to my wife and kids."

Ihaka and Firkitt went down in the lift together. Firkitt leaned against the wall, hands in pockets, looking almost amused. "Give the man some credit," he said. "That's as close as he ever gets to eating humble pie."

"You're taking this very calmly," said Ihaka.

Firkitt shrugged. "I just follow orders, I don't get involved in strategy." The lift doors opened and they emerged into the foyer. "If we carry on like this, we'll be having nude saunas together before you know it."

Ihaka watched Firkitt walk away in a cloud of cigarette smoke. It was 9.20: was it too late to call Miriam Lovell? Probably. Should he have told Charlton and Firkitt about Black's sex-on-demand sideline and the Helen Conroy shakedown? Probably.

*

The next morning Ihaka drove out to Paremoremo Prison at Albany to see John Scholes, aka Johnny B Bad, the boss of The Firm. Even though Scholes had been inside for almost five years, he still pulled the strings. Word was the guys on the outside didn't shoplift a gash mag from a corner dairy without his approval.

The meeting took place in the superintendent's office, the idea being that Scholes might be more cooperative if the other inmates, particularly members of The Firm, thought he was being carpeted by the head screw, as opposed to having an off-the-record chat with a cop. Personally, Ihaka wouldn't have bothered. Those ploys might have worked on your average crim with his dim-bulb mind and Pavlovian responses, but Scholes was anything but average.

For a start he didn't look like a hardcore criminal. He looked and sounded like a fat, jolly Englishman. You could picture him as a choirmaster in the Barmy Army, beer in one hand, Union Jack in the other, swaying and sweating as he led another scurrilous ditty. He had ginger scalp stubble, pale blue eyes, a pink complexion, a beer belly, a permanent half-smile that was no indicator of his mood or intentions and an East London accent, even though he'd run away to sea at sixteen and lived in Auckland since jumping ship twenty-two years earlier.

Scholes had one vanity, known only to his wife: a Godfather complex. He watched the movies – the original *The Godfather* and *The Godfather Part II*, not the botched third instalment – at least once a month. He saw himself as a blend of the two Dons, Corleone father and son, Marlon Brando and Al Pacino. Definitely old-school, a man of the people who hadn't forgotten his roots, but with Michael's icy acumen and inscrutable ruthlessness.

So when a businesswoman, a well-known and respected figure in the community, came to see Scholes seeking revenge – although she called it justice – on behalf of her abused daughter, he thought straight away of the scene in *The Godfather* in which Don Corleone, on the day of his daughter's wedding, is petitioned by the undertaker Bonasera.

Scholes knew it off by heart: every word, every gesture, every inflection.

Bonasera's daughter's boyfriend and another guy had plied her with whiskey and tried to take advantage of her. She'd kept her honour, but at a price: "They beat her like an animal. She was the light of my life, a beautiful girl. Now she will never be beautiful again."

Bonasera wants the punks killed, but the Don points out that wouldn't be justice since his daughter is still alive. After demanding and receiving the undertaker's obeisance, the Don promises to make them suffer as she suffered.

The businesswoman's daughter was a brilliant student, already fielding approaches from some of the biggest law firms in town. She'd met a guy at a nightclub, one of those sleek young men getting rich quick in telecommunications. On their first date he'd taken her to an expensive restaurant and behaved like a gentleman. On the second, he'd put something in her drink – probably Rohypnol, the date-rape drug – taken her to his Devonport villa and raped her. Anally.

She was so traumatized that she didn't tell her mother until three days later, when all traces of the drug would have left her system. The businesswoman couldn't bear the thought of her daughter testifying in court, the rapist's lawyer making her out to be the sort of precious little bitch/princess who wants to be a Saturday night hottie, then wakes up with a hangover and the realization she did things that are going to get her talked about for the wrong reasons, things that former head girls and future judges only do on their honeymoon and subsequent stays at five-star resorts. So instead of going to the police, the mother went to see Johnny B Bad.

Flattered by the approach, Scholes was always going to arrange for the little fuck to get a good kicking. The fact that it was anal rape took it to another level of insult and injury. The idea was to brand her and make it impossible for her to forget. Scholes decided to take it personally.

He and a couple of henchmen broke into the rapist's villa at three in the morning and dragged the rapist out of bed. Scholes shoved the barrel of his semi-automatic in the guy's mouth and told him he was going to blow his fucking head off. Then they beat him to a pulp. The rapist had lots of toys and Scholes encouraged his lads to help themselves to anything that took their fancy.

But Scholes made one critical mistake. He assumed the rapist wouldn't be foolish enough to take it any further, so he hadn't bothered to conceal his face. He was picked out of a line-up and charged with aggravated robbery. If he'd set out to get the book thrown at him, he couldn't have managed it better. He ticked every box: he had a criminal record, he pleaded not guilty, the incident took place at night and involved multiple offenders breaking into a private residence which activated the home-invasion provisions, a firearm was brandished, murder was threatened and severe injuries inflicted. He got twelve years, which meant he came up for parole after four. The cops, who couldn't believe their luck, made sure that didn't happen.

"Mister Ihaka," said Scholes, pronouncing it Eee-arker. "Nice to see you, to see you nice, as that Bruce Forsyth used to say. What a fucking quince he was. Anyway, long time no see. I trust life's treating you well."

"Can't complain. Yourself?"

"Me neither. Just goes to show, don't it? The larger gents like you and me tend to look on the bright side of life, unlike your lean and hungry geezers. I see blokes in here worrying themselves sick that if they drop their guard for a moment, some giant coon – no offence intended – will be up their arse to the back wheels in a trice. I always tell them, first off it might never happen, second, if it does, you might find it well to your taste. So what's the point in worrying about it?"

"And how many giant coon rapists have you had to fight off, Johnny?"

"Not a one, as a matter of fact. Now some blokes would take that to heart too, start wondering what's wrong with me, what have all these bitches got that I don't? But I rise above all that. I refuse to allow my self-esteem to be dependent on the opinion of others. Especially degenerate fucking poofs."

"Listen," said Ihaka, "I could talk about this stuff all day, but I'm kind of busy."

"Course you are, what with all these murders and such. So what can I help you with?"

"A couple of things. Your boys Cropper and Parks, obviously. And Blair Corvine."

"Who?"

"Come on, Johnny. I know they call it the wild west, but how often does someone put five rounds in an undercover cop?"

"Oh, him. You wouldn't credit it, would you? Five holes in the bloke and he's still above ground. I can't for the life of me understand why you're asking me, Mr Ihaka." Scholes's eyes twinkled. "I mean, correct me if I'm wrong, but wasn't there a full and frank inquiry which concluded that there wasn't a leak, and therefore a little dicky bird must have told those bikers what's-his-face was a copper."

"From where I'm sitting, it looks like you think the inquiry was full of shit."

"Oops, I better get the old poker face out."

"So why not tell me what you know? No skin off your nose."

"I'll be the judge of that, if you don't mind."

"Fair enough. I heard it had something to do with an outfit that was ripping off other bad boys."

"Did you now?"

"And that said outfit might've included a cop."

Scholes sat back, folding his arms. "What the fuck are you playing at?" He looked and sounded genuinely perplexed.

"I'm not playing, Johnny. Corvine's a mate of mine."

"I can't fucking believe I'm giving advice to a copper," said Scholes, "but here goes. It was looked into and a conclusion was reached. Everything I know about your lot tells me that's the end of it, so you'd be wise to let sleeping dogs lie."

"So it is skin off your nose? Makes sense. Bugger all happens out west if you don't want it to happen. For that matter, from what I hear, bugger all happens in here if you don't want it to happen, which suggests you gave the green light to Jerry Spragg getting his head kicked in."

"Well, if that was the case – and I'm certainly not admitting it, mind – shouldn't you be thanking me?"

"If that was the case, you would've had a reason."

"You want a reason?" said Scholes. "He tried to kill a cop. That's just fucking nuts, stirs up no end of shit."

"I'm touched, Johnny. I don't believe a word of it, but I'm touched."

"Well, that'll have to do for now," said Scholes imperturbably. "Was there something else?"

"Just the brace of murders committed by your employees."

"What's to talk about? You've stitched those lads up a treat. Case closed, ain't it? Another triumph for the brown Sherlock Holmes."

Ihaka waved. "Yoo-hoo, Johnny, I'm over here – in the real world. Christ, they might as well have done it live on the six o'clock news. We know they did it, I'm interested in why."

Scholes's eyelids drooped. "You're talking to the wrong fella."

"You must've had a bloody good reason for it, because it's costing you big-time. Your rackets are taking a major hit."

The half-smile stretched to a three-quarter. "You really think so, do you?"

"I know so. If you believe otherwise, then your guys on the outside aren't telling you the full story."

"Every leader's quandary, old son. Are the troops giving it to him straight, or are they telling him what they think he wants to hear? It's a fine line. You want them to be fearful, but not so shit-scared they don't tell you what you need to know."

"How do you manage it?"

The smile became a full-blown grin. "Well, not shooting the messenger's a good start."

"You know those fucking apes are going down for Arden Black and his sister. It's open and shut, so why not tell us what it was about?"

The smiley creases vanished from Scholes's face. "Can't help you, I'm afraid."

"Well, I could've helped you." Ihaka stood up. "I guess you're not as smart as I thought you were."

"Oh, don't you worry about me, Mister Ihaka." Scholes clasped his hands behind his head and leaned back, his chair tilting precariously. "I haven't lost the knack of knowing which side my bread's buttered on. Take those fucking apes, as you so perceptively called them. You think I give a toss about them? We're all better off with them out of the picture."

"Getting too big for their boots, eh?" Ihaka had his hand on the doorknob. "Well, glad to be of service. See you round."

"You will indeed. I'm up for parole again next week. Seeing I've been such a good lad, a model prisoner if I may say so, I've got a feeling I'm going to walk this time. But look, seeing you came all the way out here to say hello, I wouldn't want you to go away empty-handed. The apes didn't do the sister."

Ihaka gave Scholes a hard stare, but the fat man's smile was impenetrable. "Why should I believe that?"

"You came to see me because you reckon The Firm don't do nothing without my say-so, yeah? Well, I didn't fucking say so, did I?"

He arrived late and watched from the back of the room as Arden Black's coffin disappeared into the furnace, not sure what to do with his hands, seemingly wanting to shove them in his pockets but sensing it wasn't the done thing at a funeral, if you could call it that.

Ihaka assumed the latecomer had got his times or crematoriums mixed up. The forty or so others who'd gathered at the funeral home to farewell Arden obviously knew him through the café, his modelling work or his nightclub meet-and-greet gig. They were a type: skinny, vain, fashionable. The sort of people who'd rather be cool than happy. The latecomer was from another tribe. He had a she'll-be-right haircut and his manual worker's hands were chipped and scarred and lined with ancient grime. He was wearing scuffed brown shoes and a cheap, light-grey suit that looked as though it belonged to someone else. He was the only one wearing a tie, but clearly hadn't put one on often enough to get the hang of it.

Someone from the nightclub announced that Danny Howard, the manager, was putting on drinks, everybody welcome. The latecomer stood aside as the others streamed out, taking no notice of him. If he was at the wrong funeral, Ihaka thought, he would have worked it out by now. He could have slipped out unnoticed rather than being the last to leave.

Ihaka followed him out of the funeral parlour, across the road and down the street to an old, mud-splattered station wagon. He tapped on the driver's window, showing his ID.

"Detective Sergeant Ihaka, Auckland Central. I'd like to talk to you."

The guy frowned. "What about?"

Ihaka couldn't help smiling. "People keep asking me that. The bloke who was cremated back there was murdered. When people are murdered, we have to go round asking people questions until we find out who did it and why."

"Oh yeah?" The tone suggested he still didn't get it.

Ihaka got into the passenger seat. "Let's start at the beginning," he said. "Who are you?"

Even that question seemed to take him by surprise. He eyed Ihaka warily for thirty seconds. "Glen Smith, but what...?"

"See, that wasn't so hard, was it? Okay, Glen, what was your relationship with the deceased?"

"Warren? I went to school with him. We were mates. At least I thought we were."

"When did you last see him?"

"I can tell you the exact day," said Smith. "Boxing Day, 1998. We drove down from Greytown in the old man's ute, me and Warren and a couple of other guys. We dropped him off on Lambton Quay – he was meant to be catching the ferry over to Picton – and went to the cricket at the Basin. I watched the whole game, saw Tendulkar get a ton."

"Wasn't Warren a cricket fan?"

"He wasn't into sport, full stop. Like the rest of us played footy, but Warren? No way. We used to give him a hard time about being scared of breaking his nose or something and messing up his pretty face. One time he said, 'The difference between me and the rest of you guys is that I don't have to go out there and show how brave I am to get a root.' It was bloody true too."

"Did he actually go to Picton?"

"Shit no, that's when he took off. Turned out he bullshitted everyone. His olds thought he was with us, we thought he was camping with his sister, buggered if I know where she thought he was. By the time everyone realized they'd been had, he was fuck knows where."

"So you came up for the funeral?"

"No, no, I work in the market gardens out at Pukekohe – Mum sent me the death notice from the local paper." He shrugged awkwardly. "With Eve gone and Sheila – that's Warren's old girl – pretty much wiping him, I thought if I don't front, there won't be anyone from the old days. Not that he gave a shit about them, obviously. Or us."

"Did you have a sense of that back then?"

"Not at all." Smith was relaxed now; he didn't mind going back in time. Perhaps adulthood had been a let-down. "That's why it was such a bloody shock. Far as I knew, he was the same as the rest of us – pretty keen to get away from home, but it wasn't like Greytown was the arsehole of the universe. I've always wondered if the shit we gave him over the woman in the café had something to do with it."

"What was that about?"

"Well, Warren was a chick magnet, right? I mean, he just took his pick of the girls our age. He had a part-time job at a café run by this couple, Donna and Craig. Donna was pretty bloody choice, but in her mid-twenties I guess, so she was out of his league. Warren might've been too cool for school and all that, but he was still a kid. Anyway, Warren started going on and on about Donna, plus he was hanging out at the café even when he wasn't working, so a few of us were saying, 'Jesus mate, what's up with this Donna? Are you in love with her or what?' He'd be going, 'No, no, I'm just saying she's really cool,' or whatever. Then one day Donna and Craig shot through; didn't say a word to anyone, including Warren. He tried not to show it, but you could tell he was gutted. Everyone gave him fucking heaps. You got to remember he was the man, different girlfriend every second week while the rest of us were wondering where our next hand-job's coming from. The sheilas ripped into him as well, because he'd given most of them the old bum's rush at some stage. You'd have to say he handled it okay, but it must've pissed him off. Here's a guy, ever since his balls dropped he's had chicks all over him and guys envying him, now suddenly he's copping shit from everyone. So as I said, I wondered if that had something to do with him buggering off."

Ihaka was looking at it another way. Donna and Craig just up and disappear. Warren follows suit. Was it copycat, or did he know where they'd gone and go after them?

"You remember their surnames?"

Smith shook his head. "Don't think I ever knew."

"Would anyone in Greytown?"

"Doubt it. I'll ask Mum, but it's a long time ago now. Most of that crowd have scattered."

"How well did you know Eve?" said Ihaka.

"Well, she was Warren's big sister. I had a bit of a crush on her to tell the truth, but as far as she was concerned I was just one of Warren's little mates. She probably couldn't tell us apart. Christ, she bloody doted on him, though. I used to say to my sister, 'Why are you such a bitch? Why can't you be more like Eve?' You can probably guess what she came back with."

"Why can't you be more like Warren?"

"Spot on."

Ihaka never saw Finbar McGrail's old house, but from what he'd heard it was exactly what you would have expected back then: a modest family home in an unremarkable street in a suburb notable only for having more Bible-bashers per capita than any other in Auckland. Now that he'd moved up in the world, home was a gracious villa on a leafy section on the slopes of Mt Eden.

Ihaka stood on the wide veranda, waiting for someone to answer the door and having second thoughts about his spur-of-the-moment decision to drop in unannounced on the Auckland District Commander at 9.30 p.m. The door was opened by a lanky teenager in baggy surf shorts and a singlet, with a baseball cap on backwards keeping heavy-metal hair off his face. Apart from all that, he was the spitting image of his old man.

Before Ihaka could introduce himself, McGrail Junior said, "You're Sergeant Ihaka, right? I met you a few years ago when Dad took me into Central. We arrived just as you were giving someone a blast. It was quite an eye-opener."

"I remember. You were just a little squirt."

"Well, it must be seven or eight years ago now. I'm David, by the way." They shook hands. "Come in. You're here to see Dad?"

"Is he around?"

"Yeah, he's in his study."

Ihaka followed David down the corridor. "I suppose you picked up a few new words that day?"

David threw a grin over his shoulder. "I was straight onto Google as soon as we got home."

He knocked and put his head around the door. "Sergeant Ihaka's here."

From within: "Really?"

Ihaka thanked David and went in. McGrail was sitting at what looked like an old farmhouse kitchen table surrounded by stacks of documents, each a foot high. Bookshelves covered one wall and the curtains were partially drawn over the French doors which opened out to the rear of the section. Behind McGrail was a sideboard with framed family photos and some bottles and glasses on a silver tray.

McGrail got up, peeling off his reading glasses. "This is an unexpected pleasure. Can I offer you a nightcap?"

Ihaka shrugged. "Well, if you're having one."

McGrail directed Ihaka to a chair and handed him a glass of port. "To be savoured."

"As opposed to drunk?"

"As opposed to swilled."

Ihaka took a sip. "I don't suppose you get this by the cardboard box at the local Pak'nSave?"

"I shouldn't think so," said McGrail. "Nineteen ninety-four was an outstanding vintage."

"Speaking of the finer things in life," said Ihaka. "Nice place you've got here."

"We like it."

"Be worth a bit, wouldn't it?"

McGrail smiled thinly. "Have you had your house valued lately?"

Ihaka shook his head.

"You should. You'd probably find it's worth quite a lot more than it was five years ago. But I don't suppose you called in at this hour to compare property portfolios."

"I'm still curious about Blair Corvine."

McGrail looked down, pinching the bridge of his nose.

"Oh, we're back on that subject, are we? I would've thought you had enough to be going on with at the minute."

"You know I've talked to people, I've read the report, I've kept my ear to the ground, but I haven't seen or heard any mention of what Corvine told you, presumably in this very room, just before he was shot."

"About thieves stealing from other thieves?"

"And the whisper that a cop was in on it."

McGrail went through his routine: sniff, sip, swirl, swallow. "Corvine had no names, no details, just a rumour he'd heard from one of his outlaw acquaintances. As you know, Sergeant, the criminal fraternity accuses us of all sorts of things, knowing that there'll always be some useful idiot who'll give it credence. Having said that, I didn't dismiss it out of hand. I asked Charlton to look into it."

"And?"

"Well, as you can imagine, information was hard to come by because the victims weren't filing into Central to lay complaints. He established that there'd been an uptick in what one might call dog-eat-dog activity, but found no evidence of what Corvine was talking about."

On his way home Ihaka rang Detective Inspector Johan Van Roon in Wellington.

"You seen where McGrail lives these days?"

"Yeah, I have," said Van Roon. "Not too shabby, is it?"

"In my subtle way I invited him to put a ballpark figure on it. He ignored me, of course. What would you say?"

"I'm no expert, but I wouldn't have thought you'd get much change from one and a half mill."

"Fuck me, nice for some. And his beverage of choice is 1994 port, an outstanding vintage, so he tells me."

"What did I tell you?" said Van Roon. "It's all changed up there, mate. Every bastard's looking after number one."

14

Ihaka was having breakfast – porridge, boiled eggs, Vogel's with cholesterol-free spread, tea with two fewer spoonfuls of sugar than he used to have – when Helen Conroy called to say she'd tracked down the woman who introduced her to Arden Black. She'd lost touch with Margie Brackstone when Margie and her husband moved to Akaroa, where they had an apparently charming bed and breakfast.

He told her there'd be a press conference in an hour's time to announce arrests in connection with Black's murder, but so far that hadn't led to progress on the blackmail front.

"Well, it's only been a few days," said Conroy. "I know I shouldn't expect miracles, even if I can't help praying for one."

"Let me know if you hear back," said Ihaka. "I prefer to work alone, but I'm prepared to make an exception for God."

When Margie Brackstone answered the phone, Ihaka told her, "Listen carefully, Mrs Brackstone. I'm Detective Sergeant Ihaka, calling from Auckland. I need to talk to you about Arden Black, but I'm picking that's a conversation you won't want to have if your husband's around."

"Uh, no. Not at all."

"Is he there now?"

"Yes."

"Okay, here's what you do. When I finish talking, you say, 'I don't think we're really interested, thanks all the same,' and hang up. If your husband asks, tell him it was someone wanting you to take part in a survey of drinking habits, or whatever. Get yourself sorted so you can talk, then ring me at Auckland Central. What do you say now?"

"Look, I don't think so, thank you. I'm rather busy just now. Goodbye."

"I thought I'd put all this behind me," said Margie Brackstone three hours later. "I just heard on the radio that two men have been arrested."

"There's still a few loose ends," said Ihaka.

"Did Arden's death have anything to do with his love life, for want of a better term? Not that love had much to do with it."

"One of the loose ends is motive. We don't know why he was murdered. Are you okay to talk?"

"Yes, my husband's having lunch with some friends over at French Farm vineyard. I pulled out at the last minute. The only good thing about being prone to migraines is that they're very useful when it comes to getting out of things. Just as a matter of interest, how did my name crop up?"

"I asked a client of Arden's how she got involved; she put me onto Helen Conroy, who put me onto you."

"I see."

"No one else knows about this, Mrs Brackstone. As I told Helen, I can't make promises, but I'll do my best to keep it just between us."

"That would be enormously appreciated."

"So how did you meet Arden?"

"I was walking the dog in Cornwall Park one Saturday morning and ran into this woman I vaguely knew, who was there watching her little boy play cricket. It was a

210

bit awkward, really, because she'd had an affair with a friend of ours who was quite a bit older than her, and the general consensus was that she wasn't smitten by his looks and personality, if you get my drift. As it turned out, we did her an injustice because she walked out on him. Anyway, while we were chatting, Arden appeared and she introduced us."

"That friend of yours," said Ihaka. "The older bloke wouldn't have been Christopher Lilywhite by any chance?"

"Well, yes, as a matter of fact, it was. But how...?"

"Which I guess makes the woman Denise Hadlow?"

"My God," she said. "Ihaka. I was so thrown when you rang I didn't place you. You're the one who gave Chris such a hard time when Joyce was killed. Weren't you packed off to the wop-wops?"

"I'm back."

"I suppose it's all academic now."

Oh, no it fucking isn't, thought Ihaka. It's just starting to get real. "Did you get the impression Denise and Arden were an item?"

"I just assumed so. We swapped phone numbers and I rang her the next day, overcompensating, as usual, to congratulate her on a good catch. She said no, he was just a friend, someone she'd known for ages. I said something like 'He's not gay is he? That would be a waste.' God no, she said, he's straight as a die and, what's more, he's into older women. Every time I think of this conversation, I wish to God I'd ended it right there instead of making some facetious remark along the lines of 'Too bad I'm married'. She laughed and said that wouldn't bother Arden and, besides, you can still window-shop when you're on a budget, so why don't we meet for coffee at his café in Newmarket? No harm in that, I thought – my second mistake. I turned up – no Denise. Next thing Arden comes over. Denise had texted to say she'd been held up so he'd keep me company. The rest, as they say, is history."

Denise Hadlow checked Ihaka out through the peephole, which was sensible seeing it was dark and he'd hadn't rung ahead.

She opened the door, striking a pose: head on one side, knee bent, hand on hip. She was barefoot with her hair pulled back into a ponytail, wearing skintight black leggings and a precarious white singlet. He was reminded of the models in those women's health and fitness magazines which tell you how to live to be a hundred and have sensational sex all the way there.

"Excuse the outfit," she said. "I was exercising."

"I didn't notice."

"So much for Pilates then." She checked her watch. "I guess coffee doesn't keep you awake?"

"It's not a social call."

"Oh, well, in that case I'll put some clothes on." She led him through to the living room. "Make yourself at home."

Hadlow reappeared in an oversized hoodie that ended mid-thigh, shaking out her hair. She sat down opposite him, tucking her legs underneath her. "I'm afraid there's no beer."

"As I said, this isn't a social call."

"Fine." She pulled a cushion onto her lap. "Billy will be sorry he missed you. He's just gone to bed. He took quite a shine to you."

"He doesn't know me."

"Oh my God," she exclaimed. "I get that it's not a social call, but does that mean you actually have to be antisocial?"

"I was surprised I didn't see you at Arden Black's funeral."

She held his stare. "Is that what this is about? What's the big deal? I'm not that into funerals, okay? One a month is my limit. And especially with what happened to Arden – that really creeped me out."

"Why didn't you tell me you knew him?"

"You didn't ask."

"He was murdered. I'm a cop. Most people would've mentioned it."

She shrugged, affecting boredom. "I didn't realize you were working on it, and I wouldn't have had anything useful to say." She disentangled her legs and stood up in one fluid movement. "I'm having a glass of wine. Sure I can't tempt you?"

"I'm okay. I thought you didn't drink at home."

"I never said never. I never do."

She returned with a glass of white wine, settling back on the sofa. "Cheers," she said, laying on the irony.

Ihaka aimed his cellphone camera at her. "Say cheese."

Instead she said, "What the fuck?"

He put his phone away. "A guy called Glen Smith turned up at the funeral. He grew up with Arden – let's give him his real name, Warren Duckmanton – in Greytown." Hadlow raised so-what? eyebrows as if she had no idea where this was going. "He told me Warren got hung up on this woman, Donna, who ran a café with her boyfriend. Not long after Donna and the boyfriend skipped town, Warren followed suit. The reason I took your photo is that I have this theory you and Donna are one and the same. Glen can tell me whether I'm right."

Hadlow shook her head slowly, eyes wide. "This is all based on me not telling you I knew Arden, even though I had no reason to?"

"Not quite. You're the right age and you fit the bill. Glen thinks Warren shot through and never came back because his mates gave him such a hard time over this Donna, but I reckon he knew where she was and went after her. See, I doubt the Warren-Donna thing was all one-way traffic."

"What makes you think that?"

"The fact that Warren couldn't stand cricket."

Hadlow put her glass down and plonked her chin on the heel of her hand. "Right," she said, drawing the word out. "You know, it's a real privilege watching a master detective at work."

"I spoke to Margie Brackstone today. Ring a bell?"

Something stirred in Hadlow's eyes. She shifted on the sofa, ironic detachment giving way to fidgety distraction. "You introduced her to Arden, as he'd become, at Billy's cricket. I was wondering why a guy with zero interest in cricket would watch a kid's game, and I came up with another theory: Arden's the daddy."

Hadlow threw the cushion aside and swung her legs out from under her, sitting up straight. "Well, whoop-de-do, you win a set of steak knives and your choice of soft toy. Would you like the bunny rabbit or the teddy bear? So you've found out I went by another name in a former life and made up a story to fob off those nosey pricks who thought it was their business who Billy's father was. Correct me if I'm wrong, but neither of those things are against the law, are they? Which makes me wonder, why exactly are you here?"

"I'm coming to that. Arden fucked older women for money. You obviously knew that. In fact, I reckon you were in on it. That's my third theory: you were the finder. You got him together with bored women looking for excitement and prepared to pay for it; he provided the excitement, you took a cut. Everyone's a winner, baby."

"You have a very low opinion of me, don't you?"

"Convince me otherwise."

"Do you really want to be convinced?"

"I want the truth."

214

"Okay. Have a glass of wine, take a chill pill and I'll tell you the truth."

"Got any red?"

Denise was a country girl, believe it or not. Grew up on a farm in South Canterbury, just outside Pleasant Point. When she was thirteen, her parents sent her to an Anglican boarding school in Timaru. She went in an ardent believer who said her prayers every night, kneeling by her bed talking to God for ten minutes, halting, one-sided conversations a bit like the phone calls to her remote, uncommunicative grandfather up in the Mackenzie Country. Even when her parents no longer hung around to make sure she didn't just pay lip service or bug God with frivolous requests; even in the middle of winter, with her arms and legs cobbled with goosebumps and hot-water bottle cosiness two seconds away.

She came out an atheist who knew whole chunks of the Book of Common Prayer by heart and could recite them while imagining herself in a very different setting, or thinking about things good little Christian misses weren't supposed to think about, least of all in church.

The summer she left school she and two friends chipped in to buy an old bomb and toured the North Island party venues – Gisborne, Mount Maunganui, Waihi Beach, Whangamata – cancelling out five years of moral force-feeding in five weeks of stoned abandon.

Everyone said Dunedin was Fun City so she went down to Otago University, even though she had no great urge to do an arts degree, nor much idea of what she'd do with it. After waking up in another freezing student hovel next to another guy whose name she couldn't remember and whose attraction, in the cold light of day, wasn't evident, she decided life was too short to waste three years living like this. She borrowed a friend's car, saying her mother was sick, drove to Christchurch and bought a one-way ticket to Sydney. She arrived with an overnight bag, a few hundred dollars and the names and addresses of two friends of friends who possibly wouldn't mind her crashing on their couch for a few nights.

She tried pretending to be a secretary, but couldn't keep up the pretence for long enough to cut it as a temp. She waitressed, she pole-danced and eventually she stripped. That was where she drew the line, although there were various incentives to proceed further down that track. She often thanked the God she no longer believed in that there was at least one temptation she could resist: hard drugs.

She bummed around Asia, sleeping on beaches, getting really skinny and so bronzed people assumed she was Latin, living on her wits and looks, flitting from guy to guy. The trick was to pick the ones with a financial lifeline back to mom and pop in San Diego or Düsseldorf or Stockholm. She didn't overdo it, always being the one to pull the plug, always leaving them wanting more of her. That way she felt less of a user. You had to have rules: don't get emotionally involved; don't stay in one place or with one guy for more than a month; don't look back.

There was bad news from home: some glib little shit from the bank had talked her parents into getting a foreign-exchange loan to buy those paddocks down the road her father had always coveted. There'd never be a better time, he said, so max out – do up the house, upgrade the farm equipment, take that European holiday you've been promising yourselves.

The exchange rate flipped and suddenly they owed a lot more than they'd signed up for. Her father had health issues: he wasn't up to the years of hard slog needed to get out of hock. They sold the farm in a buyer's market and moved into Timaru. Now her father felt like a failure, on top of everything else.

She came home, moved in with her parents and took a waitressing job. Within three months she was managing the place. She was efficient, a hard worker when she put her mind to it, and could read situations and manage/manipulate people. And it was Timaru, after all.

One night Craig came into the restaurant. Halfway through his meal, he left the table and his date and came over to ask her out. A cool operator. They took off together, working their way north – Christchurch, Kaikoura, Blenheim, Nelson, Wellington. Craig had a cavalier attitude to money, especially other people's: run up debt, run out on debt, change towns, change names, do it all over again. If you keep moving, they'll never catch up with you.

The good folk of Greytown were suckers for Donna's and Craig's ingratiating liveliness – we like this place, we like you guys, we like to have fun. There was just one complication when it was time to go. Warren, this cute young guy who worked at the café and had a heavy crush on her, even though the local schoolies were queuing up to spread for him.

They'd had enough of small towns, so they bypassed the heartland. After they'd been in Auckland a few weeks, she wrote to Warren encouraging him to come up. She didn't mention it to Craig. In Greytown he'd had this running joke – although they both knew it wasn't entirely a joke – about her relationship with "the toyboy".

To tell the truth, she was a bit thrown when Warren turned up so soon and adamant there was no going back. It made her responsible. Having enticed him to run away, she couldn't let him become another of the lost angels, the dreamy kids who flock to the big smoke entranced by a glossy magazine narrative of instant acceptance and overnight success. You saw them sometimes teetering along Karangahape Road on hookers' heels late at night, or glassy-eyed in the needle parks.

She'd hoped Craig would put up with Warren, that they could be a couple plus one, but the way he carried on, veering from sullen withdrawal to simmering aggression, knocked that on the head. So she compartmentalized, seeing Warren on her own and not telling Craig. What was the point? He'd only get shitty. Besides, she didn't tell him who he could and couldn't hang out with.

Lying beside Craig after yet another row, face turned to the wall, the atmosphere too toxic to permit an exchange of good-nights, she'd sometimes think about Warren. The boy was becoming a man; he just needed someone to provide the finishing touches.

Inevitably someone saw them together and told tales, putting a suggestive slant on their flirtatious interaction. It wouldn't have been too hard for Craig to have believed her when she insisted nothing had changed, because he'd seen it with his own eyes often enough. But he'd reached the point of wanting to believe the worst because it provided a convenient explanation for the unravelling of their relationship. His parting words were, "Now you can fuck the little faggot to your heart's content."

"Maybe I will," she said. "No reason not to any more."

On Warren's nineteenth birthday she took him to bed. Next morning she told him it wouldn't happen again. They could be friends or lovers but not both, and friendships lasted.

But when she hit thirty and decided she wanted a child, Warren was the obvious sperm donor. He was the nicest man she knew and the best-looking, so genes-wise he had a lot going for him. He wouldn't complicate things; he'd let her decide how much or how little contact he had with the child. Plus, getting started would be fun. What she'd discovered,

218

on the long night of his nineteenth birthday, was that he wasn't too far off being the finished article.

Hadlow got refills. Ihaka's cellphone message alert went off. It was Miriam Lovell. They'd talked earlier about meeting for a drink. Was he was still up for it? He texted back, saying definitely, he'd be in touch as soon as he finished, probably half an hour or so.

"Anyone I know?" asked Hadlow. Ihaka ignored her. "Well, now you know the whole story."

"I doubt that, somehow. So you knew from the start Warren was making money off these women?"

She held his gaze. "No. He fessed up at some stage, I don't remember exactly when. I told him I didn't want to know – consenting adults and all that."

"It didn't stop you introducing women to him."

"You make it sound like a crime. It's called social inter-course."

"You got that half-right."

"Look, if I was meeting someone for coffee, I'd usually suggest Warren's place, not because I was thinking 'Oh, you look like you could do with a decent fuck, dear', but because I wanted to support his business. Okay, there might've been a few times I hoped something would happen, like if I felt sorry for them because they were married to an arsewipe who I happened to know was screwing around, or I liked the thought of some stuck-up bitch screeching at the ceiling then going home to hubby and pretending she'd been at her book club. But if the question is how many of his clients found their way to him via me, the answer is I have no idea. I didn't ask and he didn't tell."

"But you were okay with it?"

She shrugged. "They were all grown-ups. Knowing Warren, he would've delivered on his side of the bargain, and I'm not just talking about pressing the right buttons. He would've made them feel special, put some excitement and intrigue in their lives. As for the money, well, most of them would've spent a lot more on clothes and beauty treatments, and I bet they didn't make them feel half as good as he did."

"One of his clients is being blackmailed. I bet she's not the only one."

Once again her eyes didn't slide away from Ihaka's hard stare. "I'd put this house on him having nothing to do with it. Look, no one would accuse me of being naïve. I knew Warren, I knew his weaknesses, better probably than anyone. But he didn't shit on people. Being a good person was important to him."

"I wasn't necessarily thinking of him."

This time she did look away, but slowly, disdainfully. "Oh, thanks a lot. You don't expect me to respond to that, do you?"

"You might have to at some stage."

"I can do it right now. Go fuck yourself."

Ihaka nodded. "I'll put you down as refusing to answer on the grounds it might incriminate you. So if Warren was Mr Nice Guy, why was he murdered?"

"Hey, you're the detective. I'll tell you this, though: he wasn't someone who made enemies. You could accuse him of being vain and superficial, possibly even a bit emotion- ally retarded, but he didn't treat people badly. I don't know, maybe they just got the wrong guy. Maybe it was as fucked-up as that."

"Drugs is the popular choice."

She shook her head decisively. "No way. You obviously think you're dealing with some kind of sleazebag here, but you're way off. Here's an example. Warren and Chris, no contest. Warren had a much stronger sense of right and wrong."

"Seeing Lilywhite had his wife killed, that's not saying a hell of a lot."

"Except everybody but you thought he was such a pillar of society it was outrageous to suggest he might've had something to do with it. But all those fine, upstanding people, Chris's friends, would probably believe the worst of Warren, just because he was different."

"And because he was fucking their wives."

"They didn't know that," said Hadlow. "What you don't know can't hurt you."

"What happened to Craig?"

"He kept moving," she said with a dismissive gesture. "Someone was saying they saw him in Phuket."

"Okay," said Ihaka, "I need you to write down the names and contact details if you have them of every married woman you know or think or suspect Warren was knocking off. Err on the side of the opposite of caution. Start with the most recent and work back."

"Promise you'll be gentle with them?"

"I'll get one of my colleagues on it. She's a good operator." He stood up. "I'll be in touch."

She sat there, legs crossed, idly swinging a foot, looking up at him. "You don't have to go."

"What does that mean?"

"What do you think it means?"

"Are you offering me your spare room?"

"I don't have a spare room," she said.

"What brought this on?"

"Excuse me?"

"You just can't resist my charm, is that it?"

She laughed, throwing her head back. "You're not completely without charm," she said, "but those little bursts tend to be cancelled out by bigger bursts of anti-charm. But charm's overrated."

"Warren's clientele obviously didn't think so. Sounds like he had charm coming out his arse."

"Oh, he did," she said, "which kind of proves my point. If I'd wanted to, I could've had him all to myself."

"So what have I got that he didn't have?"

"So many questions," she murmured. "It's like a job interview. Warren was a sweet guy, but he lacked… substance, I suppose you'd call it. He was pretty self-absorbed, just floated through life looking terrific, pleasing himself, having a good time, being everybody's friend. But if you're everybody's friend, chances are you're nobody's best friend, you know what I mean? You, on the other hand, you're a bit of a driven man, aren't you? So what drives you? Do you see yourself as a knight in shining armour, riding to the rescue, or do you just hate people getting away with it?"

"You're telling the story."

"I remember when you were hounding Chris – well, that's how I saw it at the time, I thought you were just out of control – he'd have these rants: 'That fucking Ihaka, he's messing with the wrong man, I'm going to have his balls for breakfast, blah, blah.' He'd go on about all his friends in high places he had lined up to cut you off at the knees. One time I said something like, 'Is Ihaka too thick to realize what's going to happen?' And Chris said, 'Oh, he's not thick, he knows he's sticking his neck out, big-time.' 'So why's he doing it?' I said. He kind of shrugged and said, 'Well, I guess he must really believe I killed Joyce.'"

She paused, emphasizing what was coming next. "I admire people who go out on a limb – especially when they're right."

"So all these years," said Ihaka, "you've been burning a candle for me?"

Hadlow laughed again, perfect teeth lighting up her face. "Hey, buddy, I don't want a sympathy fuck."

"I've got to go."

The glow of amusement faded from her eyes. She got up and stood right in front of him, their faces centimetres apart. "What's the matter, Tito?" she asked, teasing but a little curious.

"I'm a cop and you're a —"

"Suspect?"

"You're involved. And this is serious shit."

"Not so keen on going out on a limb these days?"

"It's got to be worth it."

She grinned lazily. "Oh, you have no idea."

"I'll see myself out."

Ihaka sat in his car staring at himself in the rear-vision mirror. He said out loud, "What the fuck are you doing?"

He got out of the car and retraced his steps. Hadlow answered the door, trying to keep a straight face, a smile tugging at the corners of her mouth. "Forget something?"

"There's just one other thing."

"Yeah, yeah," she said. She pulled him inside, pushed him against the wall and fitted her body against his. An arm slithered around his neck, pulling him down into a kiss from which there was no escape. Not that he tried.

15

Tito Ihaka sat in a commandeered office at Auckland Central deciphering Miriam Lovell's text: "Gess u gt tyd up lst nite. Say la v bt a heds up wdve bn nice."

Last night was a bit of a blur, but he was pretty sure he hadn't been tied up. He would've remembered that. He couldn't argue with the rest of it, though.

It wasn't in Ihaka's nature to dwell on what-might-have-beens or wallow in regret. He knew that the correct, proper, professional thing to do was walk away from Denise Hadlow, so that's what he did. But on giving it further thought, he decided he didn't give a shit what was correct, proper and professional, because there were only so many Denise Hadlows in a man's life. That's how it worked: you made a choice, you went in with your eyes open, and then you lived with the consequences. You didn't blame it on her feminine wiles or a moment of weakness, because you weren't Joe Vanilla from the suburbs who should've been at home watching some wankathon on TV with the wife and kids.

Even so, it was an uneasy morning after, partly because he hadn't played fair with Miriam, partly because he was sailing close to the wind. Even if he believed every word Denise had said – which he didn't – she was a person of interest in two murder cases.

Partly too because Denise wasn't quite what he'd expected: not better or worse, different. He was expecting a serious sack-artist with lots of energy and very few inhibitions. She was certainly accomplished, but her lovemaking was leisurely and affectionate, almost tender, rather than theatrical. As he slipped into unconsciousness, having set his phone alarm for 6 a.m. so that he'd be up and away before her son awoke, she'd burrowed into him. "Billy's playing cricket on Saturday," she'd murmured. "Why don't you come along? He'd be really stoked."

But it was mostly because he knew he was missing something. Talking to her, he'd had the feeling that an answer, maybe even the answer, was there in his head, in among the jumble of information, intuition and suspicion. But his mind wouldn't give it up. Now he could feel it sitting there, taunting him, the way a cat sits on a fence taunting a dog. You want a piece of me? Well, come and get it. But when you get there, it's gone.

If he hadn't gone back, he might've had it; it was that close. If he'd gone home, sat out on the veranda with a glass of wine and methodically thought his way through it, it probably would have come to him. But once Denise Hadlow got her hands on him, it went the way of everything else.

Glen Smith rang, sounding pleased with himself. "I've tracked down a photo of Donna."

"Well, thanks for that," said Ihaka, "but I've tracked down the woman herself."

"Shit, really? Where?"

"Here in Auckland."

"How's she looking these days?"

You're asking me, thought Ihaka. "Not too bad at all."

"I wouldn't mind catching up with her," said Smith. "Just for old times' sake."

"I can't give you her contact details, but I'll mention it to her."

"That'd be good. I guess she put you on to Craig?"

"No, that didn't turn out so well. Last she heard he was in Thailand."

"Well, maybe he was," said Smith, "but he's back now."

"Eh?"

"Yeah, a mate of mine saw him in Auckland not that long ago. I rang round the old crowd to let them know I'd seen Warren off and see if anyone had a photo of Donna. One bloke did. He didn't even have to look for it because he'd dug it out after he'd seen Craig – he's in the photo too. See, what happened was, he went into this nightclub called the Departure Lounge, and there was Craig – he works there, apparently. He said gidday but Craig said, 'Nah, mate, you've got me mixed up with someone.' Reckoned his name was Danny something. It's been a few years and my mate had had a few, so he was thinking, shit, maybe I've got it wrong. Then he remembered the photo. He had to hunt high and fucking low, but he found it in the end. No question about it, he says. The bloke looks a bit different these days, but it was Craig all right."

Ihaka rang Jason Gundry, a detective sergeant in the Waitemata district who was overseeing the crackdown on The Firm.

"I hear Scholes is up for parole next week," he said.

"In his fucking dreams," said Gundry. "Don't worry, mate, we kept the fat prick behind bars last time round, and we'll do it again. Just been reading our submission as it happens – he hasn't got a shit show."

"What if I said we should do a deal, offer to let him walk?"

There was a long silence. "You're shitting me, right?"

"No, I'm serious. I'm pretty sure he can help us out with a couple of these murders. I saw him the other day. You know Scholes, he always puts on a front, but he's had enough."

"Fuck you, pal. You know bloody well we're talking about a real piece of shit here. You won't get any help from us, I can tell you that right now."

"Well, if you're going to be like that, I guess I'll just have to get McGrail to acquaint you fucking bogans with the facts of life."

Beth Greendale poked her head around the door to say that Christopher Lilywhite's daughter was in reception.

"What does she want?"

"She wouldn't say."

Ihaka groaned. "Here we go again."

But the fire had gone out in Sandy Lilywhite. "I owe you an apology," she said, unable to look him in the eye. "I've just seen Inspector Charlton. He told me what my father did."

Ihaka came out from behind his desk. "Why did he do that?"

"He says the investigation's reached the point where there's a risk of a leak and he didn't want me to hear it second-hand."

Ihaka nodded. "He's got a point. I'm sorry you had to find out, but you don't owe me anything."

"You were right all along," she said, "and my father tried to destroy you. My brother and I said some terrible things."

"What happened, happened. There's no need to apologize for believing your old man – any kid would do the same. And for what it's worth, I think the guilt got to him."

"Why are you defending him?"

"I'm not defending him," said Ihaka. "I'm just saying he repented. In my book that counts for something. It's certainly a lot better than not giving a shit."

Sandy shook her drooping head, as if Ihaka's forbearance had undermined another comforting assumption. "Don't you even want to say 'I told you so'?"

"Oh, I've said that to a few people around here, don't worry about that. Can I ask you a question? You've probably already answered it, but did your father tell anyone he'd talked to me?"

"Sergeant Firkitt asked me that. I don't know, I'm afraid. All I can tell you is he was hardly talking to anyone at that stage. He'd told everyone who needed to know and been visited by the people he wanted to see, and he really just wanted to be left alone."

"What about you?"

"Well, not as such. Denise Hadlow rang to speak to him that afternoon and I was so steamed up I just blurted out that you were there. Apart from that, I didn't mention it to anyone."

"Did Denise ever get hold of him?"

"She said she'd try again. I was out for a while that night, so she might have. Why do you ask?"

"If your father was killed because he was talking to me – and right now there aren't too many other theories – then anyone who knew that is a suspect."

Denise Hadlow emailed through a list of eleven names, none of which Ihaka recognized. He briefed Beth Greendale, and sent her off to talk about sex and blackmail.

He invited Ron Firkitt out for a sandwich, his shout. Firkitt shook his head. "No way. If you're paying, I'm having more than a lousy fucking sandwich."

He was as good as his word, loading his tray with a sausage roll, a beef and mushroom pie, a slice of bacon and egg pie, a smoked chicken panini, a cream bun and a Coke. Ihaka had a chicken salad sandwich and a short black.

As they sat down Ihaka said, "So much for the theory that smoking kills your appetite."

"Oh, I probably won't eat half this shit," said Firkitt, "but you've got to show willing. So what's this in aid of?"

Ihaka told him about Arden Black's gigolo sideline and Helen Conroy being blackmailed.

"Two questions," said Firkitt. "Why the fuck didn't you tell us earlier, and why the fuck are you telling me now?"

"I wanted to keep a lid on it for the same reason that women like Helen Conroy – and I'll bet she's not the only one – are vulnerable to blackmail: if it gets out, there's a reasonable chance her marriage will fall over, her kids will get screwed up and half the people she knows will treat her like she's the Whore of Babylon. She doesn't deserve that."

"You're a great big softie, aren't you?" said Firkitt.

"You know," said Ihaka, "I've always thought the difference between us and the scumbags is they don't give a shit what they do to innocent people."

"She's not innocent."

"That's between her and her husband. Anyway, I'm telling you now because it's getting too big for me to freelance."

Firkitt nodded. "You going to tell Charlton?"

"I have to, don't I?"

"He's down in Wellington today, probably getting his arse punted around the Beehive. Look, why don't you let me tell him? The thing with Charlton, timing is everything. If you give him bad news at the wrong time, he'll rip you a new arsehole. I can read the bloke, so I'll slip it in his ear when the time's right – or as right as it's ever going to be." Firkitt paused, baring his wrecked teeth. "Of course, you've got to ask yourself: is this just a ruse on Firkitt's part to really fucking drop me in the shit?"

Ihaka shrugged. "I don't think it matters either way. There's something else. I'm bringing in Denise Hadlow this afternoon; I want you to interview her."

Firkitt's eyes narrowed. "Why don't you do it?"

"I'm compromised."

"You mad fuck. How bad?"

"Bad enough."

"Don't blame you, mind you. She's got the X factor, that sheila. What about that one on the plane? You get anywhere with her?"

"Well, we had a drink the other night."

"What the fuck is it with you?" said Firkitt, scowling. "I mean, you're a fucking lard, you're as ugly as a pugdog's bumhole…"

"Not to mention being a brownie."

"Hey," said Firkitt, "I don't go there any more, all right? I don't say that stuff. I still think it, of course, but I don't say it."

"As you do."

"Course you do. Christ, some of your mob are the biggest fucking racists in the country, except it's not racism when whitey cops it."

"Be fair. We've got a lot of ground to make up."

"I'll have to tell Charlton about that too. Better he finds out now than down the track. So what are you going to tell this bird, that you've been pulled off the case again?"

"I'll tell her the truth."

"Will you now? Okay, I'll do it, I'll interview her but I'll do it my way. It won't be pretty."

"We're way past pretty."

"She'll hate you for it."

"As someone said to me just this morning: c'est la vie." Ihaka stood up. Firkitt had scoffed everything but the cream bun. "I'll leave you to your pudding and go and get things organized."

"Just because I'm giving you a hand here, doesn't mean anything's changed," said Firkitt. "You understand that, don't you? I'm still going to get you."

"Fair enough."

"And I still think you're a cunt."

"Then we're on the same wavelength, because I still think you're a cunt. And I still think your mate Charlton's a cunt. Huge cunts, the pair of you."

Firkitt shoved half the bun in his predator's maw. "I bet you say that to all the boys."

Denise Hadlow bounced to her feet as Ihaka entered the interrogation room. "Tito, what the hell...?"

"Sit down, please," said Ihaka.

After five seconds of silent defiance she snapped, "Fine," and sat down, mimicking the bright-eyed attentiveness of a Year 10 teacher's pet.

"Last night —"

"Yeah, let's talk about last night," she said. "Did last night happen, or did I imagine it?"

"Last night I asked you what happened to Craig. You said the last you'd heard, he was in Phuket. I'm going to ask you again, and I suggest you think real hard before you answer."

"Oh, shit." Hadlow sighed heavily and dropped her chin. "Okay, I'm sorry. He did go to Phuket and other places, but he came back. Can I just...?"

"Where is he now?"

"Here, in Auckland."

"Doing what?"

"He runs a nightclub," she said. "The Departure Lounge."

"What's he call himself?"

"Danny Howard."

"Thank you."

"Can I just explain?"

"Before you do," said Ihaka, "let me explain something. In everyday life, people tell lies all the time, so a bit of bullshit here and there isn't that big a deal. In an investigation, if a cop catches you telling one lie, he's going to assume he can't believe a fucking word you've said. You understand what I'm saying?"

"I promised Craig I wouldn't tell anyone he was back. I don't make many promises, but when I do, I stick to them."

"Even if it means lying?"

"Sometimes it just works out that way," she said. "A promise is a promise."

"Let's hear it."

"Basically, Craig split because he owed money all over town. He was away for, I think, three years and came back a different person. Even to look at. He'd always been big on the weights, but he'd got into swimming and cycling so his body shape had changed. And the whole act had been toned down – he was just a lot less in your face. He wanted to start over, but some people have long memories when it comes to money, so he made me and Warren and I guess a few others promise that if his name ever came up, we'd stick to the story that he was gone, over the horizon, no forwarding address. It didn't seem too much to ask."

"So he'd got over you and Warren?"

"It wasn't an issue. We went out one night, he admitted he'd made a dick of himself, we had a laugh about it and that was that – the subject never came up again. I mean, he got Warren the nightclub gig, and he and I get on fine. In fact we get on better than we did when we were a couple."

"Changing the subject, did you speak to Lilywhite after I'd been to see him?"

"You mean in person?"

Ihaka gave her the stare. "Don't play games."

"Jesus," she said indignantly. "Touchy. Yeah, I rang him. I wanted to go and see him. He said maybe in a week or two, but as it turned out he didn't have a week or two. That was it. It was like a two-minute conversation."

"You'd rung earlier and talked to Sandy, right?"

"Yeah."

"And she told you I was there, with Lilywhite?" Hadlow nodded. "I find it hard to believe you didn't raise that when you spoke to him."

"Sorry, yes, you're right, I did. I was pretty blown away when Sandy told me, so I asked him what was going on. He said he was making his peace."

"That sort of intrigue, you've got to share it with someone. So who did you tell?"

She shook her head. "No way, it was private."

"You didn't tell a soul?"

Ihaka's stare pressed into her eyeballs like a pair of thumbs. "Apart from Craig," she said. "He was the only one."

"Why him?"

She shrugged. "Because we told each other stuff. I've never been one to confide in women. I don't know what that says about me." There was no response to her collusive smile. "And he knew the background."

"The affair?"

"Yeah," she said. "The whole scenario appealed to his sense of humour. He used to ring me for updates."

Ihaka hunched forward. "You see where this is going, don't you?"

"What are you talking about?"

"Lilywhite hired a hitman, right? We figure the hitman found out he was talking to me and killed him to shut him up. Only five other people knew that: his lawyer, the Auckland District Commander, Sandy, you and Craig. You'd have to say there's a couple of names there that kind of jump out at you."

Hadlow frowned, still not sure how seriously she should be taking it.

"Go back to Joyce," said Ihaka. "The hitman approached Lilywhite. You don't ring up a bloke and offer to take out his wife unless you're pretty fucking sure he wants to get rid of her. Who knew that Lilywhite was cheating on Joyce? Who knew how much she pissed him off? Well, we know for a fact you did, and now we know for a fact that Craig did."

She flinched as if she'd been backhanded. "How can you do this?"

"It's my job."

"Oh, I get it." She looked away, not wanting Ihaka to see the hurt in her eyes, or pretending as much. "So last night was just —"

"Last night was last night. This morning I came in to work and found out you'd lied to me."

She gave him a bitter half-smile. "Just like that?"

"You're now a suspect in two murder investigations," said Ihaka. "At least two. We have reason to believe —"

"Oh God, now he's even starting with the cop-speak."

"— that Joyce wasn't this guy's only hit."

"You don't seriously think Craig's the hitman?" she said with a jarring laugh. "Sorry, but that's just fucking ridiculous."

"Why? Because Craig's a model citizen? Like fuck he is. He knew Lilywhite wanted Joyce out of his life, he knew Lilywhite was talking to me, he's never had enough money. I'd have to say he's looking pretty good."

"And how do I look?"

"You and Craig were a couple, you operated your little scams together and you still share secrets even though the relationship turned to shit – according to you. Maybe it never really stopped, it just went underground. If he is the hitman, you'd be a handy set of eyes and ears looking out for prospective clients. Lilywhite's a given; now we'll have to see whether you had a tie-up with the other cases."

"I can't believe this is happening." She put her head in her hands, dragging her palms down her face. "I can't believe what I'm hearing."

"Put yourself in my shoes," he said.

She brought up her chin. "Okay, let's say for the sake of argument Craig is the hitman. Why would he need me?"

"I told you. To look out for potential —"

"Why the fuck would he need me to do that? Running that nightclub, he'd be meeting potential clients every second night. He's always going on about how people latch onto him when they've had a few drinks and tell him all sorts of shit. There's that false intimacy thing, like this guy's your best buddy but actually he's not part of your life at all, so it's safe to tell him you're screwing your secretary. Warren said Craig was really good at it. He couldn't believe how patient he was."

"Jesus and bartenders," said Ihaka.

"What?"

"It's a country and western song: 'Anger, depression, tearful confessions, Jesus and bartenders hear it all.'"

"That's what I'm talking about."

He stood up. "Are we finished?" she asked. "Can I go now?"

"Detective Sergeant Firkitt's going to interview you. By the book. That's the way it's going to be from here on."

"Getting him to do your dirty work, eh?"

He nodded. "I've done my share."

Ninety minutes later Firkitt blew in to Ihaka's office without knocking, dropped heavily into a chair and lit a cigarette.

"You don't mind, do you?" he said, exhaling a metre-long plume.

"Not my office," said Ihaka. "How did it go?"

Firkitt filled his lungs again before stubbing the cigarette out on the sole of his shoe. "I got no change out of her."

"You went in hard?"

"Fucking oath."

"How did she handle it?"

"She didn't like it, but she didn't crack. Maybe it's what she says it is."

"Where is she now?"

Firkitt jerked his head. "Out there. Wants to talk to you. You're the fucking expert on women, but I don't think she wants to whisper sweet nothings in your earhole."

"I just got off the phone to Phil Malone's widow. Guess what his favourite after-hours haunt was?"

"The Departure Lounge? You're fucking kidding me."

Ihaka shook his head. "I'm not kidding. Tell me what you think of this idea."

A constable escorted Denise Hadlow into Ihaka's office.

"Behind closed doors, eh?" she said. "Scared I'd cause a scene? Scared I'd blab your dirty little secret, Ihaka sluts around with murder suspects?"

"Actually, that'd probably do wonders for my reputation. I've got a proposition for you. How would you feel about ringing Craig and telling him pretty much the truth – that the cops are giving you a hard time?"

"What would that achieve?"

"If he's not the hitman, he'll probably say something like, well, as long as you tell the truth, you've got nothing to worry about. On the other hand, if he is the hitman, he'll probably try to kill you."

"Put your life where your mouth is, eh?"

"Well, if you're so sure…"

"Yeah, well."

"Having second thoughts?"

"No, I was just thinking. Remember I said you could say Warren was a bit emotionally retarded? Same with Craig. They both walked away from their families and friends and never looked back. Craig's the least sentimental person I've ever come across, and that's coming from someone who's not exactly sentimental herself. Like if I died tomorrow, he'd be upset for a couple of hours then life would go on. So he's unsentimental. So what?"

"Something you should know: one of the cases Lilywhite put us on to involved a guy called Phil Malone, whose business partner was murdered. The partner didn't want to sell the company. Malone did. Once the partner was out of the way, Malone sold the company for a shitload. A couple of days ago, someone threw a hairdryer into Malone's bathtub. He was in it at the time. Here's the kicker: Malone used to hang out at the Departure Lounge. So will you do it?"

"You'll be there, right?"

"Yeah. And the street will be crawling with cops."

"So what could possibly go wrong?"

"Are you up for it tonight?"

"You mean am I up for it after that session with your pet gorilla?"

Ihaka nodded.

"You should take a look in the mirror, Sergeant. He wasn't half as rough on me as you were."

Hadlow made the call: "Hi there, it's me. What's up? Not great, actually. It's kind of why I'm ringing. The cops are getting really heavy, and I don't know what to do. About Chris Lilywhite. Yeah, I know he's dead, so's his wife. Remember I told you Chris had a heart-to-heart with that cop, Ihaka?

237

Well, apparently he confessed that he hired someone to kill Joyce. Now they're giving me a hard time because they reckon I might've egged him on and put him in touch with a hitman. How the fuck I'm meant to have done that, I've no idea. Also, they've found out from his bitch daughter that I spoke to Chris after he'd seen Ihaka. Why? I'll tell you why: because they're saying if Chris was killed to shut him up, the killer must've known he was talking to Ihaka. Jesus, Craig, just settle down, I'm getting to that. When I say I had nothing to do with it, they come back with well, who did you tell? I keep saying no one, and they keep saying I'm full of shit. I was down at Auckland Central all fucking afternoon getting abused and screamed at by Ihaka and this other goon, and they say they'll keep doing it till I tell them the truth. Well, the only thing I'm not telling them is that I told you. Yes, I know, I can imagine it'd be a real pain in the arse for you, but I can't take much more of this shit. I'm telling you, it really sucks. I've got a nine-year-old kid, for Christ's sake. I fucking hate it when Billy comes home from school and there are cops here, or when he has to go next door because I'm down at the police station. You there, Craig? Oh yeah, and they've also connected me to Warren. Right, they've gone all the way back to Greytown, and because I wasn't upfront about it, that's another black mark. Yeah, I know they've arrested a couple of guys. I don't know – believe it or not, they don't share that sort of information with me. Anyway, I just wanted to give you a heads-up. Sure, come round by all means, I'm not going anywhere. I think there's still a bit of that bourbon left. No, he's having a sleepover. Okay, see you soon. Ciao."

She put the phone down. "Was that all right, sir?"

"Yeah, good," said Ihaka. "Okay, this room's wired for sound and vision, so the boys in the van across the road can see and hear everything, and I'll be hooked up to them.

Just act normal. If he sees you're nervous or not yourself, he'll get suspicious. Where does he usually sit?"

Hadlow shrugged. "The sofa, I guess."

"Okay, I'll be on the other side of that." He pointed to the door leading to the stairs. "So if he's on the sofa he'll be pretty much in front of me when I come in. Whatever happens, when I come through that door, just get the fuck out of the way. You got that?"

She shrugged, giving him a look that said, what do you take me for?

"You're very relaxed."

"I don't think he's a killer, remember?"

"He's coming, isn't he?"

"I more or less asked him to."

"Why did he want to know if Billy's here?"

"Gosh, let me think. Maybe he likes Billy."

"Sentimental old Craig."

She made a sarcastic face. "You really think it's him, don't you?"

"You can feel when you're getting close," he said. "Things start to fit."

"And you have an instinct for this stuff?"

"Yeah," he said. "I have an instinct for this stuff. I don't know what that says about me."

He had Firkitt in his ear, from the surveillance van with blacked-out windows parked across the road: "Car coming. Slowing down. Gone past. Pulling up now. Lights off. Driver getting out. Single male, coming your way. Why didn't he park right outside? Cagey bastard, eh? Wearing a polo and board shorts, so unless he's got a derringer up his arse he's not carrying. Here we go. At the door now."

Denise Hadlow led Craig into the living room and offered a drink. He declined.

"There is some bourbon there."

"Still no."

"That's not like you."

"Maybe you're seeing another side of me," he said.

"Oh?" She poured herself a glass of wine. "Would that be a new side or an old side you've kept hidden?"

"Bit of both." He studied her, taking his time. "Have you ever thought about what it would be like to kill someone?"

"Jesus, Craig, where did that come from?"

"Have you?"

"No, I can't say I have. I can safely say the thought's never occurred to me." Craig was slumped on the sofa, head resting on the arm, staring at the ceiling. "Are you okay? You want a Panadol or something? You seem a bit —"

"A bit what?"

"I don't know, just not your usual self."

"What is my usual self?"

"I've known you for sixteen years, Craig: this is not your usual self." He sat up, tilting forward, elbows on his knees, hands loosely clasped. "And if this is the new you, I've got to say I preferred the old one. Can you get him back?"

"Oh, you won't be seeing that guy again."

"Can you knock it off? You're making me nervous."

"You know, at the club, it took me a while to get used to people who didn't know me from Adam telling me stuff they wouldn't tell their best friends. They certainly wouldn't fucking dream of telling their wives or girlfriends, because nine times out of ten it involved them. Booze has got a bit to do with it, but I worked out it's mainly because they can't tell their best friends. There's something going on in their lives that's eating away at them, and they've got to let it out. So they tell me. Believe it or not, I've been asked if I know anyone who could take care of a troublesome person. Permanently."

240

"What did you say?"

"'Maybe'. Which of course means, 'You bet I do'."

Hadlow sat very still, holding eye contact. "Who's that?"

"Ever since I was a kid I had this thing, this question always in my head: what would it be like to kill someone? Before we met I was seriously thinking about becoming a mercenary, would you believe? The places those guys operate, you could do any fucking thing. No one gives a fuck. Trouble is, it cuts both ways in your Third World hell holes, and that bit – other people trying to kill me – never had much appeal. When I was away, I had this brilliant idea: to become a hitman. Best of both worlds: you get to kill people, and you get paid for it. I'd be Mr Invisible. The client would never set eyes on me, and there'd be nothing to connect me to the client or the victim, so I'd be sweet as long as I didn't fuck up in the execution – if you'll pardon the pun. But you know what? If it hadn't been for you, it would've been just another day-dream, something you think about to pass the time when you're on a train for eighteen fucking hours, or hanging around some shitbox airport. When you hooked up with Lilywhite, it was like a sign from above." He spread his arms, beaming at her unnervingly. "This is your destiny, my son."

"Did you kill Joyce?"

"Uh-huh. Pretty good job, if I say so myself. The cops didn't even call it murder."

"One of them did."

"Oh yeah, good old Ihaka. Look where it got him."

"Did you kill Chris too?"

"Yep. Too late, as it turned out. The damage had been done. Bit of a fucking tragedy all round, really."

"What do you mean?"

"Well, first off, I didn't get paid for it – major bummer. And if he hadn't had an attack of conscience, or if I'd got to him in time, I wouldn't be here."

241

"You don't have to kill me, Craig. You know you can trust me."

He chuckled, a throaty, self-satisfied sound. "Darling, if I didn't have to kill you before I came over, I sure as hell do now. Look on the bright side: it'll look like a rape that got out of hand, so you'll get some action on the way out."

Craig stood up, producing a flick knife from the pocket of his shorts and popping the blade with a casual snap of the wrist.

"Go, mate, go," barked Firkitt.

Ihaka threw the door open and came in with a Glock semi-automatic in both hands. "Police," he bawled. "Drop the fucking knife. Do it now."

Craig stared at Ihaka and the pistol, rock steady, pointing at the tip of his nose. Then he slowly turned his head towards Hadlow. "You set me up," he said, his voice tinny with disbelief. "You fucking bitch."

Craig lunged at Hadlow. Standing side-on, Ihaka shot him in the chest, dead centre, knocking him flat on his back.

The front door crashed open. Firkitt came in so fast he almost tripped over Craig. He steadied himself, gulping in air. "Holy fucking Jesus."

Hadlow, eyes glazed, was pressed back into the chair with her knees drawn up and her hands balled into fists. She looked like she'd been in a car crash. Firkitt stepped over Craig to brush her shoulder with his fingertips. "It's okay, sweetie. You did good. You did real good." She looked up at him like a grateful child, her eyes clearing.

Ihaka squatted on his haunches beside Craig, the pistol dangling from his right hand. "Better get the medics," he said. "This prick might live."

Firkitt looked at him oddly. "They're right outside," he said. "I'll get them in."

As he left the room, Hadlow said to Ihaka, "Believe me now?"

He nodded, "Yeah, I believe you."

"So I'm not a suspect any more?"

"No, you're not."

"Good," she said. "In that case you can get the fuck out of my house."

16

Superintendent Finbar McGrail told Tito Ihaka to take a couple of days off. As he put it: "Creating messes is your forte, Sergeant. Best leave the cleaning up to others."

On his way home from a long weekend at his family's bach at Tauranga Bay, Ihaka dropped into Auckland Central for an update from Beth Greendale.

She'd accounted for the eleven women on Denise Hadlow's list. One was in France doing a cooking course on a barge drifting down the Garonne from Bordeaux to Toulouse. Another was living on the Gold Coast, but not picking up her phone or responding to messages. Two claimed they didn't know, indeed had never heard of, Arden Black. Greendale was pretty sure one was lying and suspected the other found it hard to keep track of the men in her life. Two pretty much slammed the door in her face.

One claimed she'd met Arden for an exploratory lunch, but had been turned off by his obvious and intense self-adoration. Another admitted to an affair, but became highly indignant when Greendale suggested Black was only in it for the money. Of the three who admitted paying for it, two were adamant they weren't being blackmailed and Greendale was inclined to believe them. They'd weaned themselves off Arden more than a year ago and hadn't had anything to do with him since.

The one who owned up to being blackmailed told a very similar story to Helen Conroy. Her last session with Black was a fortnight before he was murdered. Shortly after the murder, the blackmailer rang her with the same threats, demands and instructions.

On his way out, Ihaka bumped into Charlton and Firkitt.

"There you are," said Charlton. "I want a word with you."

Ihaka glanced at Firkitt, but he had his default expression, an unfocused glower, in place.

"I'm on a day off," said Ihaka.

"So what are you doing here?" asked Charlton.

"I was in the neighbourhood; I popped in to see how Beth Greendale's getting on."

"On what, this blackmail thing you chose not to tell us about?"

"You had a lot on your plate."

Charlton turned to Firkitt. "You hear that, Ron? It was for our own good. Wasn't that thoughtful of him?"

"That's Ihaka for you," said Firkitt. "Thinks of everyone but himself."

"An example to us all," said Charlton. He turned back to Ihaka. "What's happening?"

"I think we're starting to get somewhere."

Charlton nodded. "That's the sort of briefing I like. Short, sharp and to the point, but without omitting any relevant details. You just love flying solo, don't you? Well, Sergeant, to paraphrase what your patron saint Finbar the Devious said to me just a few days ago, if you claim ownership of a case, it's your arse on the line." He paused. "That was a high-risk operation the other night."

"He ran it past me first," said Firkitt.

245

"I'm aware of that," said Charlton sharply. "I heard you the first time. So I'm telling both of you, it was dangerously risky. What if he'd pulled a gun and shot her in the face when she opened the door?"

"That wasn't the hitman's MO," said Ihaka. "He'd always tried to make it look like something else. And we had a plan B if it looked like he had a firearm."

"What about Yallop?" said Charlton. "I seem to remember someone walked up to him and put one in his head."

"So far," said Ihaka, "there's nothing to connect Yallop to Howard – unless we found it when we searched Howard's place."

"We didn't," said Charlton. "Still, seeing as you rather miraculously managed not to kill him, he might have something to say about that and the old woman in Remuera in due course. Any chance the blackmail was a joint venture between him and Black?"

"It's possible," said Ihaka, "but my gut feeling is that Black wasn't in on it…" Suddenly Ihaka's head was awash with bright light. It was like flinging open the curtains at noon on a summer's day. The contents of the room, previously shadows within shadows, sensed rather than seen, were now in plain sight.

Firkitt saw the flash of comprehension light up Ihaka's face from the inside, like a Chinese lantern. "What's up?"

"I could have something," said Ihaka. "I need to think it through."

"Well, off you go, Sergeant," said Charlton, almost jovially. "The sooner you think it through and knock this thing on the head, the sooner you'll be back in Wairarapa."

Ihaka sat on his veranda in the late-afternoon sun, replaying snatches of conversation in his head.

Margie Brackstone asking: "Did Arden's death have anything to do with his love life, for want of a better term?"

Denise Hadlow saying, "All those fine, upstanding people, Chris's friends, would probably believe the worst of Warren, just because he was different."

Him replying, "And because he was fucking their wives."

Her coming back with, "They didn't know that. And what you don't know can't hurt you."

Him asking: "If Warren was Mr Nice Guy, why was he murdered?"

Denise replying, "Maybe they just got the wrong guy. Maybe it was as fucked-up as that."

That was it, right there. And it was fucked-up, all right.

It was 4.15. Denise Hadlow finished work early so she was there when her kid got home from school. He felt a flutter of nerves as he dialled. His scenario was clean and logical and the pieces clicked into place like a Rubik's cube, but it all hinged on the answers to a couple of questions.

"We missed you at the cricket on Saturday," she said.

"Really? What part of 'fuck off' did I misunderstand?"

She laughed. "I was – what's the word? – overwrought. Besides, you weren't coming to watch me."

"I thought you and Billy were a package deal."

"Not at cricket," she said. "He's on his own out there. I just thought it would've been a chance to see what happens when you're not being a cop and I'm not a suspect."

"Didn't we try that?"

"Yeah, but then you went and spoilt it by becoming a cop again."

"That's what I am, Denise."

"You don't have to be with me. Not any more."

"It's not over. I'm being a cop now."

Her voice went flat. "So what do you want?"

"That list you sent me. Would Lorna Bell have been on it if she was still alive?"

"Why do you want to know?"

"Just answer the question. This is important."

"Jesus, all right. Yes, she would have."

"Tell me about it."

"She came into the café when I was there. Pure coincidence. I introduced her to Warren and it was like, okay, thanks Denise, we'll take it from here. I mean, let's face it, they were made for each other."

"How so in her case?"

"She was bored out of her tree. Had been for years."

"Then what?"

"Then nothing. That was the last time I saw her. And as I told you, with Warren and his women, I didn't ask and he didn't tell."

"Okay, thanks."

"It's almost the end of the season. Billy's only got two more games."

"Summer's gone, winter's in your eyes."

"What?"

"It's another song."

She said, "What is it with these lyrics? Do you collect them?"

"No, some just stick in your head."

"I'm surprised there's any room."

"Should I take that as a compliment?"

"That's up to you," she said. "Like everything else."

Ihaka rang the superintendent of Paremoremo. "You keep a record of every visitor, right? Who they visit and when?"

"Yep, it's all here on the computer. What do you want to know?"

"Has Jonathon Bell ever been to see John Scholes?"

"You mean *the* Jonathon Bell?"

"Yeah, that one."

"Why would he have anything to do with Scholes?"

"Just a thought."

"Bell's been here, but not to see Scholes. We've got his mate Mark Wills."

Mark Wills was a wheeler-dealer who got badly burnt in the global financial meltdown. Taking a leaf from John DeLorean's book, he tried to restore his fortunes with a monster drug deal, but he fucked that up too and now he was doing time in Paremoremo medium.

"I don't know if you ever saw that piece on *60 Minutes*," said the superintendent, "about how Wills's friends had rallied around to keep the family in the family home and his kids in private schools? I suppose writing a cheque's the easy part – Bell's the only one who's ever been to see him."

"How's Wills doing?"

"Oh, he's all right. These guys can relate to someone who had a fortune and lost it, and of course he got brownie points for the drug deal if not the execution. Having said that, he does have someone watching over him."

"And who might that be?" said Ihaka.

"Let me put it this way. If Scholes didn't give a damn what happened to Mark Wills, he would've had a bumpier ride."

"I thought Wills was on the bones of his arse."

"People like Wills are never broke, are they. Don't they always have cash tucked away in trusts or offshore bank accounts? But you're quite right: Scholes isn't doing it out of the goodness of his heart."

Ihaka borrowed Firkitt's best surveillance guy, Detective Constable Jack Booth. What made Booth so good was that he was twenty-five but could pass for fifteen with his baby face and scrawny build. In baggy shorts and an extra-large

T-shirt, with a back-to-front baseball cap and a skateboard under his arm, you'd pick him as just another zoned-out juvenile cluttering up the streets. Put him in a sharp suit and an Audi, and you'd pick him as just another amoral young opportunist. Either way, he didn't set off alarm bells, even in the most paranoid heads.

After a couple of days, Booth brought in some photos of the target with a young woman. They'd had lunch together, they'd had dinner together, they'd gone home together. Ihaka sent Beth Greendale over to the Langham Hotel to go through CCTV footage from the evenings on which Helen Conroy and the other blackmail victim had made the handovers. When Beth called to say the target's girl-friend turned up both times, Ihaka decided it was time to make his move.

Jonathon Bell sat behind the antique desk in the darkened study of his Paritai Drive mansion, half-illuminated by the light from a desktop lamp. He was wearing a Lacoste polo shirt and shorts, having just come off the tennis court. Ihaka could smell the exertion from across the room.

He tried to visualize Bell before his wife's self-destruction: a rich man's year-round tan and the sleek, in-the-pink appearance that comes from avoiding the workaday chores and money worries and penny-pinching that grind down ordinary folk, leaving them dull-eyed and grey-skinned, always on the verge of a creaking yawn. Now there were grooves in his face, but they weren't evidence of character or self-denial. They were symptoms of torment, like cor-rugations in the landscape caused by subterranean turmoil. Cops often see men put on a brave face out of old-fashioned notions of propriety or manliness, and are good at sensing when the grieving is for appearances' sake. According to Firkitt, who'd seen him in the immediate aftermath, Bell hadn't stood on his dignity and hadn't needed to pretend. His grief had been raw and unrestrained.

"This had better be good," said Bell. "The chaps weren't too thrilled at having to call it off at one set all."

"Pass on my apologies," said Ihaka unapologetically.

Bell gestured with his sports-drink bottle to the dark-suited figure hovering in the background, barely visible in the gloom. "My lawyer. Well, one of them anyway."

"You and I should have a private chat," said Ihaka. "No lawyer, no notes."

Bell glanced at the lawyer, inviting his input.

"I don't think so," said the lawyer.

Bell's gaze switched back to Ihaka. "You heard the man."

"This isn't an official contact," said Ihaka. "No one at my end knows I'm here. I thought you might be interested in hearing what I know, as opposed to what we're saying."

"About what?" asked the lawyer.

"What do you think?" said Ihaka, looking straight at Bell. "It's a nice night. We could go for a stroll around the estate."

"I suppose there's no harm in that," said Bell, getting to his feet. "David, help yourself to a drink. If I'm not back in twenty minutes, send out a search party. Sergeant, if you'll follow me."

Bell led Ihaka out through a side door, around an immense swimming pool and onto an all-weather tennis court. The floodlights were still on and unflatteringly bright, turning their faces into riots of blemish and discolouration.

"Private enough for you?" asked Bell, with a wary half-smile.

Ihaka looked around. Everything beyond the bubble of harsh light had been swallowed up by the night. It felt as though they were in the middle of nowhere. "This is fine."

"Must be some secret you've got there."

"It's not my secret," said Ihaka. "It's our secret."

Bell's smile expanded. "Really? That seems pretty unlikely."

"I'm investigating a couple of murders, a guy named Arden Black and his sister…"

"Let's cut to the chase," said Bell. "What the hell's it got to do with me?"

"Nothing," said Ihaka. "Nothing at all. I just came out here to see how the other half lives." He stared at Bell until his gaze slid away. "Shall I continue?"

Bell shrugged: if you must.

"Fourteen years ago, just finished school, Arden left Greytown and never came back. There was a phone call home to say don't come looking for me, then silence. They didn't have a clue where he was. He came to Auckland and hustled around, as guys like that do. He was a handsome rascal with a thing for older women, and found he could have his cake and eat it too because some older women were prepared to pay for his company, if you know what I mean.

"A couple of months ago his sister Eve, who'd never given up hope of a family reunion, ran into someone who'd seen her brother in Sydney, wrapped around an Auckland-based TV star. She hired a private investigator to track her brother down, which he did, but Arden still didn't want anything to do with her. By this stage the investigator's worked out why all these middle-aged women in headscarves and dark glasses are trooping in and out of Arden's apartment. After he'd told Eve about it, he realized he's sitting on a goldmine because some of these women would far rather fork out hush money than have their husbands find out they're getting a seeing-to from a male prostitute every second Thursday afternoon. So he put the hard word on a couple, one of whom went and killed herself."

Bell groaned and turned away. Ihaka talked to his back.

"Her husband finds the body with a note and some incriminating photos. He jumps to the conclusion that

252

the guy in the photos, the gigolo, is the blackmailer, and wants to make him suffer. Fortunately, he's got a mate in Paremoremo who owes him big-time. Among other things, he's paying for protection so his mate doesn't end up as some big boy's fuck-toy. So he slips his mate a photo of Arden and asks him to get his gang buddies on the job. Maybe they weren't meant to go all the way, but these guys are animals – overkill's their standard operating procedure. Whatever, they get hold of Arden and bash him to death.

"The PI sees all this. He's been tailing Arden, hoping to add a few more frisky wives to his portfolio. He shoots over to Arden's apartment to grab his laptop in case he kept records of his clients. Then he realizes there's a giant fly in the ointment: the sister. When she finds out what's happened to her brother, she'll tell the cops everything. There goes the goldmine, not to mention his freedom. So he lures Eve up here, probably by saying her brother's agreed to a meeting, and does to her pretty much what the animals did to Arden, figuring we'd be only too happy to pin both murders on them, and they'd be too dumb to talk their way out of the one they didn't commit."

Bell turned back to face Ihaka. He was moist-eyed, stunned and afraid.

"You set the dogs on the wrong man, Mr Bell." Ihaka turned and walked away. "The blackmailer's name is Grant Hayes," he said over his shoulder. "He's in the Yellow Pages."

Grant Hayes had an office above a chemist on Karangahape Road. Ihaka walked in at 9.05, too early for his secretary, a hotted-up peroxide blonde. She was the woman in Booth's photos, the face Beth Greendale had spotted in the Langham's CCTV footage.

"Mr Hayes is busy right now," she said.

Ihaka showed his ID. "He'll see me." He made a show of tilting his head and peering at her. "You look very familiar. Have we met?"

The secretary giggled. "Some people think I look like Christina Aguilera."

"That can't be it," said Ihaka. "I wouldn't know Christina Aguilera if I ran over her. I'm sure it'll come to me. I never forget a face."

Her artificial half-smile blinked on and off. She pressed the intercom button. "Grant, there's a guy from the police here. A Mr...?"

"Ihaka." He was already in Hayes's office, closing the door behind him.

Hayes was at a kitset desk, drinking coffee from a paper cup and doing the crossword. He didn't seem surprised or ruffled by Ihaka's appearance. "Detective Sergeant Ihaka," he said with a salesman's smile. "What brings you to my humble workplace?"

Ihaka examined him, searching for a sign. There wasn't one. Hayes looked like a normal, well-adjusted guy. After he'd beaten Eve to death, he probably went home and watched a wildlife documentary.

"I'm here to do you a favour," said Ihaka.

"Then you're doubly welcome. It's been a while since anyone did."

"This is a biggie. It'll save your life."

Hayes shuffled his masks, settling on good-natured puzzlement. "Excuse me?"

"Jonathon Bell knows you tried to blackmail his wife, which of course was what made her kill herself. He knows he sent those cavemen after the wrong guy. If you want to die of old age, you'd better come with me. We're the only ones who can protect you now."

The frown lines on Hayes's forehead deepened, but his expression didn't waver. "I'm sorry, Sergeant," he said, half-suppressing a snort of amusement at the sheer zaniness of it all. "I don't have the faintest idea what you're talking about."

"Suit yourself," said Ihaka. "But I'll spell it out one more time anyway, because it's important you understand just how deep in the shit you are. Bell knows you sent his wife over the edge. Pretty soon The Firm is going to know you copycatted them so their guys would get pinned for Eve. How do you think they'll react? Shrug their shoulders? Say something like 'Hey, smart play, dude. Respect'? Or hunt you down and nail your dick to your forehead? I know what my money's on. You're not going to last on the outside, so if you want to stay alive, you better come down to Central and lay it all out – Eve, the blackmail, the works."

Hayes chuckled ruefully, shaking his head, like someone trying to extricate himself from a social ambush without resorting to rudeness. "This is just so out there, I don't know what to say."

"Okay," said Ihaka briskly. "You want to tell me who's your next of kin?"

"You know, that's not particularly funny," said Hayes. "If there's nothing else, perhaps you should leave."

"There's just no helping some people," said Ihaka. "But you know what? I'm kind of glad you didn't take me up on it. It'll save us a lot of frigging around, that's for sure."

As Ihaka reached for the door handle, Hayes said, "Just as a matter of interest, what would give Bell the idea I'm the blackmailer?"

Ihaka retraced his steps. He leaned forward, planting his hands on the desk. "Bell knows," he said softly, "because I told him."

17

This time John Scholes didn't bother pretending that he was pleased to see Tito Ihaka.

He rounded on the guards who'd escorted him to the superintendent's office. "What the fuck's all this then?" he said, more like a high-handed employer than a convict. "I've got nothing to say to this bloke. Where's my lawyer? We're meant to be having a meeting."

Ihaka sat down at the meeting table. "Thanks, fellas," he said to the guards. "You can leave us to it." As the door closed, he told Scholes to sit down.

"Fuck you," said Scholes. "I don't want to talk to you. I'm up before the parole board tomorrow, and I need to have a run-through with my lawyer."

"As we speak," said Ihaka, "your chances of getting in front of the parole board are somewhere between fuck all and zero. If you don't sit the fuck down, they'll be less than zero."

Scholes advanced in sullen silence. He sat down opposite Ihaka, tilted the chair back, clasped his hands behind his head, and began whistling softly. Ihaka recognized it as the theme song from the old TV comedy *Dad's Army*, 'Who Do You Think You Are Kidding, Mr Hitler?'

"Why all the drama?" asked Ihaka. "I thought parole was going to be a rollover, you being a model prisoner and all."

Scholes's look got dirtier. "Apparently your colleagues out West Auckland, being a right bunch of cunts, have muddied the waters. But you already knew that, didn't you?"

"You know, the funny thing is, a few days ago I was thinking about intervening on your behalf, maybe even having West Auckland's submission taken off the table. It just goes to show, timing is everything. Now we know why your boys killed Arden Black and we know who killed Black's sister, so you don't have a lot of leverage."

"Is that right?" said Scholes, the habitual half-smile back in place.

"It was a hit, wasn't it? And a well-paid one, I bet. Set up by Mark Wills."

The half-smile didn't waver; the eyebrows didn't twitch.

"Not quite the perfect crime, you'd have to say," said Ihaka. "We know who made the approach, we know who paid for it, the guys who did it are behind bars and, to top it all off, they smashed up the wrong bloke. I believe the technical term is a goat-fuck."

He leaned back, grinning. "Is that your poker face, Johnny, or have you just shat your pants?"

Scholes's eyes widened fractionally. "Look, this is all very interesting, not that I've got a fucking clue what you're on about, but if it's all the same to you I really would like some time with my lawyer."

"Let me ask you a question. What do you reckon the parole board's view will be if we tell them beforehand that you're about to be charged with conspiracy to commit murder? I know they sometimes get a bit of stick for being a soft touch, but I think they'd baulk at that, don't you? In fact, coming on top of Waitemata's submission, I'd say it'd be a bit of a game-changer."

"Conspiracy to commit murder?" Scholes rolled his eyes. "Do me a favour. That one ain't going to fly, Sergeant. You know it. I know it."

"Admittedly it wouldn't be a walk in the park —"

"Ah. Is that the voice of common sense I hear?"

"— but it looks like we'll have to go down that route to make sure we nail Cropper and Parks. We don't have a motive otherwise."

Scholes sat up straight, folding his arms over his belly. "That wouldn't be an issue if they pleaded guilty."

"Now there's a thought."

"Consider it done. So I take it I can rely on your positive input at the parole hearing, Sergeant?"

"Shit no."

Scholes flushed crimson, snarling unintelligibly.

"Time to get real, Johnny. Getting those apes to plead guilty would be helpful, but it's also in your interests. If I'm going to take the heat for springing you, I'm going to need a shitload more than that. Here's the deal and it's non-negotiable. You tell me exactly what happened to Blair Corvine, and I'll get you out of here."

"What about the conspiracy charge?"

"Well, if we're going to go after you, we'll also have to go after your client. That won't be my decision."

"As I said before, you and I both know what that decision's going to be, seeing as who the client is." Ihaka's reaction prompted a fat man's chuckle. "Oh yes, Mr Ihaka. See, I insist on knowing who I'm dealing with, and that Wills geezer – well, put it this way, he's neither strong nor silent."

"You might be hearing from the client again."

"Oh, why's that?"

"Cropper and Parks actually got the right bloke," said Ihaka. "It was your client who got it wrong. He knows that now. And he knows who he should've had taken out."

"How come?"

Ihaka shrugged. "Maybe a little bird told him."

Scholes whistled. "My, my, you're playing for keeps, aren't you?"

"Now this will interest you, Johnny. The reason we thought Cropper and Parks killed Black's sister is that the guy we're talking about, the guy who did kill her, saw them do Black and tried to copy it. You see what I'm saying? He went out of his way to make us think your boys killed her."

"Fucking cheek."

"I didn't think you'd be too thrilled. So do we have a deal?"

"Well, that depends," said Scholes. "I can't tell you who ratted out Corvine because I don't know. But I can certainly tell you a thing or two about Doug Yallop."

"The Prof? What's he got to do with it?"

"Oh, quite a lot, I think you'll find. But I can't do it all for you. After all, only one of us is a trained detective, and it ain't me."

"Fair enough."

"It was Yallop who got Jerry Spragg duffed up. He called it, he paid for it. Spragg came in here like he was fucking Al Capone, going on about how he'd rumbled Corvine and turned him into Swiss cheese and bragging about his connections, which I took to mean he had one of your lot in his pocket. I guess word got around that he was talking too much because next thing I've got the Prof come to see me."

"He wanted Spragg put away?"

"Oh yeah, he wanted him put away all right, but I drew the line at that. Someone gets topped, all hell breaks loose. Everything tightens up, the screws start going by the book." Scholes's eyes twinkled. "I mean, it's bad enough being in here without getting treated like some kind of criminal. So we settled on giving Spragg a hiding. A proper fucking hiding, mind, not a touch-up, a very clear message that he should keep his gob shut. Now Spragg wasn't the full quid to begin with, but he was fucking sixpence in the pound after the lads were finished with him. So Yallop got what he wanted after all – and on the cheap, which pissed me off more than somewhat, I can tell you."

"You're sure Yallop was acting for a cop?"

"As sure as eggs are eggs," said Scholes. "And in return for you getting me out of here, I'll tell you why."

"Go on."

"If I tell you now, what's to stop you welshing on the deal?"

"I don't work that way, Johnny."

"There's always a first time."

"I'm looking at the big picture here," said Ihaka. "In the long run I don't gain anything by shafting you."

"The big picture, eh?" Scholes nodded approvingly. "I like that. People who look at the big picture are few and far between, as I'm sure you know, Mr Ihaka. All right, I'll take you at your word, one big-picture man to another. I never liked that fucking Yallop – all the bollocks about being some kind of criminal mastermind – so when he was planning and packaging jobs and selling them to the highest bidder, I didn't want a bar of it. A few years ago I began to detect a pattern: all Yallop's jobs, the lads who pulled them ended up either getting collared or ripped off."

"You reckon Yallop and the cop were planning jobs, selling the blueprints, then robbing their own customers?"

"Well, if they weren't robbed, they were nabbed red-handed. A nifty little scam, you'd have to say."

"But you kept that to yourself because it thinned out the competition?"

Scholes shrugged. "It was no skin off my nose. If blokes were too fucking dim to see what was going on, it served them bloody well right."

"Corvine got a sniff of it, although he didn't know it was Yallop. He tipped off Central a couple of weeks before he was shot."

"Well, there you are. The bent copper killed two birds with one stone. He stopped Corvine getting any closer and no doubt got a pay-off from Spragg. You know why I'm in here, right?"

"Yeah."

"Well, fixing up Spragg was a barter arrangement – no money changed hands. In return for us kicking Spragg's head in, Yallop told me where I could find that piece of shit who put me in here."

Ihaka stared. "He was in the witness protection programme."

"Precisely, old son. If you needed actual proof you've got a rotten apple, that's it."

"What did you do to the guy?"

"Nothing yet. I've been in here, haven't I? It's not the sort of task you delegate."

"That was a while ago. He could be anywhere by now."

"Oh, don't you worry about that," said Scholes happily. "I've been keeping tabs on him."

"This puts me in a kind of tricky position."

"Forget about it. Not your problem. A, he's scum. B, you're looking at the big picture. Don't sweat the small stuff, Mr Ihaka."

"I can't let you kill him, Johnny."

"Don't be fucking daft, I'm not going to kill the poxy little bitch. Apart from anything else, he's not worth it. But he's bought and paid for and by Christ I'm going to have him."

Ihaka nodded. "I guess I'll just have to take your word for it."

Scholes's smile stretched. "Fair's fair."

"I need you to make a list of every one of Yallop's jobs you can think of."

"I thought you might."

"How long will it take?"

"Well, I'll need to wrack the old brain," said Scholes. "And I'm a great believer that if a job's worth doing, it's worth doing well. Come back tomorrow morning. I should have something for you by then."

"Okay." Ihaka stood up. "I'll leave you to it."

"You know," said Scholes reflectively, "it's a bit rich you getting on your high horse about what I might do to the filth who put me in here. What about the way you've set that bloke up?"

"Your guy didn't kill anyone. This one did. He beat a woman to death. Besides, I warned him."

"You did what?"

"I explained the situation to him and pointed out that his best chance, maybe his only chance, of staying in one piece was to come into Central and own up."

Scholes shook his head. "You're a fucking piece of work, you are."

Ihaka looked back at Scholes from the doorway. "Everyone gets called to account, Johnny. One way or another, everybody pays. Don't you forget it."

Scholes's notes ran to half a dozen A4 pages, an orderly exercise set down in a riotous scrawl. He'd listed fifteen crimes, arranged in three categories: those he knew for sure were Yallop's work, those he had reason to believe were Yallop's work, and those he assumed were Yallop's work because the guys who pulled the job were way too dumb to have planned it themselves.

With one exception, the perpetrators were either swiftly arrested or themselves robbed. The exception was the theft of a private collection of rare Chinese snuffboxes that was about to go on public display. Scholes picked Yallop himself for this one because it wasn't really the Asian gangs' style, plus it would be just like the Prof to have known the value of a load of old Chinese porcelain and a fence somewhere in the world who could shift it.

Ihaka was impressed. Scholes had an organized mind, impressive powers of recall and an intimate knowledge of the workings of the Auckland underworld. That didn't make him regret his decision to let Scholes loose. Yes, there might be blowback, but you made these deals because they delivered here and now. There was no point losing sleep over whether they'd come back to haunt you down the track. Some did; some didn't. There was no telling.

Scholes was a bad man, but in the dark places there are degrees of bad, and bad was better than evil. He was a parasite, but a rational parasite who operated within a set of rough rules. He adhered to the protocols in the cold war with the police, and accepted that there were limits to how ruthlessly he could prey on the community. He would be brutal, even murderous, when he calculated that the benefits outweighed the risks, but there was a residual humanity keeping him in check. Some day, greed or hubris or even boredom might drive him to cross the line, and then those who'd made murky, unauthorized accommodations with him would be tainted.

The alternative was to stick to the rules and not think about the price others paid for your clean hands. Ihaka had never been able to do that. It had set his career back and would do so again. In the end it would probably be his undoing.

He set the alarm for 3.30 a.m. so he could pore over computer files in a near-empty Auckland Central. What he found didn't make sense, so he went through the whole process again looking for innocent explanations, reasons not to believe, an inconvenient fact that undermined an otherwise obvious conclusion, even complexities and uncertainties that would take him into a grey area where there was no way forward and therefore no choice but to abandon the quest.

But there weren't any. Each time one of Yallop's jobs resulted in a quick arrest, it was the same arresting officer. Each time the breakthrough came from information supplied to the arresting officer by an unnamed informant. And each time the perpetrators were themselves robbed immediately after committing the crime, that same officer was off-duty.

Ihaka was stuck in traffic on the airport motorway when Scholes rang.

"How did you get this number?" he asked.

Scholes laughed. "What sort of question is that? I wanted you to be the first to know that I'm sitting in McDonald's waiting for my Big Mac and fries. It's not quite what I would've chosen for my first meal as a free man, but I was outvoted."

"That must be a new experience for you."

"Not at home it's not, it's par for the fucking course. So did you find what you were looking for?"

"Yeah."

"Did it make you happy?"

"No."

"I didn't think it would."

"Did you know?"

"I had an inkling. Good word that, inkling. We should use it more often. I fucking warned you, didn't I? I told you to leave it alone. So everybody pays, do they, Mr Ihaka?" This time there was a harsh edge to Scholes's laugh. "Well, we'll see about that, won't we."

Before Ihaka could reply, the line went dead.

*

They met in the St Johns Bar on the Wellington waterfront, Johan Van Roon bustling in with his cellphone clamped to his ear. He was still on the phone five minutes after shaking hands, his body language evoking an overburdened boss surrounded by mediocrities.

"Mate," he said when he got off the phone, "if you'd given us some warning, we would've had you round for dinner. Yvonne and the kids would've loved to see you. But you know what she's like when it comes to entertaining. She doesn't do spontaneous. Two days' notice, minimum."

"It was very last-minute."

"So what are you down for?"

Ihaka was tempted to make something up – that he was tidying up the Duckmanton case or some domestic issues in Wairarapa – just to salvage a few precious minutes of how it used to be.

They went all the way back to the day Van Roon arrived at Auckland Central fresh out of police college – a shy, pale, lanky first-generation Kiwi, the son of Dutch immigrants. Ihaka told the crowded station room that Van Roon was the whitest white man he'd ever seen and dubbed him the Milky Bar Kid, a label that took a few years to shake off.

Ihaka soon realized that Van Roon's choirboy Nordic features and diffident manner were misleading. He was intelligent, hard-working, loyal, eager to learn and appreciative of guidance. Without making a conscious decision and certainly without fanfare, Ihaka became his mentor. He helped Van Roon grow up and toughen up, sometimes putting an arm around his shoulders, sometimes a rod up his back. They stopped calling him the Milky Bar Kid.

When Van Roon made detective sergeant, Ihaka lost his right-hand man. He'd seen it coming, though, and had helped make it happen because he wanted Van Roon to fulfil his potential and go on to bigger things, things that were probably already out of his own reach. And being on an equal footing meant they could be mates. Ihaka had many a meal at the Van Roons' and was godfather to their oldest child, even though he'd warned them he wouldn't be a role model, wouldn't remember the kid's birthday and had a philosophical problem with the God aspect.

They'd seen very little of each other since Ihaka's banishment from Auckland. Despite the proximity, that didn't change when Van Roon was promoted and transferred to Wellington. He was flat out, Ihaka had his routine, and perhaps neither was in a hurry to find out how their respective rise and fall had reconfigured their relationship. But there was no point in having a few beers and a catch-up, pretending nothing had changed. All that there was between them, the sum total of their friendship, was back in the past, slipping out of reach.

It was a Sunday night; they had one end of the bar to themselves. Ihaka still leaned in, lowering his voice. "I came to tell you that I know what you did up there, you and Doug Yallop."

Van Roon had the beer bottle halfway to his mouth. He put it down carefully and pushed his chair back, frowning at Ihaka as if he'd expressed some ratbag opinion.

"I'm not wired up," said Ihaka. "You can pat me down if you want."

"What, here?"

"We can go into the loo."

"I don't think so," said Van Roon, standing up. "I think I'll just call it a night."

Ihaka shrugged. "If you walk out of here, I ring McGrail. After that, it's out of our control."

"You've got this all wrong."

"Then you've got nothing to worry about."

Van Roon grimaced, running his fingers through his hair, once corn-yellow, now grey/white. "Tito, I don't know where you're coming from, mate. I mean, this is crazy. It could sink both of us. We should be sticking together."

"Are we going to the shithouse," said Ihaka, "or are you going home?"

"Okay," said Van Roon with a heavy sigh. "Let's go."

They went into the toilet. Van Roon checked the stalls were empty, then stood with his back against the door.

"Strip."

Ihaka took off his shirt and dropped his jeans.

"Keep going."

Ihaka stepped out of his jeans.

"Throw them over here. And the shirt."

Ihaka did as he was told. Van Roon patted the clothes down and went through the pockets.

"Let's see the shoes."

"You've been watching way too much TV," said Ihaka, tossing over his shoes. He put his thumbs in the waistband of his boxers. "You want the full frontal?"

"Why not?" said Van Roon. "We've got this far."

Ihaka stepped out of his boxers, naked now. "It goes without saying," he said, "but I'll say it anyway: we wouldn't be doing this if you were clean."

Van Roon nodded distractedly, as if he was thinking about something else altogether. Then he pulled the door open and disappeared.

Ihaka threw on his clothes and hurried back into the bar, half-expecting to find Van Roon gone. But he was sitting at the table, head bowed over his beer.

"I suppose you want to know why," said Van Roon without looking up. "You won't like the answer. It was because of you. You remember what I was like when I joined: Billy

Brighteyes, a real fucking Boy Scout. It didn't take me long to realize I'd been sucked in. We're just another government department, full of clock-watchers and brown-nosers and guys who'd trample over their grandmothers to get one notch up the pecking order. Half the guys at the top end have forgotten why they ever wanted to be a cop in the first place, half the ones coming in at the other end are second-rate people who'll be second-rate cops, if we're lucky. But at the end of the day, I still thought we were about serving and protecting, and that we valued people who stood up for those things. But when I saw what they did to you, I stopped believing.

"I know you're high-maintenance and two of you would probably be one too many for any district, but you're a hell of a cop. You've got a real talent for it. Everybody knew that. You'd earned the right to be taken seriously about Lilywhite, but because he was in the eastern suburbs' money set, they didn't want to know. And when you wouldn't let go, they cut you off at the knees. McGrail, who for bloody years had been only too happy to gather brownie points off the back of your work, dropped you like a hot potato. Look at him now in his tailor-made suits and his BMW. Look who got his job instead of you: that slimy prick Charlton, a prime example of everything that's wrong with the organization. If you'd got that job, none of it would've happened."

Van Roon's voice wobbled and he looked away. "All I wanted was to work for you again, the old team. I'd have swapped that for coming down here as a DI any day. But I got the message. You can be the best cop in the building, but unless you play the political game and do the networking you'll end up mediating white-trash domestics out in the sticks. I made up my mind that wasn't going to happen to me."

"So you got cosy with Yallop?"

"You introduced us, remember?"

"I didn't expect you to get into bed with him. How did it start?"

"I heard Yallop had shopped a payroll job around, so I had him on about it." Van Roon's gaze slid off into a faraway stare, his tone flattening into indifference. "You know what he was like, slippery as an eel. Anyway, the idea just popped into my head. I suggested next time he sold a job, he should let me know. He'd make money, I'd get the collar. Of course he came straight back with 'What's in it for me?' I said something vague about doing favours. You know what was going through my head? This is what Tito would do, this is how he operates. Get your hands dirty, do what you have to do. Yallop said he'd think about it. A few months later, out of the blue, I got the call. Then I got another one. I wrapped up a couple of cases double-quick and suddenly I was the blue-eyed boy."

"Then he called in the favour."

"There was this private collection of Chinese snuffboxes that was going on public display. The Prof wanted inside info on the security arrangements. He said the stuff was insured up the jacksie, so it was effectively a victimless crime."

"I doubt the insurance company saw it that way."

"Well," said Van Roon, "I guess they just would've bumped up their premiums."

"So you gave him what he wanted, and then he had you by the balls?"

"Not really," said Van Roon mildly. "He came up with this scheme: at any given time, between the two of us, we'd have an idea which crooks around town were sitting on the takings from a job. As he pointed out, if you steal stolen goods from a crim, he's hardly going to dial 111."

"But as they say," said Ihaka, "it's all fun and games till someone gets hurt."

"Meaning?"

"Meaning the five rounds Jerry Spragg put in Blair Corvine."

Indignation convulsed Van Roon's face. "Fucking hell, what do you take me for? I had nothing to do with that. When McGrail told us Corvine had picked up a whisper there was a cop in this outfit that was robbing the robbers, I decided then and there that was it, no more. I never breathed a word about Corvine to anyone on the outside. Christ, I'd never sell out another cop, even a worm like Charlton."

He changed pace again, throttling back to matter-of-fact. "There were three of us in the crew – me, Yallop and Spragg. Spragg was a headcase, but Yallop wanted him on board to do the strong-arm stuff if the need arose. Word got back to Spragg that Corvine was taking an interest in our operation. I don't know exactly how it went down. Yallop reckoned Spragg, who was paranoid at the best of times, got jacked up on P and did it pretty much on the spur of the moment. I doubt that. I suspect Spragg consulted Yallop who did some digging, maybe put a tail on Corvine, and put two and two together. He was a pretty average human being, the Prof, but he was sharp, no two ways about it. And when he'd figured out what Blair was up to, he would've got in Spragg's ear. You know, 'What are you going to do about it?'"

"So that's you off the hook then," said Ihaka.

"Come on, Tito, you're better than that. Corvine had been inside Spragg's outfit for months. If I was going to drop him in it, I'd have done it much earlier."

"He wasn't making waves earlier."

"Christ almighty, when you wanted to find Blair the other week, who did you call? Me. I've known where he was all along, and a few people would've opened their wallets for that information."

"You told John Scholes where to find the guy who put him inside."

Van Roon shook his head impatiently. "No I didn't. I mentioned it to Yallop, which I know I shouldn't have, but it never occurred to me that he'd tell Scholes in return for him putting the bash on Spragg. Something else I had nothing to do with. Incidentally, the fact Yallop was so anxious to shut Spragg up is why I'm sure he was in on the Corvine hit. He was worried Spragg would implicate him."

"And you weren't?"

"Spragg was an animal who'd done way too many drugs, but he was staunch. He wasn't going to roll over. And even if he did, no one was going to take his word against mine."

"Next thing you'll be telling me Yallop committed suicide." Van Roon didn't say anything so Ihaka pressed on: "I did a bit of checking. You called in sick the day Yallop was killed. What did you do, fly up under a false name or drive? I guess you used a gun you acquired on one of your nights out stealing?"

"Look at you," said Van Roon bitterly, "sitting there in moral judgement. You should be thanking me. I saved your fucking life."

"Really?"

"Yallop got spooked when you turned up asking about Spragg and Corvine. Not surprising, I suppose. He'd heard me talking you up often enough. He wanted to put a hit on you. So, yeah, Tito, I called in sick, I drove up, I shot him, then I drove home again. And I did it for one reason only. To protect you."

They locked eyes. The stare went on and on. There was a time, thought Ihaka, when I would have sworn this guy was incapable of lying to me. Now I just don't know.

"So what now?" asked Van Roon.

"I've got some thinking to do, haven't I?"

"Listen to me, Tito. You don't have to do anything. Just let it lie. Okay, I know I went off the rails and did some shitty things but, when all's said and done, it wasn't that big a deal. No innocent people got hurt. I wouldn't say my conscience is clear, but I can live with myself. The only blood on my hands is Yallop's, and he had it coming. He egged Spragg on to do Corvine, and he was going after you. And it's all over. I got out of that toxic place and went back to being a good cop. What would be the point of blowing the whistle on me? They'll never prove a thing. You trained me well. You taught me how to put myself in the other guy's shoes. Believe me, the trail is cold."

Van Roon was pleading now, reaching back into their friendship, shuffling the emotional cards looking for a trump. "All it would do is fuck my career. You know how it works: mud always sticks. They wouldn't find anything, but that would be it anyway. They'd shunt me off into some dead-end desk job or pay me out. Even if you think I deserve that, even if you just want to wash your hands of me, think of what it would do to Yvonne and the kids. If this thing blows, they'll go through absolute hell."

"They're your wife and kids. Maybe you should've thought of that."

"Who do you think I did it for?" Van Roon stood up. "So I guess it's all over between us."

Now that he'd come to the reckoning, Ihaka felt nothing but desolation. "I don't know what it is."

"Just walk away – from the whole fucking thing."

"Including you?"

Van Roon nodded. "You're going to do that whatever happens."

"I'm sorry it had to be me."

There was shame and grief and something close to love in Van Roon's glassy smile. "It was only ever going to be you, Tito."

He walked out of the bar. Ihaka sat there with his head in his hands, thinking, so this is what heartbreak feels like.

EPILOGUE

On their way home from work, the private investigator Grant Hayes had an exchange with his live-in girlfriend, secretary and partner-in-crime Simone that fell somewhere between a negotiation and an argument.

Hayes tended to have a light breakfast and lunch and didn't eat between meals, so there was a lot riding on dinner, especially the main course. He wasn't much of a dessert man, and had decided that cheese gave him a double chin. Simone, though, regarded the main course as protein intake, necessary but nothing to look forward to. She was far more interested in what followed.

There was a chicken in the fridge which she was prepared to roast with all the trimmings, provided he went and got something nice for dessert. Hayes's opening gambit of hokey pokey ice cream with chocolate sauce, both procurable from the corner dairy, was rejected out of hand. She wanted raspberry sorbet and triple chocolate brownie, which meant going to the St Lukes supermarket, a round trip of anything up to an hour at that time of day. Fuck that, said Hayes, who was hanging out for a beer. "Suit yourself," said Simone with a cold shrug. "Takeaways it is."

Hayes dropped Simone off and headed for the mall. If he hadn't been so absorbed with saying to himself what he would have said to Simone if he didn't value her home cooking and wantonness, he might have noticed the car parked across the road from his place pull out from the kerb and fall in behind him.

Having taken the edge off his mood by treating himself to a four-pack of high-alcohol, high-priced boutique beer, Hayes hurried back to his car in the supermarket car park. In fifteen minutes, traffic permitting, he'd be sinking piss with his feet up in front of the TV while the little bitch slaved over a hot stove. As he put his purchases in the boot, something hard poked him in the back. He jerked upright, his head snapping around. There was a guy right behind him, so close Hayes felt a puff of breath on his earlobe.

The rear passenger door of the car in the next space, a Ford Falcon, swung open.

"In case you're wondering," said the guy poking him in the back, "it's a Browning 9. Now get in the car."

The gunman herded Hayes into the Falcon and got in beside him. Hayes was sandwiched between him and a fat guy with a round, pink face, ginger scalp stubble and what under different circumstances he would have regarded as an encouraging smile. There were two more in the front, big buggers by the look of them, but they didn't even bother flicking him an over-the-shoulder glance. As the car took off, Hayes felt panic sweat popping out all over, as if he was being squeezed like a lemon. Even his shins were sweating.

The gunman looked straight ahead, ignoring him. The fat man stared out the window. As they headed west on St Lukes Road, the fat man twisted around so he didn't have to turn his head to look at Hayes.

"You know who I am?"

He sounded like a Pom, but that was no help. "No. No idea."

"John Scholes is the name. Me and my mates here belong to an outfit known as The Firm. Maybe you've heard of us."

Hayes's voice stalled. Scholes didn't wait for him to finish clearing his throat.

"I'll take that as a yes," he said. "You whacked out some bird and tried to get a couple of my lads done for it. Where I come from, that's called taking a diabolical liberty."

Scholes was still smiling, but even in the state Hayes was in, dizzy with nausea, bile leaping in his throat, his body not responding to simple commands, he could tell it didn't mean anything. Actually, it did. It made it worse. If Scholes was screaming at him, threatening his life, it would mean he wanted something and there was still a chance Hayes could talk his way out of it. As it was, they were treating him like a dead man walking.

They hit the North Western Motorway.

"You were warned," said Scholes, "but you didn't take a blind bit of notice. Being inside wouldn't have been a doddle, mind, but as the saying goes, where there's life, there's hope."

Hayes managed to speak, although not in a voice he recognized. "What are you going to do to me?"

"I just told you, old son. Now shut it, because there's nothing more to say. You just get yourself ready, all right?"

Scholes craned his neck to look through the rear window at the city skyline, a glittering silhouette against a blue-black sky. "I love this fucking view," he said.

One of the others murmured assent. After that the car was silent.

They took the Henderson turn-off, swung down a side street and pulled up behind a Range Rover. Another big unit got out of the Range Rover and came over to open the door for Scholes.

Scholes got out of the Falcon and looked down at Hayes. "Well," he said, "it's goodbye from me and it's goodbye from him. Him being a bloke whose wife topped herself."

The new guy got in beside Hayes. "Who's this cunt?" he asked, with a jerk of his head.

"What fucking difference does it make?" said the driver. He did a U-turn and headed back towards the motorway.

Scholes sat behind the wheel of the Range Rover, making a call on his cellphone. "Hello, love, it's me. Yeah, all finished for the day, I'll be home in ten. What's for tea, then? Oh, a surprise, eh? I only like nice surprises. You know that, don't you? I'm sure it will be, love. Looking forward to it. Those kids behaving themselves? Yeah, tell him Dad will read him a bedtime story as long as it's not that Harry Potter, fucking four-eyed git. Why? Because those fucking books are as long as the Oxford fucking Dictionary, that's why. Don't worry, I'll make him an offer he can't refuse. All right then, love, see you soon."

Scholes dropped the phone into his jacket pocket and started the car.

This time Finbar McGrail himself answered the door. "Perfect timing, Sergeant. I was just about to have a glass of port. Come on in."

He led Ihaka down the corridor to his study and ushered him into a chair.

"Actually, I've been expecting you," said McGrail, taking care to ensure the measures were exactly equal. "When I heard you were burning the midnight oil at Central, I assumed you were onto something."

He handed Ihaka a glass.

"Thanks," said Ihaka. "Heard from who?"

"Beth Greendale. She went through and covered your cyber-tracks, just in case."

"So Van Roon was right. She was keeping an eye on me for you?"

"Paranoia doesn't become you, Sergeant," said McGrail primly. "I was conscious both that I'd dropped you into a snake-pit and that, come what may, you wouldn't ask for help."

Ihaka swallowed most of his drink. "You know what I think? The Lilywhite case was never a priority for you. It just gave you an excuse to get me back up here. You knew I wouldn't be able to resist poking into what happened to Blair Corvine. You wanted me to shake the tree and see who fell out."

McGrail moved his nose to and fro above his glass, taking his time. "So who did?"

"Why didn't you just say so?"

"You explained it rather well," said McGrail. "I didn't need to."

"You mean it gave you deniability if the shit hit the fan."

McGrail tut-tutted. "Such a cynic. Are you going to keep me in suspense?"

"Didn't Beth figure it out?"

"She had no idea what you were looking for. True to form, Sergeant, you played your cards very close to your chest."

"Jesus, you're a fine one to talk."

"Touché," said McGrail, inclining his head.

"It was Johan."

"Oh."

"That's it – 'oh'?"

"Well, bear in mind when you took everything into account there weren't that many candidates. But I'm very sorry to hear that, partly on my own account. I would've said Van Roon was a good officer and a good man. It turns out he's neither."

"It's not black and white."

"Carry on."

As McGrail refilled their glasses, Ihaka summarized Van Roon's self-defence.

"Artful," said McGrail, resuming his seat. "And perhaps not without some validity. But I rather suspect he executed Yallop to protect himself, rather than you."

"So what do we do now?"

"You've done your bit by telling me. I'm sure Van Roon pressed you to keep it to yourself."

"Okay, so what are you going to do now? He's a bright bastard, Johan, and very careful. It'll be a bloody tough nut to crack."

"He has two areas of vulnerability," said McGrail. "One is money. It's difficult for someone on a salary to conceal supplementary income or explain sudden spikes in expenditure which aren't balanced by borrowings. Conversely, it takes an almost inhuman degree of self-discipline to hide it somewhere and forget about it for a couple of decades. The other one is family. My impression would be that he'd dread the impact public disgrace would have on his wife and children."

"No doubt about that."

"So my recommendation to the commissioner will be that we offer him a choice: resign with immediate effect, or we publicly announce an open-ended investigation into his involvement with Yallop."

"And if he walks the plank, that'll be the end of it?"

"Good heavens, no. Murder is murder, Sergeant. We can't sweep that under the carpet. You'll share your theory regarding Yallop's murder with the officer in charge, Detective Sergeant Firkitt, and then let the cards fall where they may. There's nothing new in us knowing who committed a crime but having the devil's own job proving it, although Firkitt is nothing if not persistent."

McGrail went behind his desk to peer at his computer screen. "On another matter, would the Grant Hayes whom you suspect of killing Eve Diack be the same Grant Hayes who went out to the supermarket last night and never came home?"

"I hadn't caught up with that."

"I can't imagine there are two private investigators by that name. I assume you issued a ports and airports alert?"

Ihaka nodded. "I wouldn't worry about Hayes. He'll turn up eventually."

McGrail took off his glasses, breathed on them, polished them with a piece of cloth, put them back on. "Sergeant, I've known you long enough to have the strong sense that you could shed some light on this situation."

"You know Jonathon Bell had Arden Black done in because he thought Black drove his wife to suicide?"

"Yes."

"Well, I told Bell who really drove his wife to suicide."

The intensity of McGrail's scrutiny went up several notches. "Didn't it occur to you... Let me rephrase that. It obviously occurred to you that he might do the same to Hayes."

"That's exactly what I pointed out to Hayes," said Ihaka mildly. "He reckoned he could stay out of jail *and* stay alive. I warned him he could do one or the other, but not both."

"And what about Bell?" said McGrail sharply. "What sort of rough justice do you have planned for him? After all, he had an innocent man beaten to death."

Ihaka drained his glass. "Bloody nice drop, that. Last time I went after someone in that neck of the woods it didn't turn out too well for me, so I might sit this one out. I'll leave Bell to others, like John Scholes."

"Why Scholes?"

"Bell wanted blood so badly he sold his soul to the devil. I wouldn't call that getting off scot-free. I'd call it a life sentence, no remission, no parole."

"I see. Would I be correct in assuming Scholes would have a good idea of Hayes's current circumstances and whereabouts?"

"I'd say so."

"Well, at the risk of sounding like a broken record, what about Scholes? He's as free as the breeze, thanks to us."

"I'm not finished with Johnny Scholes. He belongs to me now."

McGrail felt slightly foolish, which didn't happen very often. He should have known Ihaka would be relentless. One way or another, his justice would reach all those who deserved it.

"That makes it sound like you're staying?"

"I guess that's up to Charlton."

"It's most definitely not up to Charlton. It's up to you and me."

"Well, yeah, but —"

"I know what you mean. You're thinking about how it would work. I don't think you should be concerned about Charlton. He's in your debt now, which of course is the very last place he wants to be. Having said that, Charlton's driving force is ambition. He wants people around him who get results, so that he's seen as someone who gets results. Believe me, if you want to come back, Charlton won't stand in your way. He'll swallow hard, grit his teeth and pretend it was his idea. Firkitt's another matter altogether. I'm pleased to say I have no insight into what goes on inside that head."

"Firkitt I'm not too worried about. One of these days, out of the blue, he'll take a swing at me, and then honour will be satisfied."

"In that case, welcome back, Sergeant. I think a toast is in order. Goodness me, we seem to have finished the bottle."

"Sir, I've known you long enough to have the strong sense that you will have planned for just such an eventuality."

McGrail sighed. "Unfortunately, Sergeant, you're absolutely correct. Again."

Ihaka had dinner with Miriam Lovell, who had a more robust appetite for food and wine than her slim build and vegetarian aura had led him to expect. In fact, as they started their main courses she moved the bottle of Pinot Noir closer to her, telling Ihaka that just because he drank faster than she did, that didn't mean he was going to get more than his fair share. He defused the stand-off by ordering another bottle.

As they waited for their taxis she told him, in a matter-of-fact way because she believed at their stage in life there was no point in not being upfront about these things, that she was open to the idea of a relationship but would want to take it slowly. She'd got to quite like being single and was in no rush to alter her routine. Ihaka said he could relate to that. They agreed to touch base in the morning, with a view to maybe getting together for brunch.

The next morning, a Saturday, Ihaka was awoken by his cellphone's text message alert. The text, sent from Denise Hadlow's phone, said, "Hey sargent ths is Billy. Im playing at the Domain at nine. Be real cool if you could come. Mum thinks so to."

Ihaka looked at his watch. It was 8.35. He rolled out of bed and headed for the shower.

Acknowledgements

I'd like to thank my sister, Susan Thomas, for her legal expertise.

This novel contains material from a serial I wrote for the *New Zealand Herald* several years ago. Thanks to *NZH* editor Tim Murphy for his support and to APN News & Media for permission to reproduce the material concerned.

Finally, I wish to express my sincere thanks to Creative New Zealand, whose generous support greatly facilitated the writing of this novel.

Paul Thomas
Wellington
November 2011